Thad watched several emotions flicker across Macy's face—surprise, incredulity, anger—but before she could settle on one, he added, "There would be a lot of benefits to the arrangement, for both of us. Before you say anything, just hear me out."

"No."

"No, you won't hear me out? Or no, you won't marry me?"

"No, period. Our 'arrangements' have gone far enough. Don't you understand that what you want, what we're doing—having a baby like this—makes a mockery of everything I believe in? You've reduced love, marriage and family to…to this. To nothing but emotionless agreements and practical considerations."

Thad flinched. Love, marriage and family were just as sacred to him, maybe more so. "Think of the baby," he said. "If we marry, the baby will have my name."

"So we'd be married but we wouldn't live together. Is that what you're suggesting? A marriage in name only?"

Thad cleared his throat, certain Macy wouldn't like this next part any more than she'd liked the first. "Actually, I was thinking we could live together. Just as roommates."

"But why? What purpose could there possibly be in— Oh, I get it." Her eyes narrowed. "You'd be protecting your investment."

Dear Reader,

Sometimes someone touches your life, and you know that afterward, nothing will ever be the same. It's incredible, when you think about it, that we have the power to make such a difference to those we meet. Katie, a mere child of five, made that kind of difference for me. As her Sunday school teacher, I watched her fight a battle against cancer. Her courage inspired me. Her death broke my heart. Her life gave me new appreciation for the ties that bind us all, for beauty and for love.

I wrote *Baby Business* during Katie's last year. Though its characters are entirely fictional, I hope I've succeeded in my desire to share the magic that came from knowing her.

I'd love to hear from you. You can write me at P.O. Box 3781, Citrus Heights, CA 95611. Or simply log on to my Web site at www.brendanovak.com to send me an e-mail, enter my monthly draws, join my mailing list, check out my book signings or learn about my upcoming releases.

Here's to love and to life!

Brenda Novak

Books by Brenda Novak

HARLEQUIN SUPERROMANCE

899—EXPECTATIONS
939—SNOW BABY

Baby Business
Brenda Novak

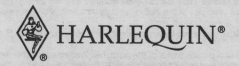

TORONTO • NEW YORK • LONDON
AMSTERDAM • PARIS • SYDNEY • HAMBURG
STOCKHOLM • ATHENS • TOKYO • MILAN • MADRID
PRAGUE • WARSAW • BUDAPEST • AUCKLAND

ISBN 0-373-70955-2

BABY BUSINESS

Copyright © 2000 by Brenda Novak.

All rights reserved. Except for use in any review, the reproduction or
utilization of this work in whole or in part in any form by any electronic,
mechanical or other means, now known or hereafter invented, including
xerography, photocopying and recording, or in any information storage
or retrieval system, is forbidden without the written permission of the
publisher, Harlequin Enterprises Limited, 225 Duncan Mill Road,
Don Mills, Ontario, Canada M3B 3K9.

All characters in this book have no existence outside the imagination of
the author and have no relation whatsoever to anyone bearing the same
name or names. They are not even distantly inspired by any individual
known or unknown to the author, and all incidents are pure invention.

This edition published by arrangement with Harlequin Books S.A.

® and TM are trademarks of the publisher. Trademarks indicated with
® are registered in the United States Patent and Trademark Office, the
Canadian Trade Marks Office and in other countries.

Visit us at www.eHarlequin.com

Printed in U.S.A.

For Katie, because I believe in rainbows, too.

And for my own five children, Ashley, Megan, Alexa, Trey and Thad, because they're the reason I believe.

CHAPTER ONE

"Is SHE the one?"

Startled, Thad Winters glanced up. Kevin, his best friend and partner in Winters-Brodey Advertising, stood in front of his desk, staring at the photograph of Macy McKinney that Thad had pulled out of a manila envelope. That same picture, showing a woman with wide green eyes, shoulder-length black hair and a mysterious Mona Lisa smile, had drawn his eye again and again—ever since it had arrived in the mail two days ago.

Was she the one? Thad could only hope. The sooner he found the right woman, the sooner he could make his way back to the man he used to be. "Who knows? They all look good at this point. It's after Rychert finishes his little background check that things start to go downhill."

Tall and pencil-thin, with a shock of dark hair that never seemed to lie down in back, Kevin shoved his hands in his pockets. He crossed to the wall of windows overlooking the jammed Salt Lake City streets—it was afternoon rush hour—twenty stories below. "Have you met her yet?"

"We have an appointment in fifteen minutes." With a glance at his watch, Thad shuffled the papers on his desk, trying to appear busy. He didn't want Kevin to stay. The interviews were difficult enough without an audience.

"So what are you doing? *Advertising* for women?" Kevin asked.

"No, a few discreet friends are asking around. That's it."

"Thank God for small favors. It's starting to look like Toys "R" Us in here." With his foot, Kevin nudged a life-size teddy bear that toppled over onto a box of chocolates. "How many have you interviewed?"

"I haven't counted. A dozen maybe. Why?"

Kevin straightened, his usually good-natured expression strained. "Because I think you're making a mistake."

The mistake was made eighteen months ago by a drunk driver, but Thad wasn't about to go into all that. Valerie's death was still too painful to talk about—ironic considering she was all he ever thought about. The memories swirled around and around in his head until sometimes he could almost touch her, taste her, smell the perfume he'd given her their last Valentine's Day.

Those memories preserved a small part of the heaven he and Valerie had known during their short marriage. They also introduced him to a whole new concept of hell. "And?"

Kevin sighed and rubbed his jaw. "Haven't you learned anything from all this?" He waved his hand at the pile of gifts.

"I've learned that it isn't going to be easy to find the one I'm looking for. And that some women can be far more aggressive than I ever would have dreamed."

"You dangle a hundred thousand dollars in front of anyone, and you're going to see their worst side. Why not give it some more time? Valerie's only been gone eighteen months. You'll fall in love again eventually."

How many times had Thad heard those empty words? Why couldn't anyone understand that he didn't *want* to fall in love again? He wanted Valerie and their unborn child.

"I'll make a note of your objection." Thad tried to keep

his voice flippant to cloak the anger that sometimes swelled, inexplicably, with the pain. "Anything else?"

Kevin stared at him a moment longer. "No, I'm leaving. But I wish you'd listen to me. This thing is destined to lead you into trouble."

"Mr. Winters?"

A sultry voice pulled their attention to the open door, where the woman from the picture stood, both hands fidgeting with an oversize leather handbag.

"I'm sorry," she said. "I know I'm a few minutes early, but something has come up, and I can't stay long. I hope you don't mind. I tried to call first but only got a recording."

Thad stood and tried on a welcoming smile. "No problem. My secretary's gone for the day. You must be Ms. McKinney."

"Yes."

He half expected her to tell him to call her Macy. But she didn't. "Ms. McKinney" was entirely too formal for what they planned to discuss.

Fine. It was better to keep things as formal as possible, he reminded himself. "This is my partner, Kevin Brodey."

Kevin's face, always an open book, showed heightened interest and a certain reluctant appreciation. He strode to her and shook her hand, and for some reason, Thad noticed that Ms. McKinney wore no fingernail polish, a simple detail that set her apart from the others who had applied. "It's a pleasure to meet you, Ms. McKinney."

She smiled hesitantly and nodded, but her gaze darted to Thad, then took in the balloons, candy and flowers that adorned half the room.

"My partner here was just leaving." Thad shot Kevin a meaningful look.

Kevin made a face at him from behind the woman and managed to haul himself out of the room.

Thad closed the door to ensure the privacy he wanted. "Please, have a seat. Can I get you a cup of coffee?"

The way Ms. McKinney's hands were shaking, she looked as if she could use something warm in her stomach. As a matter of fact, she looked as though she could use a lot more than coffee. Such as several weeks of healthy meals and someone to make sure she ate them. The woman in the photograph had a gleam of laughter in her eye and a healthy flush to her porcelain skin. But Ms. McKinney in the flesh looked tired and drawn. Dark circles underscored large eyes, hollows accented high cheekbones, and despite the classy sheath dress and matching jacket she wore, Thad could tell she was too thin.

What had happened to the woman in the picture? Was she ill?

"I don't have time for coffee, thank you." She hovered near the leather chair across from his desk, but when her gaze met his, it was as direct as any business associate's and far more piercing. "Actually, I'm not sure I should be here. It's certainly not what I want."

Thad cleared his throat, taken back by her honesty. "Then why did you come?"

"Why would anyone come?"

"You need the money."

She nodded.

"For what?"

A faint, bitter smile curved her lips. "Is it important? Do you have to approve of how I'd spend it?"

Thad crossed to his desk and sat down, steepling his fingers in front of his chin. "One hundred thousand dollars is a lot of money."

"No one knows that better than me. I'll be honest with

you, Mr. Winters, I need to raise $98,523, and I need it right away.''

The exactness of the figure surprised him, as she must have known it would. "For what?"

She smoothed her dress. "That's my business."

Thad's eyebrows rose. This gal was certainly different than the rest. Some of the others had eagerly gushed over the new house or car they would buy. One had hoped to sway him by claiming she'd donate half the money to charity. A couple of others had offered to do him sexual favors he hadn't asked for and certainly didn't want.

But then, it was difficult to find a healthy-minded individual to do what he was asking. He'd anticipated as much, which was why he insisted on certain precautions.

"I have to protect my investment," he said, studying her. "Part of that includes understanding your attitude toward the remuneration."

"Investment? Remuneration?" She made a sound of disgust and dropped her head into her hand.

Her damning judgment, though unspoken, told Thad she was probably the most normal woman he'd ever find, but it stung him enough to bring him to his feet. "I'm sorry. I can already see we wouldn't make good partners on this. I won't keep you."

Surprise and something akin to fear flashed across her face. Had she expected him to beg her, in addition to paying her so handsomely? Evidently she didn't understand what the money was for.

"Wait." She held up a hand. "I think maybe we got off on the wrong foot. Could we try this again?"

Thad remembered the two interviews he had scheduled for tomorrow and the many women he'd already rejected. They were calling him incessantly and sending him things, hoping to change his mind. He had to find someone quickly, while he could still withstand the onslaught.

And despite their bad beginning, Ms. McKinney struck a chord in him. There was something about her eyes.

"Please," she murmured.

"Fine," he heard himself say. "Why don't you sit down this time?"

She perched on the edge of her seat, her purse in her lap.

"You said on the phone that a friend of yours gave you my number."

"Yes, Lisa Shriver. She got it from her doctor, a Dr. Peters."

Dr. Peters was an old friend, and one of Thad's few confidants. They'd discussed Thad's intentions at his last physical, three months ago. Evidently Dr. Peters had decided to help him, after all. "And you called because you need ninety-eight thousand dollars?"

"And change."

"For something you won't tell me."

"It's not a big secret. It's just my business. If we decide to…to work together, I want my personal life kept as separate from yours as possible. I'm sure you understand."

He did understand, and he felt the same way, which was a point in Ms. McKinney's favor. "What do you do?"

"I'm in my second year of med school. I want to be a pediatrician."

"Now I know why you need so much money."

A faint smile reminiscent of the one in the photograph flitted across her face, then her gaze fell to the floor. "So, would you like to explain the details of what you propose, or have I lost any chance of…of being the one you select?"

Thad sat on the corner of his desk so he wasn't hovering over her. "Let's just say I'm willing to spend a few more minutes together before I decide."

Her hands knotted, but when she looked up at him, her unique beauty, and that mysterious something that haunted her eyes, struck him again. "I'm usually not difficult to get along with," she said softly. "I'm sorry about earlier."

Thad winced, surprised that even the dream of graduating from med school could bring this proud woman to her knees. "I'm not looking for an apology, Ms. McKinney."

"Macy."

Maybe they were getting somewhere at last. "Fine, Macy then. And please, call me Thad."

"I know you want a baby, Thad. Would you mind telling me why you're not able to have one in the normal way?"

He cleared his throat to dislodge the lump that nearly choked him whenever he spoke of Valerie. "My wife died in a car accident eighteen months ago."

"I'm sorry."

"She was carrying our first child, a son. The doctors couldn't save either of them."

"How terrible." They were simple words, the same so many people had used over the months, but something in the tone of Macy's voice told him she could hear the silent scream inside him. And he hated the vulnerability her knowing inspired.

Pushing off the desk, he went to the window so he wouldn't have to face the pity, thinking that he preferred the harshness of her judgment. "I merely want the child I was denied, Ms. McKinney...Macy. It's as simple as that."

"Simple?" she echoed. "Nothing about this is simple. Surely you must realize that."

"It's as simple as we make it."

"How do you plan to...I mean, how would I..."

He kept his face averted. "Become pregnant? You'd be artificially inseminated, of course. I want this to be handled as professionally as possible, in every way."

"Of course." She seemed to breathe a little easier. "And once I'm pregnant…"

He turned toward her. "You'd carry my baby and deliver it, then you'd turn the child over to me and walk away forever. And for your trouble, you'd be a hundred thousand dollars richer."

She studied him as though trying to decide what he was thinking behind the mask of his face. "What if I were to miscarry?"

"You'd be paid in installments as the pregnancy progresses, the final payment after delivery, all nonrefundable deposits."

"God, it sounds like you're buying a house," she whispered, squeezing her eyes shut.

"The terms have to be clear, Macy, or we're setting ourselves up for disaster."

Composing herself, she sat up taller. "I realize that. This is just all so…so unnatural."

Thad went back to staring down at the traffic ebbing and flowing in the street below, remembering Valerie's radiant smile the morning she woke him with breakfast in bed to say she was pregnant. Valerie was gone. Now there was no *natural* way to achieve what he wanted. But when the baby arrived, the end would justify the means. He wouldn't be alone anymore. After eighteen long months he might actually feel something again. "It's the only way."

"What if the baby isn't whole or healthy? What then?"

"Perfect or not, the child is mine. I'll take care of any medical bills. On the off chance that something should…happen to you in delivery, the money would go to your heirs."

"That's a comfort, at least."

He glanced over his shoulder at the sarcasm in her voice, and she lifted her hands in a defensive gesture. "I know, I know. We have to talk about all possibilities, make everything clear.''

"It's a business deal, Macy. The more we think of it that way, the easier it will be for both of us."

"A business deal," she repeated, then, more loudly, "When do you hope to finalize your plans?"

"The sooner the better." He thought of a baby's happy gurgle breaking the tomblike silence of the house that awaited him at the end of each day and thought it couldn't be soon enough. "Are you interested?"

Her forehead creased and she sighed. "Yes."

"Then you'll need to fill out an application." He strode to his desk and searched for the packet he'd so carefully created, the one that grew thicker every day. By the time Ms. McKinney finished with his questions, he'd know everything about her, from her shoe size to her grandparents' medical history. "You are single, right? That's imperative."

Tucking her silky black hair behind one ear, she gave him a look that said she was surprised marital status even mattered to a man who was already bending all the rules. "I'm divorced."

"Good." He handed her the questionnaire, and her eyebrows shot up when the weight of it transferred to her hand.

"I've seen shorter dissertations. When would you like this back?"

Thad wasn't sure how long it would take to fill out. No one else had gotten beyond the initial interview. Macy McKinney hadn't passed with flying colors, but he was interested enough to take it one step farther. "I'm still interviewing, so you might want to get it back to me in the next day or two."

"Fine." She glanced at her watch and stuck out her hand. "I have to go. Thank you for your time."

Thad clasped her hand in his, noting the delicate bones and soft skin. She had good doctor's hands, even though they were a bit cool to the touch. And though physical beauty was far from his primary concern, he couldn't help noticing she had other good features, too—and genes that would make a pretty baby.

"Hello?"

A woman he'd interviewed a few days ago poked her head through the door and thrust out a huge cookie bouquet wrapped in purple cellophane.

Thad stifled a groan.

"I'm sorry to interrupt," she said, her voice sticky sweet, "but I thought you might enjoy these. Aren't they darling?"

"Miss—"

"Lanna, silly. Call me Lanna, remember?"

Thad tried to suppress the twitch that started in his cheek. With Lanna came the memory of the other bold women his offer had enticed, and suddenly Macy McKinney's cool reserve looked far more appealing than it had a moment ago. "Lanna, I told you I'd call you when I made my final decision. I'm sorry that it's taking some time, but—"

"My phone's been on the blink, and I thought you might have tried to reach me." Coming into the room, she ignored Macy and shoved the cookies in his face so he could admire them. Then she set the elaborate bouquet on his desk, next to the flowers someone else had sent him yesterday.

Thad looked at the cookies and knew there would be a lot more where they came from if he didn't do something to stop Lanna and her competitors. "Actually, I'm glad you're here," he heard himself say almost before he knew what was going to come out of his mouth, "because I think I've reached a decision."

"Yeah?" Her smile broadened as she positioned herself

with one hand on his desk, bending slightly forward to show her cleavage to best advantage. "Who's the lucky girl?"

"Ms. McKinney and I still have to go over her application, but if she agrees to the background check and everything else is in order, then *she* is."

Thad glanced at Macy and saw her eyes widen. He also noted, again, the thinness of her body and the drawn look to her face. "If she passes the physical," he added.

CHAPTER TWO

THAT NIGHT, Macy's eyes traced the blue veins visible just below the surface of her daughter's translucent skin as Haley slept, curled up, in a hospital bed that nearly swallowed her whole. Her breathing was markedly shallow, but after fifteen minutes of studying the rise and fall of her small chest, Macy couldn't decide whether or not she was resting any easier than she had the previous night. That last round of chemotherapy had really taken it out of her, poor baby, but even at such a terrible price, the treatments had done little to stop the lymphoma.

Thad Winters's notion of an application lay in Macy's lap, and she thought briefly of using this time to fill it out. Who knew when Haley's vomiting might start again, when she might need to be held and rocked. The night could get long. But Macy refused to turn her attention to other things for fear death would creep in and steal her only child away.

"God, Macy, what are you still doing here?" a voice whispered harshly.

Macy turned to see her friend Lisa slip through the door. Almost like a sister, Lisa had been a part of Macy's life since she was fifteen. They'd gone to school together, weathered their dating years together, attended the same university. Macy doubted she would have survived the past few years without Lisa's emotional support. "I can't leave her. You know that," she said simply.

Lisa's face creased into a sympathetic smile, and she

pushed her glasses higher up on her stubby nose. "Haley's been in and out of the hospital for nearly a year. I know you're going to collapse if you don't start taking care of yourself."

"I'm fine." As though contradicting her words, the weariness Macy felt sank a little deeper, into her bones, but she forced a smile of her own. "And you can't talk. What are *you* doing here again? You've spent almost as much time at this hospital as I have."

Out in the hall, a strident voice over the intercom directed a Dr. Johansen to the emergency room, but such calls came so frequently they were only background noise to Macy now.

Lisa shrugged her thick shoulders. "You and Haley are family. That bum you were married to isn't here for you, but—"

Haley stirred, and Macy waved for Lisa to lower her voice. "I don't need him."

This assertion was met with a skeptical lift of Lisa's eyebrows as she wrapped huge arms around Macy for the hug she gave to everyone when she came and when she left. "There's nothing but noodles in your cupboards. Have you eaten today?"

Macy couldn't remember whether she had or not, but to save herself from a scolding, Lisa-style, she went on the offensive. "What were you doing in my cupboards? You'd better not have been cleaning my house again."

"Damn straight I was. The last thing you need to worry about is cleaning and cooking. You'll find my homemade lasagne in the refrigerator. See that you eat it when you get home."

"Damn straight," Macy echoed, thanking the fates for bringing Lisa into her life all those years ago.

Lisa set her purse down and wedged her bulk between

the bed and the wall. Her body was big, but not nearly as big as her heart, Macy thought as Lisa stared down at Haley. ''You think she's any better?'' she asked.

Macy let her gaze drop to the soft blond fuzz that was all the hair her five-year-old daughter had left, and shook her head.

''Did you call that guy Dr. Peters told me about?''

''Yeah.'' She lifted the manila envelope that held Thad Winters' twenty-page questionnaire. ''He gave me this. Can you believe it? He actually expects me to fill out an application to be the mother of his child. Maybe he should copyright it. This has to be a first. Or maybe I'm the only one who thinks something's wrong with buying a baby. For all I know, he downloaded this application off the Internet. Hell, maybe everyone's doing it.'' She frowned. ''On top of everything else, he wants me to take a physical. To be honest, I'm surprised he doesn't have me go in for some DNA testing just to be sure the baby will have the right color of hair and eyes.''

Lisa folded her arms across her full bosom, Macy's first indication that she wasn't going to get the commiseration she anticipated. ''His wife died while she was carrying their child, Macy.''

''Says Thad Winters. Some guy puts up a hundred grand and women fall all over themselves to get in line. But has anyone checked his story? What if it's not true?''

''Did he seem insincere to you?''

Macy pictured Thad Winters's rugged face, the high cheekbones, the thick brown hair, the square jaw and slightly cleft chin, light blue eyes contrasting sharply with the darkness of his five-o'clock shadow. The way he easily controlled his tall muscular body lent him a confident air. He seemed driven, focused, intense, but he didn't seem insincere.

"No, but good looks and an expensive office are no reason to trust a man, Lisa."

Her friend grinned. "He's good-looking, huh?"

Macy felt herself blush. She knew it had something to do with the way Thad Winters had affected her on a personal level, but she tried to ignore that, hoping Lisa wouldn't notice. "He's not bad," she lied.

"'Not bad' coming from you means he looks as good as Brad Pitt. And if he's *that* good-looking, he could probably get any number of women pregnant without spending a dime."

Macy wasn't sure she wanted to be convinced by Lisa's rationale. Despite his physical charms, she was angry at Thad, for reasons she didn't fully understand. He was offering her the one thing she needed. He was also exacting the highest form of payment, making her give him one baby to save another. "Maybe he thinks it's some sort of interesting game," she mused. "Maybe it arouses him to hold so much power over a woman's destiny, to have us all groveling at his feet for the privilege of bearing his child. You should have seen all the gifts—bribes, really—stacked in his office."

"I don't think so. Dr. Peters lived next to the Winters family all the years Thad was growing up and says he's never met a better man, or someone more capable of leading a successful life."

"What, does Dr. Peters make a percentage for brokering the deal?" Macy grumbled.

Lisa pulled her frizzy light-brown hair out of her eyes and scowled. "My, aren't we turning into a cynic! Thad Winters wants his own baby, and he no longer has a wife to give him one. So he's taking an alternate route. So what? He's an ad exec."

"Which means…"

"He's creative. As for the application and stuff, there's nothing wrong with interviewing, playing it safe."

"Playing it safe would be waiting until he falls in love and marries again. Playing it safe would be doing it the *right* way."

"The right way didn't work for him. What if he feels certain no woman could ever replace his wife?"

Macy considered this, wondering if she'd grown suspicious of all men because of what had happened with her father and Richard. Her father had left her mother before Macy was born. She didn't know him, had never known him. And Richard had run off almost as soon as he learned of Haley's illness, which only confirmed what her mother had taught her as a child: men don't have what it takes to stick around when the going gets tough. It's women who hang on through thick and thin. Edna was proving her words by being the one to help Macy pay her bills now that she couldn't work because of school and the time she spent at the hospital.

"I'm just saying it's normal for him to have a few questions," Lisa went on.

"A few questions?" Macy repeated. "Look at this folder. He's expecting me to write a book! Have I ever taken any drugs? Have I had unprotected sex in the past ten years? Do I drink or smoke? Have I ever sought or obtained psychological counseling? How much caffeine do I drink? I'd have to be the Virgin Mary to pass this test!"

"Well, you'd come closer than anyone else I know. You've never smoked or taken drugs. You need counseling for what you're going through right now, but you've never sought or obtained it, so you can feel pretty good about saying no to that. And you haven't slept with anyone other than your ex-husband."

After a quick check to make sure Haley was still sleeping, Macy gave her friend a look of incredulity and lowered her voice. "Aren't you forgetting that guy I went home with from Studio 9 last year? You relieved the baby-sitter I'd gotten to watch Haley that night and picked me up at his house the next morning, remember?"

Lisa grimaced. "You can't count that. Your husband had just run off with a seventeen-year-old. I think what you did was pretty understandable, considering."

For a short time after Richard left, Macy had frequented the bar scene as a way to help soften the emotional blow, but two things had slapped her awake to the realization that she was heading down the wrong path. One was the night she'd slept with a total stranger and woke up wondering where the heck she was. The other was Haley's quickly deteriorating health.

"Judging from this list of questions, I doubt Thad Winters will find it understandable," Macy said.

"Then don't reveal it." Lisa's words were spoken in her matter-of-fact way, but they were far from the brutal honesty with which she normally dealt with the world.

Macy gaped at her friend. "You're kidding, right? What's the purpose of an application if I only put down what he wants to hear?" She chewed on the end of a pen she'd picked up from the nightstand. "Besides, I agreed to let him do a background check."

"What are the odds of anyone finding out about that night? If you tell the truth, you might not get the job."

"I'm not sure I want the job," Macy said softly.

Lisa's attention turned to Haley's sleeping form, and her expression grew inexpressibly sad. "You don't have a choice, kiddo. Your insurance is paying for the hospital stay, but the transplant is going to cost over a hundred and fifty thousand dollars, and it's not covered. As hard as we've tried, we've only been able to raise…what?"

"Fifty thousand and change."

"Fifty thousand dollars. And no hospital is going to perform the operation unless you give them full payment, in advance. We've already been through that."

Reaching across the sterile, white sheets, Macy curled her fingers around Haley's small hand. Her head was beginning to ache, but it bothered her only slightly more than the burning in her eyes and far less than the ache in her heart.

"What did he say when you told him why you needed the money?" Lisa asked.

"I haven't told him about Haley yet. I didn't see any reason to bare my soul when I wasn't even sure I wanted to do this."

Lisa studied her. "And now? You're going to go for it if he chooses you, right?"

Macy sighed. Somehow, somewhere, all the lines had blurred. There was no more black or white, right or wrong, only her daughter, who needed a bone marrow transplant and Macy's determination that she get it.

"I'm still thinking about it," she said at last.

THE DIM INTERIOR of the steak house where Thad had told Macy to meet him was a cool respite from the bright April sun, making it seem later than it actually was. Macy removed her sunglasses and slid them into her purse, waiting for her eyes to adjust.

The smells of the restaurant—grilled onions, broiled meat, blue cheese dressing—greeted her more quickly than the hostess's smile, but did little to chase away the chill that ran through her blood. She was going to do it. Despite all her misgivings, she was actually going to try to convince Thad Winters, a total stranger, that she should be the one to bear his child. And her only consolation was that she'd spoken to Dr. Peters, another fellow who'd known Thad at college, and a couple of his firm's clients, and they all said the same thing: he was an honest, intelligent man who deserved to be a father. It was a shame that fate had robbed him.

Just as fate was trying to rob her now of Haley, Macy thought. But she wasn't about to let that happen—at least not without a fight.

"One for dinner?" the hostess asked.

"No, I'm meeting someone." Surreptitiously studying the tables she could see from her vantage point at the entrance, Macy hoped Thad Winters hadn't arrived yet. She needed a few minutes to calm down after her most recent conversation with Haley's oncologist. The stark realities he softly intoned always shook her to the core, where a fundamental part of her refused to believe her daughter's chances could really be so slim.

But Thad Winters was already waiting for her. He looked up from the drink he was nursing at a table nearby and spotted her at almost the same instant she noticed him. Standing, he waved to make sure he had her attention, then folded his tall form back into the booth.

"You're early," he said conversationally as she put down her bag and slid into the seat opposite him. "I take it you didn't have any trouble finding the restaurant."

"No." She felt his gaze run over her hair, knit top and blue jeans and wished she'd had time to freshen up since her afternoon classes at the University of Utah's College of Medicine. She'd returned to the hospital, instead, where Haley had been watching *Robin Hood*.

"Can I order you a glass of wine or something?" he asked.

It looked as though he was having a mixed drink, but Macy wasn't here to enjoy herself. She asked for a club soda, then pulled the application from her purse and slid it across the table. "I've answered all the questions."

She cringed as he picked up the document and began thumbing through it, partly because many of the questions were uncomfortably personal, but mostly because, in the end, she had lied about having slept with the stranger from Studio 9. Haley needed the money too badly for her to risk the truth. And she justified her falsehood by repeating over and over to herself that it was the only time in her life she'd done something so irresponsible.

When he paused about halfway through, Macy squirmed in her seat. What was he reading? Her answer to the question about having regular menstrual cycles? The one that asked about her marital history? She wished he'd take the darn thing home to go over it, but he thought of their arrangement as business. And if it was business, then this was a business dinner and a perfectly acceptable place to study the "prospectus" in which he was considering investing so much.

God, when had she become a commodity?

The moment I walked through the door of his office a week ago.

Fortunately the waitress arrived with Macy's drink, interrupting him. He set the package aside in favor of the thick, tasseled menu the young woman handed them both.

"Are you finding anything you like?" he asked after several minutes.

Macy peeked over the menu she was using to block his close regard and offered what she hoped was an at-ease smile. "I think I'll have the chicken salad."

When the waitress returned, Thad ordered her salad and a steak, medium-rare, for himself, then retrieved something from his briefcase. He glanced through it, apparently comparing it to what Macy had written on the application, and she suddenly felt as though the word *liar* hovered in the air over her head.

A frown creased his forehead. "Your grandmother died of heart disease?"

"Yes, but she was eighty-eight, hardly cut down in her prime."

He nodded. "There's no information here about your father."

"Because I don't know anything about him."

A raised eyebrow told her he expected to hear more.

"He ran out on my mother after she got pregnant with me. It seems he didn't share her desire to raise a family."

"I see." He went back to his questionnaire, and Macy suddenly wished she'd ordered something much stiffer than soda water.

"You've had a miscarriage?"

"Just after my husband and I were married, I became pregnant, but it only lasted three months."

"What happened?"

"My doctor had no idea why I lost the baby. He said it happens all the time. He gave me a D & C and sent me home." She took a gulp of her drink, feeling the tasteless fizz roll down her throat and wishing their food would arrive to divert Thad Winters's attention from her before he reached the infamous *Have you had unprotected sex with anyone in the past ten years?* question.

"It says here you've never taken any drugs."

"Right." At least her conscience was clear there.

"You've never even experimented? No pot? No acid?"

Macy thought back on all the college parties where she'd been offered such things. She'd been tempted occasionally, but she'd heard of too many bad things that had happened while people weren't themselves. Except for that short window after Richard left, when she'd drunk more than she should have, she'd always decided to protect her judgment. "No."

He nodded and kept reading. Finally, he stopped and glanced up, and Macy *knew* he'd arrived at the question she most wanted to avoid.

"You claim here that you've never had unprotected sex, except with your husband."

Macy let her gaze slide away, unable to face the ocean-blue intensity of his eyes while she lied. Instead of voicing her answer, she nodded, hoping he'd let her get away with that and move on. But he didn't. He frowned and waited until she started fidgeting with a lock of her hair.

"Do you want to change your answer?" he asked at last.

Forcing her hands away from her hair and beneath the table, where she clenched them, Macy shook her head. "No…ah…no. Why would I?"

"You gave me permission to do a background check, remember?"

"So?" She cleared her throat when the word squeaked out, wishing she could lie as easily and effectively as Richard had always lied to her.

"There's a woman by the name of Julia Templeton who claims you slept with her boyfriend once. She's a bartender at Studio 9."

Macy's jaw dropped. "You must have turned over every rock in my past to have come up with that information," she accused.

"That's what a background check does. Did you think I wouldn't bother, Macy?"

Being forced into the awkward position she was in and having embarrassed herself by trying to lie made Macy angry. "I'm sure you were most thorough, Mr. Winters. Tell me, what else did you find? That I was the slut of Hillcrest High?"

A muscle ticked in his cheek, but his voice was still civil when he said, "Were you?"

Grabbing her purse, Macy dug through it and tossed a twenty-dollar bill on the table. Then she stood up. "Enjoy my salad, Mr. Winters. I'm sorry to have wasted your time."

THAD SAT in the booth at the steak house long after Macy had left, staring at the report Rychert had compiled on Macy McKinney. It was certainly thorough. She'd been raised an only child by a single mother who'd worked for the Department of Motor Vehicles for thirty years and was now retired and living in Las Vegas. She'd attended college on academic scholarship, had dated a lot, despite her pressing studies, and had married a popular football player for the University of Utah. They'd had one daughter, who would be five years old now, and had divorced a year ago when her husband took off with a teenager who'd worked at the local McDonald's. Since her husband left, she'd enrolled in school again, for the first time since having the baby, and she was now living on student loans, plus some help from her mother, and what she could earn at home transcribing, formatting and proofreading dictated medical reports for various physicians.

Not an easy life for a bright young woman like Ms. McKinney, but one with promise. Her history pointed to an inner strength, dedication and resilience that Thad admired. Rychert had found no evidence of drug use, no alcohol abuse, though she did drink heavily for a short period after her marriage broke up, no particularly worrisome diseases or mental instability lurking in her family genes. And no sexual indiscretions beyond the claims of that one bartender at Studio 9.

Few women had a résumé so clean. Thad had thought

he'd found the one. Until she'd lied to him. Then he'd known it would never work. He refused to involve himself with someone he couldn't trust, not when it came to his child.

Sighing, he finished his drink and pushed the baked potato around some more on his plate. Sex was an uncomfortable subject for most people. With her goal of becoming a pediatrician hanging in the balance, he understood how strong the temptation to lie must have been. But understanding did little to alleviate his disappointment that, regardless of her initial candor, Macy McKinney had turned out to be no better than anyone else.

His cellular phone chirped, interrupting his thoughts. Pushing his plate away, he punched the Talk button. "Thad Winters."

"It's Rychert. Did I catch you at a good time?"

Thad looked across at the empty booth, then thought of going home to his empty house. Once he left work, he had nothing but time. He used to spend the evenings with Valerie, painting the nursery, landscaping their yard, cleaning their garage or cars. Since her death, he didn't know how to fill the evening hours. Her parents and younger sibling had moved out of state when her father retired the year after he and Valerie were married, and they rarely called. His own parents spent their winters in Arizona and wouldn't be back for a few weeks yet, which left him with a sister and a brother who lived close but had families and busy lives of their own. Sometimes he still tinkered around the house, but there didn't seem to be much point anymore. At least at the restaurant he could hear the quiet buzz of other people's conversations, the tinkle of a woman's laugh.

"Now is good," he said. "What's up?"

"Did you get the report on Macy McKinney I sent by courier?"

Thad frowned at the papers that still rested on the table, almost wishing he'd never seen them. "Yeah."

"What do you think?"

"I was hopeful until she walked out on me a few minutes ago."

There was a brief silence on the other end of the line. Then, "Well, if she's no longer a possibility, this might not matter, but I was just clearing off my desk to go home and ran across a page of the report I inadvertently left out."

"I don't think you left anything out. I've got pages one through four and nothing seems missing."

"This was the last page, page five. Somehow, it didn't get clipped to the rest."

Thad shook his glass and listened to the ice clank against the sides. "No problem. It can't possibly say anything that's going to make a difference now, anyway."

"I don't know. It goes a long way toward explaining why she contacted you in the first place."

"The money isn't reason enough?"

"Not for a babe like her. She's a class act. Single mother, med student, high achiever."

Putting his glass down, Thad threw his credit card on the table as the waitress came to collect the plates. "Greed can strike anyone, Rychert. She's a starving student. She has to pay for her schooling somehow. Besides, the part of your report I did receive says she drives an old Pinto. Sounds like she could use a new car."

"She could use a lot of things, but it's not school or cars or anything like that she's concerned about. She has something much bigger on her mind."

Now Rychert had his full attention. "Oh, yeah? What's that?"

"Her daughter needs a bone marrow transplant. Without it, she'll die."

CHAPTER THREE

PRIMARY CARE HOSPITAL was a creamy-white building located on Medical Drive next to the university hospital. It hummed with the fans and belts that ran the air-conditioning, specialized medical equipment and various office machines. The chilled air carried a hint of antiseptic, and the cloying smell of serious illness pervaded the place, but Thad tried not to notice. Instead, he focused on the petite, gray-haired nurse sitting at the receptionist's desk just inside the main entrance.

"I'm looking for Haley McKinney's room," he said when he reached her.

The nurse glanced at the clock, then eyed the huge stuffed teddy bear propped under Thad's arm. "Visiting hours are over."

"I know I'm a little late, but I won't stay long."

She looked at the bear again. "Well, her mother's with her. If you make it quick, I don't see how it can hurt anything, as long as you scrub up before you go in. Her immune system is so low, we have to be careful what germs she comes in contact with. Wait a minute. They moved her a day or two ago. Let me check her room number." She swiveled away to consult her computer. "Take this hallway to the elevators and go up to the fourth floor. When you get off, you'll see a set of doors leading to the oncology department. Right inside is a small anteroom where you'll scrub your hands and arms and face. Just make sure the outer door is closed before you open the inside one. You don't have a cold or anything, do you?"

"No."

"Fine. Haley's in room 3."

Thad thanked her and pushed away from the counter, growing increasingly uneasy with the memories this sterile environment evoked. He hadn't expected it to be quite so bad, but now that he was standing in the middle of the hospital lobby, he couldn't avoid the memories of Valerie's last days. He had spent many hours in a similar place, waiting while the doctors operated, hoping, praying, staring dumbly into space—and eventually losing everything that mattered to him.

Shooting a look at the sliding doors that led to the parking lot where he'd left his car, Thad hesitated. It wasn't too late to turn away instead of plunging right into the middle of someone else's misery. He didn't owe Macy anything. They were still virtual strangers. She hadn't even leveled with him and told him why she needed the money. She didn't want him in her personal life. There had to be someone else who could help her.

Then why did she contact me? Surely I was a last resort?

Thad winced under the responsibility that thought landed squarely on his shoulders. Dammit, he hadn't asked for this! All he wanted was a child of his own, and he was willing to sacrifice every penny of the life insurance money he'd collected on Valerie's death to avoid any further entanglements.

Still, it wasn't responsibility that drew him down the hall and away from the exit, he realized. It was the thought of Macy's gaunt cheeks, the lack of sparkle in her eyes. The mystery of what had caused those things had been solved, and as much as he didn't want to, he could feel her pain.

He understood—as few could—and that understanding wouldn't allow him to walk away.

The nurses' station outside the oncology department was deserted. Thad scrubbed up as he'd been told and closed the outer door, then stepped into the sterile ward, expecting someone to question his presence or acknowledge him in some way. But other than a hushed murmuring a few doors down, there was no one to stop him from walking down the hall and poking his head into room 3.

No one except himself. He hovered just outside until a small sweet voice caught him as effectively as a net.

"Mommy? Is that you?"

Not wanting to frighten the child by leaving his shadow falling across her door, Thad moved inside, where she could see him and he could see her. Small for her age and almost as white as the sheets she lay between, she stared at him with round eyes that were far too big for her face. Her hair had been reduced to a few wispy strands. Her bones were prominent through her flesh. And the circles beneath her eyes were so dark it looked as though they'd been painted there deliberately. No less than twenty-five IVs surrounded her bed.

The sight clenched Thad's stomach like a vise, and even though he didn't know this child, had no emotional connection to her, he ached for her suffering.

"My name is Thad, Haley," he said, smiling to reassure her. "I'm a friend of your mommy's."

"I've never seen you before," she replied doubtfully.

His smile grew. "No, your mother and I haven't known each other very long. Did she go home to get some rest?"

"Lisa made her go to the lunchroom."

"Good for Lisa. She's your mommy's friend, right?"

Haley frowned, looking unsure, but finally nodded.

"What's that?" she asked, eyeing the teddy bear with obvious appreciation.

"It's for you. But it looks as though you might not have room for him."

She scooted to the side. "He can fit. See?"

Thad placed the giant bear in the bed beside her, and she promptly began to cover him up with her blankets. "He's cold," she explained.

"It doesn't look like he'll be cold for long. What are you going to name him?"

She screwed up her face, thinking long and hard. "Scotty has a dog named Bruiser."

"Who's Scotty?"

"He lives next door to us."

"Well, I doubt he'll mind if you want to name your bear after his dog."

She smiled, and a hint of how beautiful she would be if she were healthy caused another pang in Thad's chest. He could see Macy's elegant features in her and began to wonder how her father could have abandoned such a lovely child, or how, for that matter, he could have abandoned her mother. Marrying a man capable of doing something like that didn't seem like Macy McKinney, but then, there was no accounting for love. It could blind even the strongest and wisest.

"What are you doing here?"

Thad turned to see Macy at the door, gaping at him.

He studied her for a moment, then chose his words carefully. "I have a hundred thousand dollars in the bank, Macy. There isn't any reason we can't both get what we want."

Macy's eyes darted suspiciously from Thad to her daughter and the stuffed bear, then back to Thad. "And what is it you want, Mr. Winters?"

"You know what I want. I want my baby." He nodded to Haley. "And you want yours."

Taking a business card from his shirt pocket, he scribbled down his home number and handed it to her. "Call me if you're still interested," he said, and walked out.

"WHO WAS THAT?" Lisa demanded, coming through the door to Haley's room just after Thad Winters had left.

"Guess," Macy replied. Dropping the backpack she'd been dragging around with her so she could study, she slumped into the seat next to her daughter's bed.

Lisa raised her eyebrows. "Well, he wasn't wearing scrubs or a white coat, so I doubt he was a doctor."

"It was Fad," Haley piped up. "He brought me a bear."

"Thad," Macy corrected, eyeing the stuffed animal as though she'd like to belt it. "Thad Winters."

Lisa blinked in surprise. "That was *him?* Ooooe, what a babe! You're crazy if you think a man like that has to pay a woman to do anything."

Macy rolled her eyes. "Handsome is as handsome does."

"And what has he done that's so unhandsome?"

Macy didn't really have an answer for that. He'd caught her in a lie, which had embarrassed her, but she had no right to hold that against him. He was offering her money to do something she didn't want to do, because he knew her back was against the wall. But he could have offered the deal to someone else. As Lisa had said, there had to be any number of women who would happily oblige a man like Thad Winters—for free! So what, then, had her so angry?

The desperation that forced her to act beyond her own good judgment, she decided. And the fear. But those things had nothing to do with Thad Winters, either. At least he seemed to want a baby for the right reasons. Everyone who knew him was convinced he'd take good care of a child. Besides, she couldn't expect him or anyone else to plop a hundred thousand dollars into her lap for nothing. A hundred bucks wasn't inconceivable as a charitable donation, but one hundred thousand?

"He wants you to do it, right?" Lisa asked, watching her.

Slowly, Macy nodded.

"And you will?"

Macy nodded again. She had no choice. Haley meant everything to her. She could only hope Thad was right— that his money would bring them what they both wanted. Otherwise, if the bone marrow transplant didn't work, she'd be expected to give up the new baby on the heels of losing Haley.

THAT NIGHT Macy tossed and turned until she wanted to scream. The nurse had insisted she go home and get some rest, had convinced her that she'd be no good to Haley if she didn't. But sleep eluded her, despite the weariness she dragged around like an old blanket. Her shoulder ached from hauling her heavy textbooks everywhere she went, and all she could think about was Thad Winters and his offer, and what the money might do for Haley. She had to believe the bone marrow transplant would finally make her daughter well. She couldn't face the alternative.

The telephone on her nightstand glowed beneath the silver sheen of moonlight filtering in through her window. Macy knew Thad's card lay beside it, nagging at her, keeping her from relaxing enough to sleep.

Impulsively, she propped herself up and flipped on the lamp. "All right, dammit," she grumbled, squinting against the light to read the number on his card while grabbing the handset. "This is it. There'll be no going back now for either of us."

Sleep slurred Thad's voice when he finally answered. "Hello?"

"Mr. Winters?"

He seemed to come instantly awake. "Macy."

"I'm sorry to wake you, but I couldn't put my mind at ease until I accepted your offer."

She heard some rustling, as though he was sitting up or readjusting his bedding. "You're going to do it?"

"Yes."

He exhaled audibly, then silence fell for several seconds.

Macy broke it. "How soon do I go in for my physical?" she asked, wondering what the next step was. Did they sign contracts? Did she visit his doctor or hers? Did she tell Haley what she was doing or wait until the baby made itself apparent?

"I'll get you in tomorrow."

So it would be his doctor. She should have known. Of course he'd want as much control over the process as possible.

"There's only one thing," she added.

"What's that?"

"I want the money as soon as I'm pregnant. All of it. Haley needs the bone marrow transplant right away. If I miscarry or something, we'll just have to do it again."

"We'll see what the doctor says," he responded.

"Okay." She felt suddenly awkward. She was going to have this man's baby, yet she didn't know what to say next. "I'm sorry about the...the lie at the restaurant," she blurted. "I was afraid you'd turn me away. Something like that looks so bad, and I was scared for Haley—"

"I know."

"Actually, I'm sorry I went home with that guy, too. I

don't remember what happened, but I'm not proud of it.''
Macy silently cursed herself for volunteering more information than was necessary, but she couldn't seem to stop
the words. ''I've never done anything like that before. Or
since,'' she added.

''Your husband had just left.''

''Yeah. I guess my ego was still smarting from the beating it took. I mean, I lost Richard to someone in a cheer-
leading uniform, for crying out loud.''

He chuckled. ''If that's all it took, he wasn't worth keeping.''

Macy thought of that for a few seconds. Richard had
some redeeming traits. He was generally optimistic and
fun-loving, but it hadn't taken her long to get over him.
Their marriage had never been what she'd hoped it would
be, mostly because living with a man like Richard was like
trying to raise another kid. ''Maybe I did something that
made him turn to other women.''

''Don't you mean girls? There's no excuse for that.''

''She wasn't his first.''

''Some men are like that. It's not right, and it's not the
woman's fault, either.''

Macy smiled. ''The parents of the girl he ran away with
were pretty upset. She used to baby-sit for us when she was
younger. It was all horribly embarrassing.''

''I can imagine. Did they turn him in for statutory rape?''

''No. She was already a troubled teen. They made him
promise to marry her as soon as our divorce was final.
That's all.''

''Did he?''

''Yeah. I had to track him down so he could be tested
for Haley's transplant and she answered the phone. They're
living in Colorado now, where her family is originally
from, but I could hear her arguing with him in the back-

ground. I didn't get the impression things were going well.''

"It's no wonder." Thad fell silent for a moment, then, ''I take it Richard wasn't a match for Haley's transplant?''

"No, neither was anyone in his family.''

"That's too bad.''

"It is, especially because of the way genetics works. A family member has a much greater chance of being a match.''

"Did it bother you to have to talk to him again?''

"No. Since Haley's become so ill, that's all I really care about.''

"I take it he pays no child support.''

"Not much. He sent almost a thousand dollars when I told him how much the transplant would cost, but he goes from job to job and can hardly support himself, let alone help us on a regular basis.''

Thad swore softly, and Macy found it strangely comforting. Talking to him on the phone so late at night made her feel like they were the only two people on earth. There was something intimate about it, something that encouraged the sharing of secrets, or at least the honest truth.

"Don't you ever miss him?'' he asked.

"Richard? No, not anymore. Every once in a while I wish for his support to bolster Haley and me through this, but then I realize that I'm deluding myself. He doesn't do negative emotions well. If he were around, he'd be going to pieces, and I'd have to be the one supporting him. I spent the first few months after he left hating him because he could abandon his own child while she was so ill, but in retrospect I think he left because our marriage was already in trouble and he couldn't bear to watch what was happening to Haley.''

"Such a sensitive guy.''

"Sensitive, maybe, just not very strong."

"Sounds like you're better off without him."

"Yeah." She yawned and sank into her pillows. "Well, I'd better go. I have class in the morning."

"And a doctor's appointment, if I can get you in."

Macy sighed. "Right."

"I'll call them first thing and leave a message on your answering machine. Do you have a way to check it from school?"

"I do."

"Great."

"You want me to call you after I see the doctor?"

"There won't be any need. I'll be going with you."

HONKING, Macy rolled down the window of her old blue Pinto and pulled to the curb, where Thad was standing outside the doctor's office waiting for her. "I'm sorry I'm late," she said when he leaned inside. "I'd forgotten that I had a test today at school."

The scowl she'd seen from halfway down the street cleared to a degree, but he still looked tense. "No problem. I was just afraid you didn't get my message. I checked us in. Hurry, they could call your name any minute."

He directed her to the back lot, where she parked. Then he joined her as she came around the redbrick building. They walked stiffly side by side, taking care not to brush against each other or come too close. The enormity of what they were about to do nearly overwhelmed Macy again, as it had several times already that morning. They were strangers, about to create a baby! A human being! Another life! Yet they'd never so much as touched or smiled or laughed with each other.

What they were doing had to be wrong, didn't it?

Macy watched Thad from the corner of her eye, wondering what he was feeling as he strode purposefully toward the front entrance. Dressed in a crisp shirt and expensive-looking tie, he'd obviously come straight from work, though he'd left his jacket in the car or back at the office. Narrow hips, accentuated by the tailored cut of his pants, extended into long legs and leather loafers with tassels. He'd rolled up his shirtsleeves, revealing sun-bronzed fore-arms covered with a sprinkle of dark hair. His hands were large and had too many nicks and scars to look as though they belonged to a pencil-pushing ad executive, but his nails were short and clean. Macy expected him to be wear-ing a Rolex watch or some other expensive brand, but he wore a simple sports watch.

"It's on the second floor," he said, holding the door for her.

Macy glanced at the sign on the wall that listed all the offices in the building. "Are we seeing a general practi-tioner for this part?"

"No, Dr. Biden's a gynecologist. She can do the pap smear and everything else today, which will save us some time."

Pap smear? Did he just say 'pap smear?' Macy looked at him in surprise. *Since when had men become so com-fortable with this kind of stuff, so knowledgeable?* She felt sure Richard wouldn't have known a pap smear from a mastectomy, but it was the "everything else" Thad had mentioned that worried her. She'd lived a pretty tame life, sexually speaking, but after that one incident with the man from Studio 9, she had never been tested for AIDS. The thought made her uneasy.

"How did you decide on the doctor? Was this your wife's OB or something?"

He nodded, and Macy felt a prick of sadness for all he had lost. She could easily picture him escorting his wife to the bank of elevators along the far wall of the turquoise and lavender lobby, just as he was doing with her.

The bell sounded and the doors *whooshed* open as a pregnant woman, who looked almost due, waddled up from behind, along with her husband or significant other. They all entered the elevator together, and Thad punched the button for the second level, then turned to the couple. "Dr. Biden's, or another floor?" he asked.

The man put his arms around the woman and pulled her back against him. "Dr. Biden. We're gonna have our first soon."

"Congratulations."

"Do you know if it's a boy or a girl?" Macy asked.

"We weren't going to look at the ultrasound pictures, but Ronny here couldn't wait, so he looked, and then I hated being the only one who didn't know, so I looked, too." The woman gave her husband a playful punch. "It's a girl."

"What about you two? You have any kids?" the man asked.

Thad said no at the same time Macy said yes. They glanced at each other and reversed their answers, but before they could explain, the elevator arrived and disgorged them all outside the door to an office labeled Dr. Joan Biden, OB–Gyn.

"Good luck," the pair mumbled, and hurried inside, having obviously lost interest in a couple who didn't even know if they had any children.

Macy smothered a sigh and followed Thad inside. If it was this uncomfortable when she wasn't pregnant, what was it going to be like to be seen with Thad when she looked as if she had a basketball stuffed under her shirt?

A hundred grand, she silently chanted. One hundred thousand dollars for Haley's transplant. She could tolerate anything for Haley's sake. She just hoped Thad wasn't planning to accompany her to every doctor's appointment. And, oh God, what about Lamaze classes? Would he insist on those?

"Ms. McKinney?"

Macy jumped up when the nurse said her name and tried to snag the clear cup she held out before the inevitable, "We need you to give us a urine sample, please." But the words came, anyway, like a prerecorded message, and Macy felt her cheeks warm. Peeing into a cup was no big deal—except for the presence of Thad and his rapt attention. Was he going to be in the exam room when she graduated to stirrups and pelvic exams?

Refusing to look at him, Macy mumbled her compliance and ducked around the corner into the washroom. She had to talk to *Mr.* Winters about letting her do the doctor and hospital visits on her own, she decided. What if an unfamiliar nurse mistook their relationship and invited him into the delivery room? Worse, what if he *expected* to be present, to cut the cord and everything?

Suddenly, Macy realized there were a lot of aspects about their "business" deal they had yet to discuss. Just how involved Thad planned to be was top on her list.

CHAPTER FOUR

THAD PASSED OVER a *Woman's Day, Good Housekeeping* and *McCall's* magazine in search of a *Sports Illustrated* or even a *U.S. News and World Report,* but to no avail. He finally settled for *Family Circle.*

The doctor's reception room was decorated in pink with silk flowers, a picture of a ballerina and a curio cabinet filled with Lladro. It looked more like a woman's boudoir than a doctor's office, but Thad was surprisingly comfortable in the feminine surroundings. He'd visited Dr. Biden's many times with his wife. They'd done the ultrasound here and saw their baby suck his thumb. They'd sat in the doctor's private office and discussed Valerie's due date and delivery options. They'd joked with the nurses.

After his experience at the hospital yesterday, where the memories of Valerie had crowded in so close he could barely breathe, he'd expected a return to Dr. Biden's to be painful for him. Instead, he felt the stirrings of excitement. This was the first step toward filling the vacuum Valerie's death had created.

Settling back to wait for Macy, he thumbed through several low-fat recipes without any real interest. Then he found an article on how to make Play-Doh at home, and he sat up straighter. This was valuable information. He had no intention of his child missing out on anything for lack of a mother, so he pulled out his day planner and jotted down the instructions. He found several other articles he felt would benefit him, too—"Ten Nourishing Meals Kids Love" and "The Top Family Vacations in America"—and made a mental note to subscribe to a family magazine when he got back to the office.

Thad had long since finished with *Family Circle* and moved on to *Elle*, when the nurse finally appeared.

"Mr. Winters? The doctor would like to speak with you now."

His heart skipped a beat as he stood and followed the pink-smocked woman down the twisting corridors. The exam had taken a lot longer than he'd expected. Did that mean Dr. Biden had found something wrong with Macy McKinney?

Sitting on opposite sides of a wooden desk strewn with folders and charts, Macy and the doctor were waiting for him in the small cluttered office Thad had visited before.

Macy shifted uncomfortably when he took the seat next to her but said nothing.

"I can't believe I let you talk me into this, Thad," Dr. Biden said, giving him a rueful smile.

Thad grinned at the middle-aged doctor. "You felt sorry for me, remember?"

"I still feel bad about what happened to Valerie, but I should have taken you more seriously when you called me a few months ago. What sounded good in theory makes me a little nervous in practice."

"Don't you think I'm ready to be a father?"

She looked at him over her wire-rimmed bifocals. "You're ready. I just don't know if the world's ready to accept your means."

"I wasn't planning on giving the world a choice. Haven't you been reading any of the latest self-help books? I'm supposed to take my destiny into my own hands, see what I want and plot the journey that will take me there."

"You sure plot a direct course," the doctor grumbled. "What happened to 'Good things come to those who wait'?"

He shrugged. "Fate hasn't been particularly kind. Forgive me if I refuse to leave my future to chance. And if you feel too much guilt or have to wrestle with your conscience, I'm sure I can find someone else who'll help me."

"I was afraid you'd say that." She sighed, and folded her long slender fingers in front of her. "All right. I'd rather be a part of the whole thing than see you go elsewhere. Call me a sentimental fool, but after spending nearly eight months with you and Valerie, I want to see you happy. I just hope this does the trick."

Happy? Thad knew that having a child would never ensure his own happiness. There'd be good times. There'd be bad. He just needed to forge some kind of bond with the living before he drifted through any more days without caring about anything.

"How did the physical go?" he asked, noting Macy's silence.

"Other than being a little run-down, Ms. McKinney seems to be in perfect health. I've given her some prenatal vitamins she's going to start taking right away, which should help build up her blood. Of course the results of the lab work won't be back for a few days, so I'll know more then, but everything looks good."

Thad wondered how much personal information Macy had shared with the doctor. From Biden's manner, he doubted she'd mentioned Haley's illness, but the way Macy kept glancing at her watch told him that her daughter was very much on her mind. He needed to get Macy on her way. "If everything turns out all right, what's our next step?" he asked, rising.

"We need to set an appointment coinciding with Macy's

ovulation. You can come at the same time and donate the sperm. We'll treat the semen with a solution that sort of turbo-charges it, then we'll do the insemination. Fortunately neither of you have a history of infertility, so I doubt we'll have to do it more than once. You're not having any problems with impotency or anything, are you?"

Thad had to clear his throat before he could answer, and saw Macy smile for the first time.

He focused on the doctor. "No, I...um, everything's in working order, I think. I mean, I don't have any reason to believe I won't be able to...you know."

"Okay. Have you ever had a sperm count taken?"

He shook his head.

"Well, we should do one. It's always best to know exactly what we're dealing with up front."

"Fine, great. Just say when." He took a deep breath and shot another glance at Macy, whose mood appeared to have miraculously improved in the past thirty seconds.

"Is that painful?" Macy asked innocently, just when he thought the doctor was going to let him off the hot seat. "The sperm count, I mean?"

"No, not at all," Biden replied.

"How, exactly, does it work?"

Thad wanted to roll his eyes. Macy was in med school, for Pete's sake. She was doing this to bait him. But Dr. Biden took the question at face value. She launched into a full explanation of the sperm recovery process, and thanks to Macy's probing questions, left nothing out—including the little room stocked with girlie magazines where he'd be expected to provide a sample.

The details embarrassed him enough to make him sweat. He loosened his tie, waiting for the doctor to come to a conclusion, then took Macy by the arm. "Call me when you get the lab results,'' he said, and dragged her out before she could ask anything else.

"THAT WAS FUN," Thad muttered when the elevator doors closed, sealing them off from the rest of the world.

Macy smiled her toothiest smile. "I thought so."

"And you wanted to make me squirm because…"

"Because misery loves company, of course. Why should I be the one to suffer all the indignities?"

"Hmm, that would probably take a rocket scientist to figure out, but let me take a stab at it—because you're the one who's getting paid for it?"

Macy's eyebrows rose at the sarcasm in his voice. "So the implacable Thad Winters doesn't like suffering indignities, huh? Well, I figured it out. You think you're paying me so incredibly well, but actually I'm only making $15.43 an hour. And that includes nothing for the pain of childbirth."

"But I bet it does include nights when you'll be doing nothing but sleeping. Am I right?"

"Obviously you've never been pregnant. It's not easy to sleep when you're pregnant."

The elevator doors opened and they headed through the lobby and out into the mellow noon sun. Salt Lake had its share of snow in winter, but its gentler seasons couldn't be more temperate or beautiful.

When they reached her car, Thad leaned against the driver's-side door to prevent Macy from opening it. "So what's your point?" he asked.

"My point is, you're not doing me some big favor."

"I thought we both understood the favor was mutual. Where else are you going to get the money, Macy?"

Macy ran a hand through her hair, disgruntled that she liked the way her name sounded on Thad's lips; he said it in such a casual way, as though they knew each other well. For all his preoccupation with having a baby in this unconventional way, she found him attractive. And that made her more nervous and cross than anything else. "I have no other options. You know that."

"Then we're in this together, right?"

She nodded. "Yeah, we're just two peas in a pod."

He grinned, transforming his face into a boyish version of himself, and Macy had the sudden impulse to duck into her car, peel away and not look back. She'd thought he was handsome with a scowl. Heaven help her if he smiled very often.

"It won't be as bad as you think," he promised.

"How do you know?"

"Because we're going to work together to make sure it isn't."

"Giving the team a little pep talk, eh, Coach?" she asked, unconvinced.

"I'll give the team whatever it needs, just so long as I can depend on you. You're not going to back out on me, right, Macy? If the lab results come back clean, you'll see this through?"

Macy stared into sky-blue eyes, alight with Thad's peculiar brand of intensity, and nearly swayed toward him. She needed to feel a pair of masculine arms around her, wanted the embrace of a mature man with strength to spare. But now wasn't the time or the place to succumb to primal urges. Thad might have the strength and maturity she craved, but their initial interview had been enlightening enough to tell her one thing for certain: he was in love with a ghost.

Standing straighter, she vowed to keep shouldering her load on her own, like the trouper everyone said she was. "I'm in it for the long haul," she promised, partly because her love for Haley would allow nothing else, and partly because she was hoping he'd smile again.

In that, he accommodated her. "That's better," he said, and stepped away so she could go. But Macy had the sneaking suspicion he'd just drawn her a little farther into his web, and he knew it.

"WHAT ARE YOU still doing at the office?" Kevin demanded, sticking his head into the room. "It's after midnight."

Thad pushed away from the computer and rubbed his eyes. He'd long since removed his tie, rolled up his sleeves and unbuttoned the collar of his shirt, but he longed for a pair of old jeans, a T-shirt and a greasy hamburger. "Macy McKinney needs the money right away. I'm trying to come up with an agreement that will protect my interests if I give it to her."

Kevin came into the room. "So she *is* the one."

Thad nodded, his mind still submerged in the glowing text on his computer screen. "Hang on a minute."

Rolling his chair back to the keyboard, he started typing again, revising, *"Macy McKinney, hereinafter known as 'Birth mother' hereby agrees to appear at each and every doctor's appointment scheduled for the upkeep and maintenance of the pregnancy,"* to *"Macy McKinney, hereinafter known as 'Birth mother' hereby agrees to allow Thad Winters to accompany her to each and every doctor's appointment scheduled for the upkeep and maintenance of the pregnancy."*

There, that ought to keep him informed of what was going on, he thought. He'd hear the heartbeat, see the ultrasound, make sure Macy was gaining enough weight.

But doctor's appointments were only once a month. How could he ensure she'd look after herself during the other times? He couldn't exactly specify how often she had to eat and rest, could he? He considered inserting a clause on basic health care, wondering if she'd agree to a stipulation that she exercise half an hour every day, when Kevin cleared this throat.

Thad looked up to find his partner reading over his shoulder.

"You're kidding, right?"

"No. Why would I be?"

"You're going to hand the woman a hundred thousand dollars, have her sign this contract and expect a baby in nine months?"

Thad scowled at the censure in Kevin's voice. "Not exactly in that order. I'm going to make sure she's pregnant first, have her sign the contract, then give her the money."

"And after she signs it, are you going to pinkie-swear, too? What do you do if she breaks your little contract? Say she miscarries and refuses to be inseminated again. Or she changes her mind, for whatever reason, and aborts the baby. You can't exactly sue her. Think about it. You don't have a legal contract. Last I checked, you couldn't 'sell' a baby in America. That doesn't mean it doesn't happen, but it does means any contract trying to enforce your rights won't be worth the paper it's written on. She'll end up with the money, and you'll end up with nothing."

Thad stretched his neck, trying to relieve the tension that had built up in his shoulders. Kevin was right about the contract. Deep down, he'd known it all along. But he'd slogged through the verbiage of what he'd like to guarantee, purposely ignoring the harsher reality. Because he *was* going to give Macy the money. He couldn't do anything else, would never risk her daughter's life by demanding she perform first.

"Bottom line, the money's your only guarantee, buddy,"

Kevin continued. "You should work it out to where she gets very little until the baby is born."

"And if she needs to pay for a bone marrow transplant for her little girl, who is lying in a hospital right now, dying of cancer?" Thad asked.

Kevin stared at him. "So *that's* why she came."

"Right again."

His partner shook his head. "You're screwed."

"Not yet."

"You are if you're going to rely on a written contract to get what you want."

"That might be true." Thad massaged his temples. Another thought had flitted through his mind while he'd been working on the contract, but he'd resisted it. It returned to haunt him now. It wasn't a guarantee exactly, but was probably the closest he was going to get.

"There is another way," he said slowly, the idea taking more definite shape in his mind. "It comes with its own share of risks, but..."

Kevin shifted his weight. "You're making me nervous, friend. You're already in this thing over your head."

"Then I'd better start swimming." Thad gave Kevin a rueful smile and snapped off his computer. "And I think I just figured out how."

Kevin groaned. "God, Thad, tell me it's the backstroke."

"Not even close."

MACY WAS EXHAUSTED. She'd originally planned to finish out the block so she didn't fall behind in her classes, but finals were only three weeks away and she didn't dare take the time away from Haley to study.

Neither could she fail, not if she wanted to become a pediatrician someday.

Setting her keys on a side table in her living room, she

punched the Play button on her recorder and listened to Lisa tell her, in no uncertain terms, to eat the Chinese food she'd dropped off earlier. The next call was from her mother. Where was she? Why didn't she keep in closer touch?

Her mother knew she couldn't afford the long-distance bills.

The last message was from Dr. Biden's office. The lab results were in. Everything had come back normal.

Well, she wasn't going to die of AIDS, at least.

Macy kicked off her shoes and sagged onto the couch, too tired to even consider heating up something from the refrigerator. She hoped Dr. Biden's vitamins were as good as the doctor claimed, because she'd given her body little else in the past twenty-four hours. What she needed more than food was sleep, but she was too keyed up. They hadn't been able to find a bone marrow donor yet, and they had to have a near-perfect match or Haley's body would reject the new stem cells. And she'd be worse off than before.

The telephone rang, but Macy just looked at it, too tired to haul herself up to answer.

The recorder came on, and Thad's voice carried into the room. "Macy? I haven't heard from you for the past two days. Is everything okay? Call me when you get a chance."

He hung up just as Macy threw a pillow at the machine and nearly knocked over the lamp. She and Thad needed to talk, but she didn't want to talk to him tonight. She could take only so much in a single day.

Climbing to her feet, she traipsed into the bedroom and brushed her teeth before pulling on her nightgown and climbing into bed.

At least when Richard ran off, he left her with the few pieces of furniture they'd acquired during their marriage. She still had the oak dining set, the sofa and an old recliner in the living room, Haley's white bedroom set, a pull-out

couch in the den and a queen-size water bed for herself.
They were all garage-sale items, but the house she was
renting made up for the style and elegance its furnishings
lacked. She lived in the Avenues, near the university, where
the houses were all unique, old and charming. Some dated
back to the 1800s. Tall, shady trees lined the streets, and a
mansion that had once belonged to Brigham Young or another of the city's founding fathers sat on almost every
corner. Macy longed for the day when she could buy one
of the large Victorians she liked best and remodel it to suit
her tastes.

Someday, when she was a doctor and Haley was well...
For now she liked her old-fashioned little house.

The phone rang again, and Macy picked it up without
thinking. "Hello?"

"There you are. You had me worried. Is Haley okay?"

Thad again. Macy bit back a sigh and cursed the brain
synapse that had shot her hand out for the receiver. "She'd
be better if we could find a bone marrow donor, but she's
hanging on while we look."

"Can anyone do it?"

"It's not like giving blood. It's painful, and it's difficult
to find a perfect match."

"Can I be tested?"

"Sure, but you'll have to fill out a questionnaire. Have
you had unprotected sex in the past ten years?"

"God, you love turning the tables on me, don't you?"

"I'm sorry. I'm tired."

"I can hear it in your voice. How's school?"

"I missed another one of my classes today but at least I
made it to pharmacology. I'm not sure I'll remember anything about the lecture, but I took enough notes to give my
hand a permanent cramp." She stretched her right fingers,
remembering her frenetic pace.

"What about the class you missed?"

"I bummed the notes off a fellow student."

"That's good."

"It's better than nothing. Finals are coming up."

"I bet you're excited about that."

"I would be if I thought I was going to pass," she said, but she didn't want to talk about school. "Will you really come in and be tested as a donor for Haley?" She knew the chances of Thad's being a match were one in a million. All of Haley's friends and family had been tested, with no luck. But it felt good to know he was willing to do what he could.

"Of course. Maybe if I go through a little pain and suffering of my own, you'll feel better compensated for childbirth."

Macy smiled, and climbed out of bed to open the window. A cool spring breeze stirred the curtains and ruffled her hair. "A woman would be untrue to her kind if she didn't point out that there is nothing as bad as childbirth, but I'm grateful, so I'll keep my mouth shut."

"I appreciate that, though I'd argue for circumcision as a close second."

The scent of lilac filtered in from the bushes in back, and Macy relaxed on her bed, letting the down comforter swallow her. "You'd have a hard time getting any support for that argument. Newborn boys don't have much of an advocacy group, while we woman are a vocal and determined lot. We're not about to lose any praise for our high pain threshold."

He chuckled. "Then I won't upset the balance by disagreeing. When can we get together? There are some things we need to talk about."

Macy yawned. "I know."

"Tomorrow?"

Fighting the increasing weight of her eyelids, she struggled to vocalize a reply. Sleep beckoned and she sank into it, despite Thad's voice in her ear. "Macy?"

"Tomorrow's...fine."

"Go ahead and get some sleep then," he said, and strangely enough the sound of his voice was like a kiss on the forehead, soothing her into unconsciousness.

MACY AWOKE to the sound of sizzling bacon and the mouthwatering aroma of potatoes and onions. *Oh good. Richard's making breakfast for Haley. I can sleep a little later.*

Richard! What was she thinking?

Macy shot out of bed as reality came crashing down on her addled mind like fifty tons of brick. She had classes today. Had she overslept? Would she have time to stop by the hospital and say hello to Haley, as she always did?

She shot a fearful glance at her alarm clock, which registered a mere six o'clock, and groaned. The buzzer wasn't even supposed to go off until six-thirty. So who the heck was in her kitchen, banging around?

Lisa, of course. Somehow she knew Macy hadn't eaten last night, and this was her revenge. Lisa knew everything.

After stumbling into the bathroom and brushing her teeth, she made her way to the kitchen, yawning and scratching her tousled head. "Jeez, Lisa, the least you could have done was warn me. Then I could have told you that I didn't eat the Chinese food because I'd grabbed something at the hospital cafeteria."

So what if it was only an apple.

"Lisa?"

"Good morning." Thad stepped around the corner into the hallway wearing a T-shirt, a pair of worn, snug-fitting blue jeans—and a smile that could melt butter from a mile away. "Have a seat. Breakfast will be ready in a minute."

CHAPTER FIVE

"HOW DID YOU get in here?" Macy demanded, anger chasing the dust and cobwebs of sleep away.

Looking shamefaced, Thad frowned. "You said we could talk today."

"I don't remember inviting you over for breakfast. And I certainly didn't give you permission to break into my house." She shoved a hand through her hair, ignoring the fact that she was standing, barefoot and wearing an old, rather prudish hand-me-down nightgown of her mother's in front of one of the most handsome men she'd ever met. "Because I agreed to have your baby, you think you own every minute of my life until the baby is born? Wrong! That's not what you're paying me for, Mr. Winters. What you get for your money is a child, not nine months of absolute control over me and my time."

He rested his hands on his hips and studied her for a moment. "Is that your last word on the matter?"

"Yes!"

"Damn, there goes the daily-exercise clause."

"The what? What did you just say?"

He chuckled and turned back to the kitchen and the bacon sizzling there. She followed him.

"Don't get all worked up, Macy. I was afraid I'd miss you if I didn't come early, and when I couldn't rouse you at the door, I checked under the mat. The key lying there was like an invitation to come in. You really should hide it somewhere else.''

"God, now I know how the average burglar justifies breaking and entering," she complained.

"The average burglar doesn't fix you breakfast. Surely that's a sign I come in peace.''

"I'd rather sleep than eat. You just robbed me of half an hour," she said, but she had to admit that the food smelled particularly good. When was the last time she'd eaten something for breakfast that hadn't come out of a box?

His smile grew crooked. "Don't worry. I've created a schedule for you that includes daily naps.''

Macy ground her teeth. "You're kidding, right? What planet are you from? Didn't you hear what I just said?''

"Hey, I'm not trying to control you. I'm just being help-ful," he said, turning the bacon.

"You're protecting your investment. Don't cloak it as something noble.''

"Maybe, but I've done quite a bit of reading, and all the specialists agree that it's important for a pregnant woman to get enough sleep. And exercise," he added, glancing quickly at her face as if to gauge her reaction.

"That isn't exactly late-breaking news. But in case you've forgotten, I'm in med school. I have finals in three weeks, and I have a daughter who's fighting for her life at Primary Care Hospital. The last thing I have time for is a nap.''

Captivated by the food in spite of herself, Macy came up behind him to see what he had cooking on the stove. She found a pan on every burner: fried potatoes, pancakes, eggs and, of course, bacon. She hadn't been grocery shop-ping in weeks. He must have brought the food with him.

"Have you invited friends?" she asked as he flipped a

large golden pancake. "Who do you think is going to eat all of this?"

"A pregnant woman is supposed to have four servings of—"

Macy held up a hand. "Stop! Don't say it. I'm not pregnant yet."

"It's important that you build up your strength. You've been running on empty too long." His gaze drifted down over her nightgown, all the way to her bare toes. "Don't you think you should get dressed?"

She gave him a saucy toss of her head. "You're the one who broke into my house. What did you expect? That I'd be showered and ready for the day at 6:00 a.m.? Or does seeing a woman in her nightgown make you uncomfortable?"

"Only when it's as alluring as the one you've got on now," he said, but he couldn't keep a straight face, and Macy had to laugh with him.

"Okay, so they're not going to ask me to be on the cover of the next Victoria's Secret catalog."

"I was making fun of the nightgown, not what's underneath."

Macy wondered if that meant he liked her figure. Then she told herself it didn't matter, anyway. The few curves she had left would soon be distorted by the pregnancy. In nine months, Thad would have his baby, and she'd be left with the physical and emotional wreckage.

"I need to ask you something," he said, reaching into her cupboard for two plates.

"The blood work came back. Everything's fine," she told him.

He threw her a glance over his shoulder. "That's great. But what I want to know is a little more personal."

Macy responded with a snort and took a seat at the table,

where a glass of orange juice was waiting for her. "What could that fifty-pound questionnaire of yours have missed?"

"I'd like to get a better understanding of your love life," he said, sliding a plate of food in front of her.

"Love life? Doesn't my nightgown say it all?"

He grinned. "A man wouldn't need much of an imagination to picture what you've got under that schoolmarm nightgown. A few more pounds and you'd have a knockout figure."

Macy's cheeks grew hot. Fortunately, Thad seemed as embarrassed by what he'd said as she was. He turned his back on her and prepared his own plate, then kept his gaze on his food as he sat down across from her to eat.

She sampled her scrambled eggs and found them unusually good. "All right. Ask me anything. You already know about that guy from Studio 9. How much worse can it get?"

He took a swallow of his orange juice. "Are you interested in anyone in particular? Is there a boyfriend, or someone else, who might object to what we plan to do?"

"No."

"You're not carrying a torch for someone?"

"Do you mean Richard? Are you asking if I still have feelings for him?"

"From what I've gathered, he was popular, well liked in college. There had to be some reason you fell in love with him."

"I fell in love with his boyish charm and his easy smile and his optimism. Unfortunately, once we were married, I realized that wasn't enough. I wanted someone with a little more depth of character and grew disenchanted before he ever left. I'm not holding a torch for him."

"And there's no one else? I won't be stepping on any

toes in the next few months or messing up a relationship that's important to you?''

''I'm not in love, and I don't see myself getting involved with anyone in the foreseeable future.''

''Because of what your ex did?''

''Isn't that reason enough?'' To her complete surprise, Macy finished the last of the food on her plate and sat back, feeling better than she had in weeks, despite Thad's probing.

''You don't seem like the type to judge all men by Richard's actions.''

''I'm not. I just have my hands full right now. I mean, where would I meet someone? In the oncology department at the hospital? All of Haley's doctors are married, or they're a good twenty or thirty years older than me, and they're the only ones I really talk to.''

''You could meet someone on campus. Wouldn't your life be easier if you had a partner to come home to?''

She finished the last of her juice. ''Not if I was pregnant with your child. That kind of thing could get a bit awkward, don't you think? Especially if you plan on breaking into my house on a regular basis. What would I tell my boyfriend? 'Oh, don't mind him. He just stopped by to make sure I'm eating the recommended daily allowance.'''

Macy glanced at the clock over the stove. ''I've got to get in the shower,'' she said. ''I know we haven't covered everything, but we'll have to talk later. I have lab today, and I want to stop by the hospital. If you'll just pile the dishes in the sink, I'll do them when I get home as my contribution to this little party. Then I'll call you.''

''Wait.'' Thad caught her by the wrist. ''I'm actually going somewhere with all this.'' He let her go, looking distinctly uncomfortable as he glanced out the window, then back up at her face. "I want to give you the money, up front, for Haley…"

"That's the only way I'll go through with the insemination," she said, still holding her plate.

"I know, but it's foolish of me to take that risk. The money is my only security. What if…" He ran a hand through his hair. "Well, let's just say there are a lot of things that could go wrong."

"You don't think I'll come through if Haley dies," she said, unable to hide her pain. That he thought Haley might die made it all the more possible, for some reason. He was just one more person who had no faith, while she was counting on a miracle.

"There are other things that could go wrong, too." His voice was gentle, and so was the look in his eyes, but his words scared Macy. She had to have the money, and she had to have it soon.

"What if I give you my word?"

"In a perfect world, that would be good enough, but I'm afraid…"

"I know. We're virtually strangers. Considering that, you'd be unwise to trust me. So—" she took a deep breath "—what do you suggest?"

"Another business arrangement, one that would give me a small degree of protection."

Macy felt a moment's trepidation, but she had to ask. "What is it this time?"

"I want you to marry me."

THAD WATCHED several emotions flicker across Macy's face, surprise, incredulity, anger, but before she could settle on one and reject him, he added, "There would be a lot of benefits to the arrangement, for both of us. Before you say anything, just hear me out."

"No."

"No, you won't hear me out? Or, no, you won't marry me?"

"No, period. Our 'arrangements' have gone far enough. Don't you understand that what you want, what we're doing, makes a mockery of everything I believe in? You've reduced love, marriage and family to…to this. To nothing but emotionless agreements and practical considerations."

Thad flinched. Love, marriage and family were just as sacred to him, maybe more so. That was why he was trying so hard to preserve a vestige of what he'd had with Valerie. But he couldn't explain that to Macy, or anyone else, for that matter. It exposed a part of him that was wounded and raw with need, a result of the pain, betrayal and anger he felt at his wife's death.

"Think of the baby," he said, stepping back from the flame of those dark emotions. "If we marry, the baby will have my name. And since I will be its father, what could be more natural than that?"

She'd gone to the sink to rinse off her plate. When she spoke, her back was to him. "And how do I explain our relationship to Haley?"

"I've met Haley already. We simply tell her that we've fallen in love and are going to be married. Think about it, Macy. I've gone over every angle, and this is by far the best way for everyone involved. If we don't marry, what will you tell your daughter about the pregnancy? That it was the water?"

Her shoulders slumped as though she was suddenly weary again, but after a moment, she stood straight and turned to face him. "And when you disappear from our lives and take her brother or sister with you, do I simply say that it's nothing? Just one more man who doesn't want us?"

A normal man would be crazy not to want Macy, Thad thought. She was bright, ambitious, determined, full of passion. And he'd never seen a more beautiful woman. For the first time since his wife's death, he'd actually felt the stirrings of desire when he saw her this morning, braless and without makeup, her hair mussed from sleep. It was probably just his body's way of reminding him how long it had been since he'd held a woman in his arms. But he had felt...something.

"We'll cross that bridge when we come to it," he said, not wanting to address the issue of divorce right now, when Macy was gazing at him with those incredible eyes. "A lot has to go right before we get that far."

She glanced at the clock again, as though she wished she could turn back the hands, then pinched the bridge of her nose. "So we'd be married, but we wouldn't live together. Is that what you're suggesting? A marriage in name only?"

Thad cleared his throat, certain that Macy wasn't going to like this next part any more than she'd liked the first part. "Actually, I was thinking we would live together here, at your place. Just as roommates."

"But why? What purpose could there possibly be in— Oh, I get it." Her eyes narrowed. "We're back to protecting your investment by controlling my life."

Thad pushed his plate away and stood up. "I know this whole thing sounds terrible, Macy. I wouldn't do it if—" *if I wasn't so damn desperate* "—if I thought there was another way. But I'm not trying to control you. I just thought you could use someone to look after the house and yard a bit, make you a hot dinner on occasion, drive you to the doctor. You wouldn't have to move or change anything. Does that sound too much like torture?"

"I don't know," she said. "What I'm going through now is torture. I can't imagine it getting any worse."

"Then trust me." He smiled. "And I'll write you a check for the full amount the moment we say 'I do.'"

She sighed and shook her head. Then she kneaded her temples. "You'll sleep in the guest room," she said at last, "and pick up after yourself, and steer clear of my friends and family, and stay away from Haley. If she doesn't know you, she can't be hurt when you leave."

"Okay."

"And you're not going to watch Dr. Biden put me in stirrups. Neither are you going into the delivery room. I'll have the baby on my own, then turn it over to you."

"But I want to see my baby being born."

"Sorry, that's the deal," she snapped. "You can take it or leave it. It's up to you."

Because of Haley, Thad knew, if he pushed, he could have it all. Macy was bluffing. The businessman in him, the negotiator, told him so. But the courage shining in her eyes, and the sacrifice she was willing to make for her daughter softened his heart. In that moment, his respect for her grew.

"That's good enough," he said, and once the words were out, he couldn't take them back. An agreement was an agreement. The businessman in him said that, too.

He could only hope she'd relent.

"YOU'RE WHAT?"

Macy held the phone away from her ear to avoid her mother's bloodcurdling screech. She was on campus, in between classes, with a flood of other students milling around, six of whom were in line to use the pay phone after she finished. "I'm getting married," she repeated.

Shocked silence greeted her on the other end of the line as Edna absorbed the news, then, "But this is so sudden. You've never mentioned dating anyone. Who is he?"

Macy watched the trees dotting the rolling campus sway in the wind that funneled down from the canyons above. "His name is Thad Winters," she said, pushing her hair back, out of her face. "He's an ad executive here in Salt Lake."

"Is he successful?"

"Mom, why would that be one of the first questions you ask? Does it really matter?"

"You don't think it's important, dear, after Richard?"

Macy chuckled. "I see your point. Okay, I think he's successful. He has some nice office space on South Temple."

"He has what?" her mother asked in surprise, and Macy wished she could take back her words. How odd it must sound for her to talk about his office, instead of something more personal, like his home. "Where does he live?"

He could live in South Jordan, Murray, Ogden, Sugarhouse, anywhere in the Salt Lake Valley, for all Macy knew. She hadn't seen him since he'd made her breakfast the day before, and she hadn't thought to ask him on the telephone last night when they'd set the date for their wedding. "Um, in a nice house," she replied vaguely.

"So you and Haley will be moving in with him?"

"No, he'll be moving in with us."

"But your house is so small. What if you decide to have more children?"

"That's a very good possibility. He really wants a baby." At least that was God's own truth.

"Right away?"

Macy nearly laughed at the question. They were getting married next Saturday, and she was being artificially inseminated the following week. "I think so, yeah."

"Then why keep your house?"

"It has charm."

"And probably termites."

"I like it," Macy replied. "It's close to school and the hospital. Do you know how hard it is to get a rental up here?" Her mother didn't share her taste for old architecture. Edna liked the new ranch-style homes they had in Las Vegas, where she lived, but Macy refused to let her mother convince her to move out of the Avenues, old plumbing and electrical be damned.

"Listen, Mom, I have to go. There are people waiting to use the phone."

"But you haven't even given me the date and time of the wedding, or where it's going to be."

And you haven't mentioned when you might be coming to town to see Haley. Typical. "It's going to be in your neck of the woods, actually. We were hoping you could be there."

"You're coming to Vegas to get married?"

"Yeah, next Saturday. Our plane gets in around nine in the morning. We'll come by or call you when we get there. It all depends on how Haley is doing and whether we'll be in a huge rush or not."

Silence.

"Hello? Mom, did you hear me?"

"Macy, are you pregnant?"

"No." *Not yet, anyway,* she silently added, and relinquished the phone.

"DON'T LOOK AT ME like that. You're the one who got me into this," Macy told Lisa, who was sitting on her couch, drinking a large Coke and finishing the rest of a McDonald's Combo Meal.

"I told you to have Thad's baby and get paid for doing it, so you could help Haley. I didn't tell you to marry him. That's crazy. What are you going to do after the baby?"

"Uncontested divorce. And I'll have to sign over full custody, of course."

Lisa's breath hissed through her teeth. "I thought you guys were going to stay out of each other's personal lives."

"I guess we've decided that if we're going to have a baby together, there's just no practical way to keep our distance, not with Thad giving me the money up front. Having me marry him makes him feel more secure. Anyway, he has a point about the baby not being born a bastard. I'll have a name to put on the birth certificate, and I won't have to write 'single' on every form the doctor or hospital hands me."

"So he'll be living here?" She used a french fry to motion at the cramped but comfortable living room.

"Yeah, it's a point in his favor that he doesn't expect me to uproot myself, not with Haley in the hospital."

"Well, I think he sounds like a nice guy."

"We'll see if you still think so in nine months."

Feeling a pang of hunger at the smell of Lisa's food and regretting her decision not to get something when they went to McDonald's after leaving the hospital, Macy kicked off her shoes and wandered into the kitchen. "Do you want any ketchup for those fries?" she called.

"No, I'm almost done."

Macy opened the refrigerator to survey her meager possibilities, and stiffened in surprise when she found it teeming with food. Fresh fruits and vegetables filled the drawers, a gallon of milk and a gallon of freshly squeezed orange juice sat side by side, and lunch meat, a loaf of whole-wheat bread, a large, ready-made salad and a giant jar of pickles were arranged neatly on the shelves. A note was taped to the milk, written in a bold masculine hand, outlining the nutritional requirements of an expectant mother.

"Damn him!"

"Who?" Lisa followed her into the kitchen, her wrappers and McDonald's sack crackling as she wadded them up for disposal.

"Thad Winters."

"What's he done now?"

Macy pushed the refrigerator door open wider so Lisa could see for herself.

"What a jerk!" she exclaimed. "He went and bought you at least a hundred dollars' worth of groceries. I can't think of anything worse."

Rolling her eyes, Macy slammed the fridge door. "It's the fact that he stocked my fridge without asking me. Doesn't that strike you as a rather personal, not to mention, controlling, thing to do? He has no right to do stuff like that."

"I'd call him on it, if I were you," Lisa teased.

"This isn't funny. I don't think he should feel so free to make himself comfortable here."

"He's going to be living here in a few days!"

"That's just it. He's not living here yet. I still have five days. And I want every one of them." She turned her back on the offending refrigerator and reached above the sink to make herself a cup of coffee, but she found a note there, too. "Caffeine causes birth defects," it said in big block letters.

Lisa started laughing so hard she had to sit down.

"I can't believe you," Macy complained. "You've been on his side from the beginning."

"I'd love to see what he's done to the liquor cabinet."

"You know I don't have a liquor cabinet. The most I ever drink is an occasional glass of wine."

"Then tell him you have some Jack Daniel's stashed away and let him knock himself out trying to find it. That would be a fitting revenge, don't you think?"

The telephone rang, but Macy made no move to answer it. At this hour, it had to be Thad…or the hospital. Her heart skipped a beat at the second possibility, and she dived for the receiver. "Hello?"

"Macy?"

Thad. She made a face into the phone, but was actually grateful it wasn't the hospital. "I see you've been in my house again."

"You had nothing but baking soda in your fridge. How can a person survive on baking soda?"

"Okay, that's it." Macy set the phone on the table and marched through the living room to the front door, where she promptly removed the spare key from under the mat and shoved it into the pocket of her jeans.

"Hello? Macy?" Thad was saying when she picked up the phone again.

"I'm back."

"Where did you go?"

"To remove your invitation to enter my house."

He whistled. "It's a good thing I know you like me. Otherwise, my feelings might get hurt."

"Yeah, you sound pretty broken up."

His laugh rumbled in her ear, and she pictured him lying back in an easy chair, watching the television she heard droning in the background. "I guess I called at a bad time. I just wanted to see if you'd like to go with me when I buy your ring tomorrow. I mean, you're the one who has to wear it for nine months."

"No." He was buying her a ring? Macy hadn't even thought about those kinds of details. Was there something she should be doing to prepare for Saturday? How far were they going to take this sham of a marriage? "I have to study for finals," she said, letting go of some of her anger.

"So, any kind of ring is fine?"

"Just get me a cheap band. I don't care what it looks like."

"Okay. I'll call you tomorrow."

"No, don't. We can talk about whatever else we need to talk about on our way to Vegas. My mother is planning on attending the ceremony, by the way."

"That should prove interesting. Anyone else?"

"No. She and Haley are the only family I have, besides a bunch of cousins who live in Oregon. I doubt any of them are going to want to fly down for a pretend wedding, but I had to invite my mother. Occasionally she drives out here to see Haley, not as often as you might think a grandmother would come to see her sick granddaughter, I might add, but I didn't want her to land on our doorstep one day to find me married and expecting."

"Right. Well, I'll let you get some sleep."

"I'm not going to bed yet, Thad. I'll stay up all night, if I want to," Macy said, bristling again.

He chuckled. "Take it easy. I wasn't ordering you to bed."

"Just like you're not ordering me to eat plenty of fresh fruits and vegetables and to stay away from caffeine? Lisa and I were just saying what a good thing it is that you didn't find the booze I have stashed away."

"What booze?"

It was Macy's turn to laugh. "If you had a key, you could let yourself in and find out. Good night!"

"Good girl," Lisa said when she hung up. "I bet he's shaking his head right now, thinking he'd better give you your space."

"Oh, yeah? I bet he's plotting another break-in," Macy replied sourly.

CHAPTER SIX

AN HOUR LATER, after Lisa left, Macy called Thad back.

He groaned as he answered. "Macy? You didn't call just to wake me up, did you?"

She piled her pillows high and laid back in her bed, pulling the comforter to her chin. "No, but there's an idea."

"Not a very good one."

"Because pregnant women need their rest?"

"Because hardworking ad executives do. What is it?"

Macy fidgeted with the curly telephone cord and stared at the ceiling, noting a few cobwebs that needed to be wiped away. Everything needed to be cleaned. She hadn't had much time for housework during the past few months. But it was eleven now, past the time to worry about such things, especially when she couldn't unwind enough to sleep as it was. "Where do you live?" she asked him.

"Why? Are you planning some sort of revenge?"

"Maybe."

"Then I'd like my refrigerator stocked with beer, pizza and ice cream."

"You didn't put any of those things in my fridge."

"I'm not the one who looks like I'll blow away in the next strong wind."

Macy frowned. "Do I look that bad?"

There was a pause, and his answer when it came, was

gruffer than usual. "No. You're a beautiful woman. Surely you must know that."

Beautiful? That soothed a small place inside her. "You didn't answer my question," she reminded him, changing the subject.

"Which question was that?"

"I want to know where you live. I had to tell my mother you have nice office space because I couldn't say anything about your house. I don't even know what part of town you live in."

"I live on Mount Olympus."

Mount Olympus was full of nice older homes, not nearly as old as those in the Avenues, but most of them dated back to the 1970s. A few were new, built on in-fill lots. All were pressed into the side of the Wasatch Mountains. After a heavy snowfall, it sometimes took a vehicle with four wheel drive to reach the higher streets.

"So you live in a house as opposed to a condo or an apartment?"

"Right, but can we talk about my house tomorrow, preferably when I'm awake?"

"You're going to call me, after all?"

"No, I'm going to come pick you up so you can help select your ring."

"I thought I told you no about that."

"*No*'s not one of my favorite words. Just bring your schoolbooks. I'll quiz you in the car."

Macy hesitated. "I don't know…I don't want to leave Haley. I usually study there at the hospital."

"I'll bring you to my house afterward. You'll be able to describe it to your mother in detail."

Edna could call any day. Macy thought it best to be prepared. "Okay," she relented. "Pick me up at the hospital at four. Since we're going to be married, maybe it wouldn't hurt to let Haley see you hanging around a time or two."

"Have you told her yet?"

"No."

"Do you want some help?"

The worry of how Haley might react to the sudden appearance of a man in her life had kept Macy from saying anything so far, but time was growing short until the wedding. Perhaps the lie of their marriage would be more convincing if Thad was there to help break the news. After that stuffed bear he bought Haley, she might even be pleased. "Maybe we should tell her together."

"Sounds like tomorrow's going to be a busy day."

"It's not every day you try and reconstruct your fiancé's past in the space of a few hours."

"I'm a simple man," he promised. "Good night, Macy. And stop worrying, okay? Everything will be all right."

Macy had no idea how he could say that, with Haley in the hospital, losing her battle against cancer. But he seemed so confident she was almost tempted to believe him. "Do you really think so? Do you think Haley's going to make it?"

There was a long pause. "I hope so," he said.

"HELLO."

Macy looked up to see Thad standing at the entrance to Haley's hospital room, wearing a shirt and tie and double-pleated trousers. He was carrying a shopping bag from a retail store.

"You just come from work?" she asked, closing her pharmacology textbook.

"No, I stopped by Crossroads Mall first." His gaze passed over her, then centered on Haley, whose small face registered pleasant surprise. "Look, Mommy, it's Thad!"

"It is, sweetheart," she agreed. "He told me he was going to come today."

He approached the bed. "I wanted to see how you and Bruiser are getting along."

"Good!" Haley announced, putting one frail arm around the stuffed bear that still shared her bed. "He sleeps with me at night and sometimes in the day, too."

"I'm sure he likes that. I brought you something else." Thad pulled a gift-wrapped box from the bag and set it next to her.

"Another present!" she squealed in delight. "What is it?"

"Open it and see."

Smiling from ear to ear, she started tearing off the rainbow-striped paper, her pain and discomfort seemingly forgotten. "A baby doll! Look, Mommy, Thad gave me a baby doll!"

Macy smiled at her daughter's excitement and Thad's obvious pleasure at being the cause of it. "Press its tummy," he told her.

Haley obeyed, and the doll started to suck the pacifier lodged in its mouth. Her grin lit up, and she pulled the doll to her chest and hugged it tightly.

"Now you have to come up with another name, huh, Haley?" Thad suggested.

She nodded, screwing up her mouth in concentration. "I think I'll name her...Haley."

He chuckled. "At least that'll be an easy one to remember."

She pressed the doll's tummy, pulled the pacifier out, put it back in, pulled it out. While she was busy playing, Thad turned to Macy.

"You ready for this?" he murmured.

The palms of Macy's hands had grown sweaty the moment Thad had walked into the room. She wasn't ready for any of it, but Haley's cancer wasn't going to wait for a better solution. Taking a deep breath, she nodded.

"Haley?" she said, drawing her daughter's attention. "Do you think your baby can keep you company for a little bit while Thad and I go out?"

Haley's brows knitted. "Where are you going? Can I come, too?"

"You know you can't, sweetheart. The doctors won't let you leave the hospital just yet, not until you're well. But we won't be gone long, and Lisa said she'd come be with you. She should be here any minute."

"But where are you going?"

"We're going to a jewelry store to pick out a pretty ring for me."

"A ring?" She looked from Macy to Thad in consternation.

Thad reached out and took Macy's left hand. "This is a special ring, Haley. It's called a wedding ring, and your mommy's going to wear it on this finger here." He wiggled her third finger. "People do that when...when they get married. Do you know what that means?"

Haley's eyes rounded as she stared up at him. "Does it mean you're going to be my daddy?

Macy's gaze flew to Thad's face. He wasn't supposed to get too close to Haley. He was only temporary. But neither of them had counted on Haley's open heart and immediate acceptance.

The muscles in his jaw clenched. His Adam's apple bobbed, then he cleared his throat. "Yeah, I guess that's what it means," he said.

Dropping the doll that had moments ago meant so much to her, Haley reached both arms out for Thad, and he bent down awkwardly and accepted her tight embrace.

THAD WAS ANGRY. He tried to hold it deep inside him, the way he'd done ever since Valerie died, but after what had just happened with Haley, it was almost impossible to bury. Why he was so upset, he couldn't say, but judging from the way Macy wouldn't look at him, the rigid set of her shoulders, she was angry, too.

"I'm not sure this is going to work," he said, pulling his Lexus to the side of the road before they even reached the jewelry store. "I must have been deluding myself."

Macy fidgeted with the pocket of the cargo pants she wore with a long-sleeved jersey. "What are you talking about? Haley needs the operation. I'll make it work. I don't have a choice."

He sighed and tapped the steering wheel with his forefinger. Since the beginning, he'd wrestled with a certain amount of guilt about using Macy's desperation to get her to do something she otherwise wouldn't. He'd tried to justify it by telling himself what he wanted wouldn't hurt her or anyone else. He knew he'd be a good father to their child.

But Haley's response to him today made him face the fact that it wouldn't be as simple as he'd hoped. A child was dying, for Pete's sake! How could he take advantage of that? He'd lost his own child. He knew what it was like. "You might not have a choice, but I do."

She looked at him from beneath her long, dark lashes, and Thad marked the fear lurking there, the same fear he'd feel if Haley were his child.

"So you're going to back out? Find someone else whose situation doesn't prick your conscience?" she asked bitterly.

"Maybe someday." He shrugged. "Who knows? But that will take a while because I'm going to give you the money."

"You're what?" Her mouth dropped open and her wide eyes blinked at him.

He rubbed his chin and looked away. "I'm going to let you out of our deal, but you can have the money, for Haley."

She turned to stare out the windshield and Thad did the same. The cars whizzed past them on North Temple. It was a wide, busy street, lined with businesses on both sides. The jewelry store where he'd planned to take Macy wasn't far.

"I don't know what to say," she said at last.

"You don't have to say anything. Do you want me to take you back to the hospital?"

Thad guessed Macy was thinking about facing Haley again and having to explain why there was no ring on her finger, because she shook her head. "Just take me home," she said, and he started the car and merged back into the traffic.

THE HOUSE was so quiet he could hear the clock ticking over the fireplace. Normally Thad filled every room with sound, from the stereo or television, the second he walked through the door after work, but today he sat on the leather couch and just listened to nothing.

He'd packed up the majority of Valerie's personal items, her clothes, jewelry, perfume, things like that, and stored them away in the basement, but her touch was everywhere. They'd wallpapered the living room together. She'd chosen the furniture and created a rather rustic decor, which went well with the French doors along the back that looked out on a wide deck and the mountain beyond. She'd insisted he rip out the carpet and lay hardwood floors—something he'd never done and didn't know how to do. They'd bought the supplies and stayed up late every night for a week, figuring it out, drinking coffee, laughing at something on the television that blared over the thump of Thad's hammer—or cursing when he made a mistake and they had to rip out half the floor. He'd taken those nights for granted, never knowing how much he'd miss them.

Coming to his feet, Thad walked down the hall and opened the door to the nursery he and Valerie had furnished. It was decorated in purple, yellow and turquoise. Valerie had painted the furniture and made the drapes. He'd painted the walls and put up the molding.

Eyeing the rocking chair sitting in the middle of the floor, he wondered if he'd ever have a baby of his own. He made a good living, but one hundred thousand dollars wasn't a sum he could easily raise, not with the overhead he was carrying at the office.

At least the money might help to preserve Haley's life. He prayed it would.

The telephone rang, calling him back to the living room. "Hello?"

"Thad? It's Debra."

His sister. "Hi, Deb. What's up?"

"I'm making fajitas tonight. Just thought you might want to come over for dinner. Gary and his wife will be here."

Thad almost refused. When Valerie was alive, they'd spent a lot of time with his sister and her husband, and his brother and his wife, going out to eat, playing games, seeing movies. They only lived about twenty minutes away and seemed to fit easily into the flow of each other's busy lives. But now that he was on his own, he didn't fit in so easily anymore. And he didn't enjoy getting together with his family quite so much. It made the gap in his life seem wider, more difficult to fill. Still, he refused to sit home and continue wallowing in self-pity.

"Sure, what time?"

"Give me another hour."

"I'll be there." Fortunately, his family didn't know anything about Macy or his plans to have a baby, so there wouldn't be any uncomfortable details to explain.

MACY SAT at the kitchen table and tried to focus on her studies, but she couldn't pull her thoughts away from the check sitting in front of her. One hundred thousand dollars. Thad had written it, just as easily as though he'd made it out for a mere ten or fifteen bucks, and handed it to her as she got out of his car. Then he'd wished her well and driven off, giving Macy the impression he never expected to see her again.

She took a deep breath and let it go. He was gone. There would be no marriage, no pregnancy, no disappearing acts at the end of nine months. And Haley would have her operation—provided a donor was found. Macy should be thrilled.

Then why was she feeling so miserable?

Picking up the check, she leaned back in her chair and studied Thad's signature. Not very legible, it was nonetheless as bold and confident as he was. Yet there was kindness in him, too. How many men would have given a woman they barely know a hundred thousand dollars to save her dying child? Possibly a few of those with money to burn. But how many would sacrifice what they wanted most in order to do so?

Thad was rare, special.

Folding her arms on the table to make a pillow for her head, Macy stared across the floor at the kitchen cabinets, remembering his notes. She'd found one more under the sink, warning her about the potential dangers of using certain cleaning supplies while she was pregnant.

With a grudging smile, she crossed to the refrigerator

and stared inside it at the food. She felt guilty, and guessed that Thad regretted the day he'd met her. He wanted a baby, but that was far from what he'd gotten. One thing had led to another until he was entangled in her and Haley's lives, despite her bluntness when they first met, the fact that she'd lied on her application, and the truth about Studio 9. Thad came off as tough and in control, but considering the exceptions he'd made for her all along, he was really a softy. A big softy.

For a moment, Macy felt jealous of his dead wife, whoever she had been. To have the love, the devotion of a man like Thad Winters—what would that be like? She could only imagine. Richard's best assets were clearly visible for all to see, his handsome face, his easygoing nature. If you looked for anything deeper, you were in for a sad disappointment.

Going back to the table, Macy picked up the phone and dialed Thad's number. When he'd dropped her off, she'd been too emotional, too confused to say much. He deserved a sincere thank-you and somewhat of an apology. But when his recorder answered, what came out of her mouth surprised even her. "Let's do it," she said, and hung up.

THE TELEPHONE RANG. Thinking it was her alarm clock, Macy's hand fumbled over books and papers, searching for the shut-off switch, until she realized she was still at the kitchen table, her studies spread out before her.

"Hello?" she said, finally answering.

"Was it you who left that message on my recorder?"

"Thad?" She squinted against the overhead light to check the time on the wall clock. Almost midnight. "You didn't call just to wake me up, did you?" she asked.

"No, but there's an idea."

"Not a very good one."

"Because hardworking ad executives need their rest?"

She laughed and rubbed her face where the book she'd fallen asleep over had left an imprint on her cheek. "Because soon-to-be-pregnant women do. It's also important that they eat plenty of fresh fruits and vegetables and avoid certain cleansers. At least, those are the helpful hints someone taped up around my house."

"That someone knew what he was talking about."

"I think I'm beginning to trust him."

There was a long pause. "That's an encouraging thought. Are you serious about what you said?"

"About having the baby?"

"Yeah."

Macy bit her lip. She wasn't sure. She was probably making the biggest mistake of her life, but she couldn't accept Thad's gift without trying to give him what he wanted in return. God willing, they could both come out of this happy. And he'd make a wonderful father. At least she knew that now. "Yeah, I am," she said.

"It could get messy—for both of us."

"I know. Somehow, we'll work it out."

"What about Haley? I realized today how hard this could be on her."

"Haley has very little chance of making it," Macy admitted for the first time, squeezing her eyes closed against the pain that truth brought her. "We may not have to tell her anything. And if she does…go, at least she'll die thinking she had a dad. I didn't realize how much she missed that."

She could hear him breathing softly on the other end of the line. "So we'll just take it one day at a time?"

"That's all we can do." Macy closed her books with her free hand and stacked them neatly on the table. "What…what gender do you want, anyway? A boy? I think they can spin the sperm or something like that to improve your chances of getting what you want.''

"No. I'll be happy with either. I think I've taken enough into my own hands, don't you?''

"Probably.''

"Okay. Well, I'll see you tomorrow then. We'll go to the jewelry store.''

He hung up and Macy sat staring at the phone. He'd let her off the hook, written her a check for the full amount, but was she smart enough to leave it that way? No! She'd called him back. Now she'd be married on Saturday and pregnant by the following weekend.

With a loud groan, she smacked her forehead. What an idiot!

CHAPTER SEVEN

"JUST A PLAIN BAND. That's all I need."

Elevator music played in the background as Macy stood on the thick-piled, royal-blue carpet of Mateland's Jewelers looking at the wide variety of wedding sets in glass cases. A salesman in a suit and tie, his hair slicked back off his high forehead and a plastic smile on his face, stood behind the counter, waiting for some indication as to what might interest them.

"What kind of wedding ring did you have with Richard?" Thad asked.

Macy didn't look up. "Oh, it was gorgeous. But like him, it didn't last."

"I thought diamonds were forever."

"Not if you pawn them. I needed money for formula and diapers. Richard was between jobs again."

Thad cocked an eyebrow. "Was that the first disillusionment of your marriage?"

"Hardly," she scoffed.

"Certainly the lady deserves a very nice ring after such a bad experience," the salesman suggested in a soft British accent. "But I'm sure I won't get any argument about that out of you, will I, sir?"

Actually, Macy bet he'd get a strong argument from her *fiancé*. How much would Thad want to spend to put a ring on her finger for nine months? He was a businessman. He wouldn't want to waste money on such frills, and she highly doubted he'd fall easy prey to cheap sales tactics designed to prick his conscience into purchasing something pricey.

"What did it look like?" Thad pressed, ignoring the salesman.

"It was a large marquis, nearly a carat, on a plain gold band."

"Sounds nice."

"Yeah, but we put it on credit. I'm still paying for it."

He whistled and shook his head. "That's got to hurt."

Macy shrugged, and he moved closer, hovering over the glass. "Would you pick something similar if...you know..."

"If you could afford it?" she teased.

At this, the salesman quickly whipped out a credit application. "Money need not be an issue, sir," he said confidently. "With just a little information and nothing down, you can finance the whole thing."

"Good news, honey," Thad said, grinning. "What do you say we try this one?" He pointed to a large, pear-shaped diamond. The accompanying wedding band had small, inlaid diamonds going all the way around.

Macy raised her eyebrows. "Don't you think that's a little out of our price range, *dear?*"

"Nothing's too expensive for the woman who's going to be *my* wife," he assured her.

The salesman's eyes started to gleam. "Oh, very nice choice, sir," he said, using a key from the ring at his belt to unlock the case. "The quality of this diamond is top-notch, clearly top-notch. Just look at the clarity."

He took it from its plush velvet box and handed it to Macy. She slid the ring on her finger. It was beautiful. One of the loveliest rings she'd ever seen. "How much?" she asked, awestruck despite the practical impossibility.

"Don't worry about price. You leave that up to me," Thad said with a wink.

He was certainly doing a good job of pretending to be the devoted fiancé, but Macy couldn't quite believe he'd go to so much effort for the sake of a salesman they'd likely never see again.

"Do you mind telling me what kind of game you're playing?" she whispered when the salesman stepped away to answer the phone. "Why aren't we looking at *plain* wedding bands? Are you *trying* to disappoint me? 'Oh look, honey, isn't this beautiful? We'll take the simple band, please.'"

He smiled. "It's no game. I'm just looking for some leverage, that's all."

"What kind of leverage? What are you talking about?"

"I want to be part of the birth."

"No! I already told you no!" She took off the ring and set it on the counter.

"But 'no' sounds so final—"

"And it's not your favorite word, I know. I'm sure you're in good company, but that's my answer."

He picked up a simple, inexpensive gold band and put it in one palm, the pear-shaped diamond in the other. Moving his hands up and down like a scale, he said, "He comes to the birth," and raised the diamond. "He doesn't come to the birth," and raised the band. "Not a difficult decision, huh?"

Macy propped her hands on her hips. "I can't believe this. Here I was, thinking you were an okay guy, but you're a creep. You're trying to buy your way into my delivery room."

"Don't say it like that. Makes me seem like some kind of pervert. I want to be there when my child is born! What's so wrong with that?"

The salesman cleared his throat to let them know he'd returned. Embarrassed, Macy glanced up at him, then back at Thad. The diamond was tempting, but she wasn't about to budge on the delivery issue. She already felt as if she'd sold her soul.

Pointing at the gold band, she told the salesman to wrap it up. "He doesn't go to the birth," she said pointedly to Thad, and walked out to wait in the car.

"I DON'T UNDERSTAND why offering to give you a six-thousand-dollar ring to let me come to the birth would make you so angry," Thad said as he drove her home.

Macy stared out the window. "There are some things money can't buy. Hasn't anyone ever told you that?"

He scowled at her. "I was merely offering you a very generous trade. But if you don't want to look at it that way, enjoy your gold band."

"I will," Macy sniffed.

"Fine."

They drove in silence down the narrow, tree-lined streets of the Avenues, the light of early evening flickering as it alternated with dappled shade. When Thad pulled to the curb in front of Macy's narrow yellow house, she got out and slammed the door without saying goodbye. He watched her go up the walk and try the door. She checked her pockets and searched under the mat. Finally, she came back, looking sheepish.

"I'm locked out," she said.

"And the key that was under the mat?" He smiled innocently.

"It's in the pocket of the blue jeans I wore the other day."

"Because..."

"Because I wanted to keep you out. You know that. You're just trying to rub it in."

"You took the key because I stocked your fridge." He shook his head. "You make a lot of sense." Jamming the gearshift into park, he turned off the car and got out. "Should we try a window or something in back?"

"These windows are the old thick panes. They shove up and have a lock on top, and they're all fastened. Living here alone, I check them pretty often."

"And the back door?"

Macy shrugged. "We could try it. But I'm pretty diligent about locking that, too."

"You make the rounds every day making sure both doors and all windows are locked, but leave a key under your front mat? That's as smart as turning down a six-thousand-dollar diamond ring for no good reason," he grumbled.

"Enough about the diamond. I'm starting to regret it without your help," she said under her breath.

"So you cut your nose off to spite your face. Let that be a lesson to you."

"I'm sure you'll offer me something else in the next nine months."

"Now that I know you're open to a trade, I might. But it won't be a six-thousand-dollar diamond."

"So now you're going to punish me?" she asked, raising her eyebrows.

He gave her a wicked look. "Don't give me any ideas."

The house was locked up tight, every window, every door. Thad stood in the small overgrown backyard, gazing at it. "I think the bedroom window would be the easiest to crawl through," he said. "Do you want me to break it?"

"No!" Macy cried. "I don't want you to break anything. It's after six o'clock. I wouldn't be able to get someone out here to fix it before dark. Just take me to the hospital. I'll wait for Lisa to get off work. She has a key.''

''Where does she work?''

''At Smith's Supermarket on Redwood Road. She's a cashier.''

''Want me to take you there?''

''No, she might not have it with her.''

''But Smith's doesn't close till eleven.''

''That's okay. I'm pretty sure she gets off before that tonight. Besides, I was just going to get my backpack and head to the hospital anyway. Getting locked out will save me from having to study.''

''Then why don't you sound more pleased about it?''

''Because in two weeks I'm probably going to flunk out of med school.''

''NOW THAT YOU'RE not angry with me anymore, do you want to swing by my house before I take you to the hospital?'' Thad drove with one hand slung over the wheel, looking casual and relaxed with his tie loosened and his collar unbuttoned.

Macy still hadn't seen his house, but her mother hadn't called, and she was beginning to think she wouldn't hear from Edna until the wedding, which took some of the pressure off. On the other hand, she knew very little about the man she was going to marry on Saturday. It would be nice to fill in some of the blanks. ''Who said I'm not angry anymore?'' she asked, propping her elbow up on the window ledge and turning to watch his face.

He grinned. ''Come on, I'm too endearing to be mad at for long. Besides, in nine months you'll be rid of me.''

Macy suspected that that was at least half the problem.

''Want to call the hospital and check on Haley first?'' he asked, brandishing his cell phone.

She dialed Primary Care Hospital. When the switchboard came on, she gave them Haley's room number.

"Haley and Bruiser's room."

Macy smiled at the sound of her daughter's sweet voice. "Hi, honey, it's Mommy."

"Hi, Mommy."

"How are you?"

"Fine. Dr. Forte brought me a new Pokémon sticker book and…oh! Miss Angela's here." Her preschool teacher from last year. Miss Angela had stopped by the hospital a few times already. Haley loved to see her. She knew just how to entertain a five-year-old.

"Are you two going to be okay without me for a little while?" Macy asked.

Haley didn't answer. She was too preoccupied with her guest. "Haley?"

"What, Mommy?"

"I'm going to be another hour or so. Will you be all right until then?"

"Sure. Miss Angela's brought a whole stack of books with her. *Chicka Chicka Boom Boom* and *Tikki Tikki Tembo* and…. I bet she's going to read to me."

A lump swelled in Macy's throat at the sudden, overwhelming gratitude she felt toward this relative stranger. Just knowing someone unexpected was there, however temporarily, to share the burden of keeping Haley's quality of life good took a tremendous load off Macy's mind. She swallowed hard, trying to keep the tears from her voice. "Tell Miss Angela Mommy is very…" *grateful* "…very happy she could come."

"I will, Mommy."

"I'll see you soon, sweetheart."

Macy punched the End button and set the phone on the console between the seats, keeping her face averted so Thad wouldn't see the emotion shimmering there. She'd gotten pretty good at withstanding the bumps of life. But let anyone show her a kindness, and she wept.

"What is it?" he asked softly.

She sniffed. "Nothing. Miss Angela is there, Macy's old preschool teacher. She'll keep her busy until I get back. She's a...she's a wonderful person."

His fingers closed over hers, startling her into looking at him. She watched through her tears as he raised her hand to his mouth and kissed it.

It was a simple gesture, full of sweetness, one that told her he understood, in a way those who have never suffered a soul-rending loss could ever understand. And for that brief moment, she felt as if she'd plugged into an outside energy source. His fingers were strong and sure and caressed hers gently. Too soon, he let go.

Macy was tempted to cling to him. He hadn't given her enough time to recharge the empty space his touch had momentarily filled. But her self-preservation instincts kicked in at the same moment, and she managed to keep her hands fisted in her lap. There'd be hell to pay in nine months if she leaned on this man. Better that they carry their own burdens.

The drive to Thad's house took a good thirty minutes. With the Winter Olympics coming in 2002, city officials had decided to give Salt Lake a complete overhaul. Road construction blocked most major roads and freeways, snarling traffic and raising tempers.

Finally they turned off Wasatch Boulevard into a nice residential neighborhood, where the traffic eased.

"We're almost there," Thad said, speaking for the first time since he'd kissed her hand. He slowed for some boys playing football in the street, rounded the next corner and pulled into a curving driveway leading to a double garage.

The accompanying house was white with green trim and looked as though it had been built about the same time as the rest of the neighborhood, thirty years or so ago. Only a fresh coat of paint and a new roof set it apart.

"This looks like a nice place," she said, getting out to follow him down a brick path to the deck at the back of the house.

"It has potential. The yard is big and goes partway up the mountain. Valerie and I wanted to plant a vegetable garden over there." He pointed to a spot that was simply grass on one side, by the back fence. "She wanted a small herb garden, too, and wildflowers near the old gazebo." He paused, as if the memories pressed too close, then finished quickly, "And we planned some major remodeling for the house itself."

"You didn't get it done?"

"No. We stopped the roof from leaking and did a few other things, but we never added on the fourth bedroom and extra bath. And I've lost interest."

Macy didn't say anything, thinking it better to let him retreat. She waited as he unlocked the door, then stepped into a room he and his wife had obviously finished. Hardwood floors gleamed beneath Oriental rugs, wainscoting covered the bottom half of the walls, and beige-and-white-striped wallpaper finished the effect, topped off by a thick crown molding. She could easily imagine his wife poring over wallpaper books, trying to find the perfect complement to the green leather sofa and burgundy-plaid side chairs. "Wow," she said.

He gave her a wry grin. "Valerie was quite a decorator."

Valerie must have been a lot more than that. Thad looked both proud and lost when he said her name.

He showed her the rest of the house, all except for what lay behind one door next to the master suite. From the floor plan, Macy guessed it was another bedroom. Maybe Thad thought it was too messy. He'd already shown her his office, where he had a large desk, a computer and a couple of file cabinets, but perhaps he needed extra storage space. Probably there were files strewn everywhere.

Or maybe he'd created some sort of shrine to his dead wife.

That thought gave Macy the creeps, so she blamed it on an overactive imagination and shrugged it off.

"What kind of music do you like?" she asked when they returned to the living room.

He nodded toward a CD cabinet. "Pick something while I make us dinner."

"Actually, I'd better get back to the hospital. Haley's used to me being there most of the time."

"Miss Angela's with her, remember? I'm sure they're doing fine. The hospital would beep you if there was a problem."

Macy looked down at the pager she carried everywhere, double-checking what she already knew—the screen was blank. "Yeah."

"Then let's eat. It won't take long."

Bottles clinked in the kitchen. A fridge door opened and shut several times. Meanwhile, Macy put on a Garth Brooks CD and wandered around the living room, looking at the prints on the walls, the wood stacked in the brass holder next to the fireplace, the oak pendulum clock on the mantel. A table behind the sofa held a lamp, several *Popular Mechanics* magazines and a picture of Thad with a woman who had long brown hair and liquid chocolate eyes. Her skin was tanned to a honey gold, and she wore a one-piece bathing suit that showed off her incredible figure. They were on a boat or something—on their honeymoon? The wind was playing havoc with their hair, but Thad stood behind her, his cheek next to hers, his arms around her middle, and they were both laughing into the camera.

God, they looked happy.

Checking to make sure Thad was still occupied, Macy picked up the photograph so she could examine it more closely. The woman had a light dusting of freckles on her face, full lips, a pert nose. She was nothing short of beautiful. Macy tried to picture her pregnant, carrying Thad's baby, and suffered a small twinge of envy. This woman had had it all. Few were so lucky.

Only, Valerie's luck had run out. A drunk driver had—

"What would you like to drink?" Thad asked, poking his head out of the kitchen.

Macy nearly dropped the picture. His gaze lowered to what she held, then returned to her face. "That's Valerie, my wife," he said simply.

"I thought so." She put the laughing couple back where she'd found them. "She was lovely."

He retreated into the kitchen. "Sprite okay?" he asked a few moments later.

"Fine." Rounding the couch, Macy sat down. The soft leather gave beneath her weight, molding to her and smelling the way good leather did. It was obviously an expensive couch. Far better than anything she'd ever owned. She leaned her head back on the soft cushion and closed her eyes, giving herself a minute to rest…. *She was playing with Haley when she was a baby, blowing on her stomach to make her laugh, and Richard was there, handsome as ever, taking a video of Haley's first birthday.*

THAD CARRIED two plates piled high with the leftovers his sister, Deb, had sent home with him the night before into the dining area off the living room, then returned for their drinks before noticing that Macy had fallen asleep on the couch. He considered waking her so she could eat. He was certain she wasn't getting enough nutrition in her diet. But she looked exhausted. The bones of her face were more prominent than ever, the dark circles beneath her eyes more pronounced. She was running herself ragged. It was better that she sleep.

He retrieved a quilt from the linen closet and covered her, then read the newspaper while he ate. She was still sleeping when he finished, so he went out to the car to get his briefcase. He'd brought some work home he needed to finish. But an hour later, he was done and Macy was still down for the count.

Again he considered waking her. He knew she wanted to get back to the hospital and feared Haley might need her. They'd been gone nearly three hours already. But Macy had snuggled into the quilt and was sleeping so soundly. Obviously she needed the rest.

He wrote her a quick note, telling her to call his cell phone when she woke up, and left it on the coffee table in front of the sofa. Then he found his car keys and slipped quietly out the back.

CHAPTER EIGHT

"I THOUGHT MOMMY was coming," Haley said when Thad walked into her room.

"She fell asleep, so I thought I'd keep you company. I thought maybe we could color together or something until she wakes up."

"You know how to color?" she asked doubtfully.

"Definitely. I'm an ad executive. I do a lot of coloring, though most of it's with words and not crayons."

He pulled a package of changeable markers he'd bought at K-Mart out of his pocket, along with two Blue's Clues coloring books, and wheeled the table she normally ate on over to the bed. "When did Miss Angela leave?"

"Just a little while ago."

"What did the two of you do?"

"She read to me. And she did some finger puppets. I liked the puppets best." She lifted her hand, wriggling first one finger, then the other, her voice climbing to a high pitch. "'I'm building a house of straw'... 'Well, if you don't let me in, I'll huff, and I'll puff—'"

"'And I'll blow the house in,'" Thad finished with her.

"You know that story?"

He smiled. "Any self-respecting adult knows *The Three Little Pigs*. Have you heard *The Three Bears*?"

"The one with Goldilocks?"

"Uh-huh."

"Yeah."

"Then I consider you a well-educated five-year-old."

"But I hate porridge," she added.

"That's okay. So do I. I like cold cereal."

"Me, too."

"What's your favorite kind?" He opened one of the coloring books and began to turn the pages, looking for something he'd like to color. She did the same.

"Fruity-Os."

He wanted to grimace, but managed to keep a straight face. "Fruity-Os are good. What about Life?"

She shrugged. "Life's okay, I guess."

"Always had a good ad campaign, anyway," he said, but she wasn't listening. She'd landed on a picture of Blue at a birthday party and was breaking out the markers.

"It's fun to color with you," she announced after a few minutes of concentration. "I'm glad you're going to be my daddy."

Thad felt the same panic he'd experienced the first time she'd said something like that. But he smiled through it, telling himself she was just a sweet little girl, *someone else's* sweet little girl. He couldn't let himself get too close. Not when he'd be walking away in nine months.

"Look!" she announced, proudly showing him a multicolored Blue next to a purple birthday cake.

"That's fabulous! Maybe you'll grow up to be an artist."

She smiled proudly and went back to work, but after a few minutes, Thad noticed her slowing down. Squinting, her breathing irregular, she finally slumped over her work.

"What's wrong?" he asked, a prickle of fear climbing his spine.

"My head hurts."

"Do you think I should call the nurse?"

"No," she said, but Thad headed out of the room, anyway. He wasn't going to take any chances.

"Nurse?" He waved to a woman sitting behind the desk at the nurses' station.

She stood and came right away. "What is it?"

"Haley says her head is hurting. I was wondering if maybe she should be checked."

The nurse followed him into the room to find Haley crying. Whipping out a thermometer, she took the child's temperature, then frowned and shook her head. "She's running a fever. I'm going to call the doctor."

A few minutes later, an older, gray-haired man with a stethoscope around his neck entered the room.

"I'm Dr. Forte," he said, nodding in Thad's direction.

Haley didn't seem to notice that the doctor had arrived. She was hugging herself and rocking.

"I'll beep her mother," Thad said, hoping he hadn't made a grave mistake letting Macy sleep. "Where's the number?"

The nurse gave it to him and he beeped Macy, then sat next to Haley's bed, anxiously watching the doctor finish his exam while the nurse rushed around, getting some kind of medication started through what she called a central venous catheter. "What's going on?" he asked.

"She's got another blood infection," the doctor replied. "We're getting her on some antibiotics."

Thad took Haley's hand to let her know he was still with her, hoping to give her some comfort amid the pain. The moment he touched her, she reached out and clung to him. "Stay with me," she pleaded. "Don't go."

THE SCENE THAT GREETED Macy when she hurried into Haley's hospital room more than an hour later nearly knocked the wind out of her. The nurse had intercepted her long enough to tell her everything was okay, at least for now, but she'd still expected to find her daughter crying, wondering where her mommy was and why she'd been gone so long, or maybe suffering quietly while Thad paced the room, anxious for reinforcements.

Instead, she found her fiancé lying next to Haley on the bed, his arms holding her close, both of them sleeping peacefully.

Lisa was sitting at the foot of the bed, wearing her blue checker's smock, reading a magazine.

Macy let the panic she'd felt during her mad rush to the hospital go in one deep breath, and just stood there, trying to stop shaking. Another close call, but Haley had managed to survive.

Lisa's sympathetic smile told her she understood.

Macy indicated Thad with her head. "I'm in real trouble here, aren't I?" she whispered.

Lisa followed her gaze. "If you call that trouble. It could also be a once-in-a-lifetime chance at happiness."

"Maybe." Macy shoved her hands in the pockets of her cargo pants. "He came here tonight on his own, you know, to baby-sit for me so I could sleep."

"That's pretty amazing."

"Yeah, considering he barely knows us."

Lisa put the magazine aside, gathered her purse and used her hands to push herself out of her seat. "He's got a lot of compassion in him." She lowered her voice even further. "Maybe you should rethink your relationship at some point. Not look at it as so temporary."

Afraid Thad might awake and overhear their conversation, Macy waved her friend out into the hall. The nurse on duty glanced up and smiled as they emerged, but when she realized they didn't need her, she went back to her work.

"I admit he has a certain appeal," Macy said softly, "but I don't think it would be wise to look at our relationship as anything but temporary. He's still in love with his dead wife.''

''Time is on your side, Macy.''

''There's nothing on my side right now, except how fiercely Haley is hanging on to life. Besides, you should see what I'm up against. His wife was—'' she let her breath whistle through her teeth ''—wow!''

''Pretty, hmm?''

''More than that. You can tell just from looking at her photograph that she was well-adjusted, fun-loving—the all-around everything kind of woman.''

''You got all of that from a picture?'' Lisa scoffed. ''It's easy to idealize the dead, Macy. She's not here to prove anyone wrong.''

Macy motioned for Lisa to keep her voice down. ''Don't you think *he* idealizes her?'' She jerked a thumb over her shoulder. ''I can't compete with that.''

Lisa grunted. ''I don't care what you say—no one's perfect.''

''That might be what your mind tells you, but his heart speaks a different language.''

''I think Thad Winters is smarter than you think.''

Macy stared at the tops of her white sneakers for a moment, considering, then changed the subject. ''When did you get here?''

''Just a few minutes ago. The store was slow, so they let me go a half hour early, but things had settled down around here by then.''

''Did you meet Thad?''

''No, he and Haley were already asleep when I arrived, but the doctor said you were on your way, so I waited.''

Macy refrained from saying that Lisa took an awful lot for granted about a man she'd never even met, because, somehow, her friend was usually right about people. ''I'm

glad you were here. It's good to see you, and—'' she resisted the temptation to squirm ''—I need the key to my
house. I'm locked out.''

Lisa didn't say anything, but her raised eyebrows were
enough to make Macy defensive.

''If Thad hadn't let himself into my house on at least
two different occasions, I wouldn't have had to remove the
key,'' she said, exasperated to find Lisa's reaction very
much what Thad's had been.

''Yeah, you were up against a wall.'' Lisa dug around
in her purse. ''Anyway, I have to go. Here's your key.
Fortunately I put it on my ring or we'd have to go to my
house now.'' She handed Macy the key, then enveloped
her in a giant hug.

''Sometimes I feel so lost,'' Macy admitted, wondering
how she was going to survive if Haley died. ''I just keep
spinning and spinning, and then I get dizzy and scared.''

Lisa peeked around the corner at Thad and smiled. ''I
have a feeling that's all about to change. You just need an
anchor, kiddo.'' Giving Macy's arm a little squeeze, she
left, her thick-soled shoes squishing as she disappeared
down the hall.

SOMEONE WAS SHAKING him.

Thad blinked and looked around the dimly lit room, trying to place his surroundings. Machines, tubes, a sink…a
small child in his arms. Haley.

He smiled at the memory of how brave she had been
throughout the blood-infection ordeal and wanted to kiss
her sweet, bald head, but her mother was standing over
them.

''You can go home now, I'm here,'' Macy murmured.

Thad gently extricated his arms and sat up, shaking his

left hand to bring the blood back into it. "Have you talked to the doctor?"

She shook her head. "The nurse."

"Is everything okay?"

"They think so."

He sighed. "That was really scary."

"I'm sorry it took me so long to get here. I was sleeping so soundly when my pager went off, it just became part of my dreams. The recurring vibrations took nearly twenty minutes to wake me. That's never happened before."

"You've probably never been so tired before."

"Then I had to wait another half hour for a cab, and the drive here took twenty minutes. I thought I'd never make it."

"Haley was a trouper," Thad said, trying to reassure her. "Fortunately, the antibiotics started working right away, too."

"Good." She didn't ask how he came to be holding her daughter, and Thad didn't volunteer an explanation. What had happened in those last few minutes before he and Haley had dropped off into the oblivion of sleep had touched him in a profound way. He didn't understand how or why, but being there for a suffering child who needed him had soothed away some of the residual pain in his heart as effectively as a good massage eases stiff muscles.

"It's late. I'd better get going," he said, covering a yawn and climbing to his feet as carefully as possible so he didn't wake Haley. "What about you?"

"I'm going to stay here. They'll bring me a rollaway if I want."

Thad nodded, hesitant to leave for fear he'd wake in the morning to learn that Haley had died in his absence. Standing vigil over a child so sick made one afraid to blink for fear she'd slip away. "What about your classes tomorrow?"

"I'll go, if Haley's feeling okay. Lisa gave me her key to my house, so I can get in and pick up my books."

"Who will be here with her?" He nodded toward Haley.

"Lisa sometimes comes by in the mornings."

"I could stop by, too, you know, just to check on her. The office is just down—"

"I know, but that's okay." She cleared her throat. "I really don't think it's wise for the two of you to get too attached."

"Right." He wondered if she was angry that he hadn't woken her, that he'd come to the hospital himself. "Well, there's still the problem that you don't have a car here. If you'll give me the keys, I'll take a taxi to your house and bring your Pinto back."

She looked as though she might argue, but after a moment, handed him the key to her house. "My car keys should be on the counter. Just park close to where we parked last time and put the keys under the floor mat when you get here."

"All right." He grinned at her. "Right after I make a copy."

She rolled her eyes. "Just don't leave me any more notes, okay?"

KEVIN HELPED HIMSELF to a beer, then nudged the refrigerator shut with his knee. "I can't believe you're going through with it. You're going to marry a complete stranger—one with a sick kid."

Thad took a pull of his own beer and grabbed a bag of corn chips out of the cupboard. "Yep, tomorrow."

Kevin shook his head, then sauntered back into the living room to sink into one of the plaid chairs that flanked the couch. Thad followed him, traded the chips for the remote and settled back on the leather couch to flip through the zillion or so channels on his satellite system.

"You don't have any problem with that?" Kevin asked when Thad didn't say more.

Thad had lots of problems with marrying a stranger, a woman he didn't love. But he had bigger problems facing the emptiness of his life without doing something to fill it. "No."

"Jeez." The pop of Kevin's mouth on his beer bottle sounded amidst the ringing bell of a game show.

Thad flipped to a sports channel.

"You're crazy, you know that?" Kevin persisted.

Thad shrugged. "Sometimes you gotta take a few chances in life."

"Me, I prefer to bungee jump or sky dive. It's safer."

"You've never been married." Hell, Thad doubted Kevin had ever really been in love. He liked anything with long legs and half a mind to show him a good time, so long as they didn't get clingy. He feared commitment, didn't understand how fulfilling it could be.

"I figure I'll save that ball-and-chain stuff for later."

"If you don't feel the need to share your life with someone you really care about, then I guess there's no reason to pursue marriage."

"That's not why you're marrying this Macy lady."

"I've already had a fulfilling marriage. Now I'm looking for a child."

"Shit, man, that's just hard to understand." Kevin shook his head. "Why don't you become a Big Brother? Then you can schedule time with the kid when you want to, work when you want to. It's perfect."

Baseball was on ESPN. Thad liked most sports, especially football and basketball, but nothing, except perhaps golf, was more boring than baseball to watch on TV. He kept his thumb on the channel changer.

"Whoa, slow down," Kevin said when a bunch of young girls wearing bikinis and dancing on the beach flashed on the screen.

MTV. Hardly the type of program Thad was looking for, but he set the clicker down to let his friend watch.

"So is there any way to talk you out of tomorrow?" Kevin asked.

"Do we have to mow the same grass over and over?" Thad demanded. "I mean, you didn't come over for this little impromptu bachelors' party to intentionally turn me into a homicidal maniac, did you?"

When he finally dragged his gaze away from the bouncing breasts and gyrating hips on television, Kevin looked surprised. "What? Am I driving you crazy?"

Thad chuckled. Sometimes he wished he could be as unaffected by the ups and downs of life as Kevin was. Or as simply entertained. There'd been a time when he'd been as wild as they come, but he was no longer interested in short-term relationships that went nowhere. He liked to think the change was proof of his maturity and wondered when, or if, his partner would ever grow up. "I'm going through with it, okay? I'm going to marry Macy tomorrow, and I don't want to talk about it anymore."

"It's your life, buddy," Kevin said, a bit defensive now.

Thad picked up the remote and settled on a rerun of *Seinfeld*.

"What's she like?" Kevin asked after a few minutes.

"Who? Macy?"

"No, the woman next door. Of course, Macy."

"She's going through hell right now—"

"I know that already. I didn't say, 'What's her situation like?' I said, 'What's *she* like?'"

"You've met her."

"Once."

"Yeah, well. Besides being attractive, which I'm sure you noticed, she's softhearted, fiercely loyal and a real fireball if you piss her off. Mostly, though, I'd have to say she's…fair."

"Like fair to middlin' or what? What the hell does that mean?"

Thad scowled, trying to control his temper. Hadn't he just told Kevin he didn't want to talk about Macy? "Fair-minded," he clarified, thinking about her message on his answering machine that night she'd called and said, "Let's do it." He'd given her the money and let her off the hook and she'd jumped right back on again—out of a sense of fair play, he suspected. "She might be too fair-minded for her own good."

"Sounds like a nice lady." Kevin took another long drink of his beer and wiped the condensation on his shirt. "When you divorce, mind if I take her out?"

Thad cast him a withering glare. "You ever touch her and I'll kill you."

Kevin laughed uproariously. "Aha! That tells me more than everything you've said tonight, you tight-lipped bastard."

Finally Thad laughed, too. "She's going to hate you," he said.

"WHAT DO YOU MEAN I should buy a dress for the wedding?" Macy ambled through Dillard's department store at Fashion Place Mall with Lisa at her side. A song by Savage Garden played in the background, over the public-address system. The store smelled like expensive potpourri, a medley of perfumes and new clothing. "You said we were coming here to pick up some shoes you special-ordered from Nordstrom's.''

''Can't we kill two birds with one stone?''

''Are you kidding? I haven't been able to work for eight weeks. If my mother has to pay my rent another month, she'll probably disown me. I don't have the money to buy chewing gum, let alone a wedding dress.''

''Then it will be my present to the lovely bride.''

''I don't want any presents. This isn't a real wedding.''

''According to law, it will be real. That's good enough for me.'' Lisa drained her Coke and tossed it in a trash bin.

Macy hitched her purse strap higher on her shoulder. ''For crying out loud, Lisa, I could wear my blue jeans for all it's going to matter to Thad or anyone else.''

They slipped past a woman with a double stroller, who was pleading with her two toddlers to stop whining. Briefly, Macy wished that having Haley act up in a mall was the worst of her problems.

''What will your mother think of you standing at the altar in pants?'' Lisa demanded.

''She'll be glad to see I'm not out squandering money while I'm eating on her meal ticket.''

''Jeez, you make her sound cheap sometimes,'' Lisa said.

Macy laughed. ''At least I'm not seeing a shrink and dredging up every parenting sin she's ever committed. And I am grateful that she's helping me out right now. I just hate being so indebted to her, especially when she makes an issue of it every time we talk.''

''That reminds me, she knows our flyers and posters weren't bringing in the kind of money you need. How does she think you're going to pay for Haley's operation?''

''I haven't told her that I can yet. When we find a donor, I'll just say the insurance relented.''

If we find a donor hovered in the air, but Macy was glad Lisa didn't go there.

"That's good. Not very believable about an insurance company, but the best you're going to do under the circumstances."

"Do you think she'd rather hear the truth?"

They both looked at each other and laughed. "Nah."

Lisa pulled Macy toward the escalator. "Well, since I'm staying in Salt Lake with Haley and will miss the big 'I do,' I want to send something from me along with you. And I want it to be a dress."

When Lisa made up her mind, there was no use fighting her. But Macy tried one more time. "You've already done so much for me, Lisa. Don't put me any further in your debt."

"Hey, now you're making me sound like your mother. If I want to buy you a dress, I will. We've been friends since forever. There've been a lot of times when you've been there for me, too."

Macy had been hurting so long she didn't remember a time when she'd been someone else's strength, except Haley's. "I hope that's true," she said. Then she glanced at her watch. "Only problem is, the mall's closing soon."

Lisa squeezed her shoulders. "Then we'd better hurry, because we're going to find something that will knock Thad's socks off."

"As far as I'm concerned, his clothes stay on," Macy retorted.

"Come on!" Lisa's eyes sparkled mischievously. "Don't tell me you haven't wondered what all that lean muscle would look like *al fresco.*"

"I haven't thought about it," she lied.

CHAPTER NINE

HUES OF MAGENTA AND GOLD streaked the sky when Macy opened the door to see Thad on her doorstep, his car still running, at 5:30 a.m. They had to be at the airport by six to make their flight, so she didn't invite him in. She let him take the hang-up bag and small suitcase she had waiting by the door to the car while she gathered up her schoolbooks. Studying was hardly the type of pastime she'd choose on her wedding day, even though this wasn't a real wedding, but time was short.

"I'm glad to see you haven't gotten cold feet," Thad said as she shoved her backpack in the trunk where he'd put her other luggage and climbed in the passenger's seat. Wearing a long, straight denim skirt with a short-sleeved sweater, she crossed her legs and waited for him to come around the car.

An old Journey tunc was playing on the radio. The heater hummed, taking the chill out of the morning air, but Macy shivered despite the warm interior. In a matter of hours, she was going to marry a man who was paying her to have his baby. *This* man…someone she'd met by appointment.

How crazy was that? Sometimes she couldn't believe she'd let this wedding farce come so far, but when she went over the events of the past two weeks, somehow it all made sense.

Macy didn't know if that was a good sign or bad. She'd

been through a lot in the past year. Maybe the stress had affected her thinking.

"My feet *are* cold," she admitted as he backed out of the driveway. He was wearing a pair of khaki pants and a golf shirt that fit him almost as well as his tailored suits, maybe better, but Macy tried not to notice. "As a matter of fact, I'm terrified that we're making a huge mistake, but…"

He paused before shifting the transmission into drive and glanced over at her. "But?"

She looked into his eyes, ice-blue and fringed with thick black lashes, and faced the truth. "I don't want to tell you no."

His eyebrows darted up and he rocked back as if she'd shot him. "That's probably the nicest thing anyone's ever said to me."

"Well, 'no' isn't your favorite word." She swallowed, her throat dry.

"Right."

"And I'm just trying to be accommodating." Embarrassed, Macy pretended to straighten her shirt, noticing for the first time that the slit designed to allow her legs some movement was cut up a little high. She smoothed the two sides together until his hand closed over hers, warm and sure. A little flutter in her chest indicated she'd like it if he'd lift her hand to his lips and kiss it again, but the devilish grin that broke across his face told her he wasn't thinking along the same lines.

"Would this be a good time to ask to come to the birth?"

Pulling away, Macy punched him in the arm for principle's sake. She was going all soft and gooey, like taffy left too long in the sun, and he was still pursuing his agenda. "At this rate, I'm not even going to tell you when I'm in labor."

"With the amount of luggage you brought, I thought maybe we were going away for the whole nine months!" Chuckling, he put the car in drive and gave it some gas, and the Lexus purred down the street. "What's in those bags? Did you forget that we're coming back tonight?"

"No." Macy turned her attention to the houses and yards flitting by her window. "Lisa bought me a dress for the wedding, so I brought it. My mother will be there, and I thought we should keep up appearances, at least for the first few months. I don't want to tell her what we're *really* doing. She'll think I've finally lost it."

He glanced over at her. "I brought a suit."

Coming to a stop at the intersection of Fourteenth and I, he paused. "Do you want to stop by the hospital and see Haley before we head to the airport?"

"Do you think we have time?" she asked. Part of her wanted to include Haley and pretend this was a joyous occasion. She knew how much it would please her daughter, and there'd been so little to be happy about in the past year.

The other part insisted the less Haley saw her and Thad together, the better.

He glanced at his watch and turned left. "I think so. I bought her a corsage so she'd feel like part of the wedding, at least in a small way. It's in the back seat if you want to take a look."

Surprised, Macy turned and lifted the lid off what resembled a cardboard hatbox. Inside she found a beautiful bouquet of white roses, a boutonniere and a small corsage, all packed carefully in tissue paper. The distinctive smell of fresh-cut flowers wafted through the car, and she smiled. "How thoughtful of you," she said, genuinely impressed.

He winked at her. "I have my moments."

HALEY WASN'T AWAKE when they arrived. Macy kissed her forehead to rouse her, and her daughter began to blink and stretch, slowing coming around.

"Mommy?"

"Hi, baby. Thad and I just stopped in to say goodbye. We're on our way—"

"To get married?" She rose up on her elbows. "It's today?"

Thad leaned on the railing of her bed. "And since you're our flower girl, at least in spirit, we brought you something every flower girl must have."

Her eyes widened. "What?"

"A corsage, of course, so everyone can tell that you're part of today's big event." He presented her the flowers with an impressive flourish, and Macy marked his incredible sales ability. The corsage could have been a toothpick, and Haley would have felt just as special wearing it.

Had *she* been fooled by an act, too?

For a moment, fear grasped Macy hard. She was passing one of those milestones in life that would either leave her immeasurably glad or filled with regret. Which was it? Would the operation cure Haley? Would she be able to walk away from the baby when it came? There was no way to answer those questions, but as she watched Thad with her daughter, she knew she was going to take a leap of faith.

"Isn't it pretty, Mommy?" Haley asked, sounding awed.

Macy nodded. "I'll be holding a bouquet that looks very much like it."

"A bouquet?"

"Flowers, like yours."

Thad held the corsage to Haley's chest. "When you wake up for the day, since it's pretty early now, just have one of the nurses pin it on your gown here. Then you'll be a genuine flower girl."

Delighted, Haley reverently touched one of the soft petals. "Can't I wear it now?"

Macy laughed. "I doubt she'll be going back to sleep any time soon. She can wear it if she wants."

Reaching into his pocket, Thad pulled out a couple of safety pins. "I brought some special pins so you won't get stuck," he said, fastening the corsage to her hospital gown.

Wearing the flowers as proudly as a badge of honor, Haley puffed out her chest.

"I'll get a picture of the two of you," Thad suggested, stepping back to use the disposable camera he'd brought with him.

"No! You, too!" Haley insisted until he finally went for the nurse and the three of them posed for the camera.

"IS THERE ANYTHING I should know before I meet your mother?" Thad asked. They'd been on the plane for nearly forty-five minutes and would be arriving in Las Vegas soon. Macy had studied the entire way, first delving into a thick textbook entitled *The Science of Medicine*, then leafing through another called *Pharmacology*. Just reading the titles was enough to bore Thad to tears. He hadn't thought to bring some work from home, so he'd read everything shoved into the pocket of the seat in front of him, including the emergency-procedure card and a portion of the *Salt Lake Tribune*, but that had taken him less than ten minutes. The next thirty-five had passed at a snail's pace. "Did you hear me?" he prodded when Macy didn't answer right away.

She reached up to turn off the overhead air vent, which was making a racket similar to Darth Vader's breathing apparatus, and pushed her reading glasses back up on her nose. "What did you say?" she asked absently, bowing over her book again.

"I asked if there's anything I should know before I meet your mother."

"Like?" She looked at him over the rims of her reading glasses, her silky dark hair falling forward, very preppy and very cute, and something tightened in Thad's chest. Something he didn't want to acknowledge, let alone explain.

But then he caught a glimpse of the page she'd been studying and his stomach nearly revolted. What was that? A kidney? Jeez!

He looked quickly away. "Like how we met," he said, trying to divert his mind. "You know, the normal stuff. I think it might be smart if we work off the same cheat sheet, don't you?"

"I don't plan on leaving you alone with her. Just let me do the talking." She went back to reading and Thad sighed, bouncing his knee and tapping the arm of his seat to keep himself busy.

Finally, Macy looked pointedly at his hand. "Do you have to go to the bathroom?"

"No."

"Then could you hold still?"

He let his finger tap a couple more times, just to bug her, then quit. But he was so restless he couldn't sit still. He shifted in his seat, trying to find a place for his long legs in the eighteen inches of space the airline allotted him. "What if she wants to know how I proposed?" he asked. "What will you tell her?"

"Don't worry. I'll explain that I've started a new rent-a-wife business and you're my first customer."

"Clever," he said with a grimace.

"Sorry, bad joke." She grinned, looking far from repentant, and that…that *thing* in Thad's chest tightened again.

"Why don't we say we met on a blind date?" he asked. "People love to hear success stories that started out as a blind date."

"Because it makes them feel better about playing matchmaker."

"We could say that you know someone at school who set you up with me. We met over dinner and fell in love at first sight. A mother would have to be impressed with a story like that. What could be more romantic?"

Macy looked at him, then quickly averted her eyes. "Nothing," she said softly, and went back to her books, but Thad didn't mind her preoccupation anymore. His proposed lie had just reminded him how temporary their relationship really was. He no longer felt like talking, and Macy must have lost her zeal for study, because it was a long time before she turned the page.

"SO THIS IS your fiancé." Macy's mother stepped back, one critical gray eye almost squinting as she looked Thad over.

Standing next to him in the middle of her mother's modest living room with Champ, her mother's German shepherd, sniffing and circling them both, Macy took a deep breath and held it. She had no doubt Thad would pass muster. He was pouring on the charm, saying all the right things, admiring Champ and scratching him behind the ears.

Macy didn't think there was a woman alive who could resist Thad now. Even her little dynamo of a mother. What made her nervous were the lies. In nine months, she'd be calling her mother to report another divorce, and Edna would probably be disappointed Macy had lost him. She felt like a failure in advance.

"Why didn't you call me?" her mother was saying, patting her carefully arranged white hair. "I would have picked you up at the airport."

"It wasn't any trouble to rent a car, Mrs. Phillips," Thad said.

"You're going to be my son-in-law. Call me Mom," she insisted, smoothing her skirt. Dressed in her Sunday best, Edna had obviously taken pains to prepare for their arrival. "I understand about the car, of course," she went on. "You'll need it for after the wedding. A young, handsome man like yourself won't want to waste time visiting with an old lady like me, not when he could be starting his honeymoon." Edna smiled slyly, as though they shared an inside joke, and Macy resisted the urge to roll her eyes. Little did Edna know her honeymoon consisted of latex gloves and doctors. Nothing to get excited about, but Thad must have smiled, at least enough to appease Edna, because she waved them to the rust-colored sectional that crowded the room.

"Sit down. This came about so quickly, I can hardly believe it's happening. You know, when Richard left, I told Macy there'd be someone else."

Macy remembered their conversations being more about the unreliability of men and how Richard had been a perfect example and what could she expect? But she kept her mouth shut. At least her mother seemed to be putting forth an honest effort.

"She was so heartbroken," Edna continued, taking the worn brown chair facing the couch, on which they'd settled, and crossing her legs in ladylike fashion. "She could scarcely function. And then, when we found out why he'd left! It was humiliating." She looked thoughtful for a moment as Champ went to sit near her knee, obviously hoping to receive a little absentminded scratching. Macy hoped her mother had finished with the subject, but then she went on,

"Of course, we should have seen it coming. He always did have a wandering eye—"

"Mom, we don't need to go into all that," Macy interrupted. "I'm sure Thad doesn't want to hear about my first marriage."

Edna looked slightly offended, but when Thad said nothing, she gracefully conceded the point. "You're right, dear. Let's not ruin this day with bad memories. Okay, tell me, Thad, how did the two of you meet?"

Macy opened her mouth to answer, but despite her confidence on the plane and the one plausible scenario Thad had suggested, her mind drew a blank. "Well...we...we met..." She glanced at Thad, and he jumped to her rescue.

"...on a blind date," he finished, and started to embellish the story from there.

Reluctant to relinquish control of the conversation to him—this was *her* mother—Macy tried to interrupt, but Edna was hanging on every word, nodding and smiling and soaking it all in. Besides, it was as good a story as any. Giving up, Macy sat back and listened.

"The moment I saw her picture, I wondered if she was the one," he said. "There was something mysterious about her smile that appealed to me. I kept going back to that picture."

His voice sounded almost wistful, and so damn sincere. Macy told herself never to believe another thing he said. She also decided her mother had heard enough.

"So it was love at first sight," she cut in, finishing for him as a muscle started to twitch near her eye, "and here we are." She stood to indicate that she was ready to leave, but Champ was the only one who followed her lead. "What chapel should we go to? Any ideas, Mom?"

Edna blinked up at her. "My, you are in a hurry."

"Well, Haley's sick, in case you've forgotten." She

hadn't meant to say it, especially with such sarcasm. But the words, and the emotion behind them, simply slipped out.

"What do you mean, 'in case I've forgotten'?"

Macy hesitated. She didn't want to get into it, not with Thad here. Not ever. If only she could close off the hurt, put it in the same place she'd put the pain when Richard left. "Nothing. Never mind. Let's go."

Her mother didn't move. She'd dropped her friendly, social aura and was staring angrily at Macy. Champ, sensing the hostility, swung his great head back and forth between them, tail wagging uncertainly. "How dare you come here and accuse me of not doing my part for Haley. Here I am, living on a pension, yet I've paid your rent for the past three months!"

Pandora's box... "I appreciate that, Mom, and I plan to pay you back, like we agreed, as soon as I can get back to work. But Haley's been in the hospital a long time, and you've only been to Salt Lake twice. You rarely call. Even when you do, half the time you don't ask about her. I feel like she and I are fighting this battle alone. You say that men don't stay. They don't last when the going gets tough. You even told me you knew all along that Richard would run out on me—" Macy stubbornly forced a swallow past the tightening of her throat "—but sometimes it feels like you've abandoned us, too."

Shocked silence. Thad's face was inscrutable. Edna looked as if she'd just been slapped. It was hardly what Macy had planned to say when she saw her mother today. She'd expected a quick, uneventful visit, more pleasant than not. Instead, she'd started World War Three. And blame it on raw nerves, exhaustion, stress, hurt, disappointment, whatever, it was too late to change that now.

"Always finding fault. That's what children do these

days. What a parent gives is never enough, is it?'' Edna demanded. "I try and try, sacrifice things I'd like to have so I can send the money to you, and it's still not enough.''

"I'm sorry Haley's illness has put a dent in your pocketbook,'' she said. "I'm certainly not asking for more money.''

"How dare you sit in judgment of me! I'm your mother. You have no right!''

Thad stood and put his arm around Macy, who had started shaking and couldn't figure out how to stop. "I think we'll go now,'' he said, herding her to the door.

"She wants me to suffer right along with her,'' her mother called after them. "That's what she wants!''

"No, she just wants your love, much more than your money,'' Thad said under his breath as they reached the porch, but only Macy could hear him.

Champ dashed out behind them and nudged her hand with his wet nose, but a moment later her mother yanked him back by the collar and slammed the door.

"I'm sorry,'' Macy muttered, keeping her face averted as Thad drove down the Las Vegas strip looking for a wedding chapel. The day was warm, almost hot, and the sky clear and blue. "Ours is a business deal. I'm sure you weren't expecting to be dragged into an emotional maelstrom.''

He glanced over at her. Her emotions were so raw, he could watch them playing beneath her expression like fish gliding silently near the surface of a lake. "Should we go back to your mother's?'' he asked. "Maybe you'd feel better if you had a chance to put things right.''

Macy shook her head, one crystal tear falling from her dark lashes. She wiped it away in a quick, impatient gesture. "It's too soon. She won't listen. And I don't know what I'd say, anyway. I don't understand why she doesn't seem to care about Haley. She used to dote on her."

"It takes a strong person to watch what's happening to Haley," he said, remembering his own hesitation as he stood in the hospital lobby that first night. "Maybe she's afraid."

"Maybe she is. But then, so am I. And if Haley can't count on her family, who can she count on?"

Me. Thad almost said the word before he caught himself, before he reminded himself that his involvement in their lives was only temporary. "What about Richard's family?"

"They live back East. She gets a Christmas card every year and a birthday present. That's it."

Thad reached over to take Macy's hand, knowing he couldn't fix the hurt. He could only try to comfort her, but she pulled away. "I never would have said what I did if you hadn't been there, telling my mother all those lies."

"You wanted me to tell the truth?"

"No, but did you have to go on and on?"

"I was telling her what I thought when I first saw your picture."

"I heard." She pulled a face. "I had a mysterious smile that kept drawing you back."

Thad maneuvered their rented Taurus to the curb of a busy street just off the main strip. A small white chapel with a single spire and a large sign that read Weddings was just up the road. "I wasn't lying about that," he said.

CHAPTER TEN

MACY DIDN'T RESPOND. They sat for a moment, staring at the chapel.

"Are you ready for this?" he asked at last.

She took a deep breath and nodded.

"I'll go make sure they're open and that they have room. Do you want to come along and see if you like this place? Because there are plenty of others."

"No, it doesn't matter. Let's just get it over with."

"Okay." He got out and strode down the wide sidewalk to the green door of the wedding chapel. They'd passed several competing places as they'd driven through town. Some had a storefront, others resembled a plain house or the lobby of a hotel. A few actually appeared to be churches, but they all looked as if they were having some sort of identity crisis. Decorated with the exterior lighting of a casino, the signing and placards of a retail store, and the interior colors and furnishings of a cheap hotel, none were especially attractive. But this one wasn't as bad as most.

At first the small lavender lobby was empty, but as soon as the bell tinkled over the door announcing Thad's presence, a young chunky girl of about eighteen appeared from somewhere in the back and took her place behind a cash register. "May I help you?"

Thad told her what he wanted. She gave him instructions

on how and where to get the marriage license and charged him a hundred thirty dollars, in advance, for the ceremony.

When he returned to the car, Macy was reading a book entitled *Hematopathology*.

"Time to get the license," he said. "But it should only take a few minutes."

She nodded, seemingly immersed in her studies.

He came around the car and drove to the county courthouse, where he had her go in with him. No blood tests or birth certificates required, just one form of picture ID. They both flashed their driver's licenses and were back at the Sunnyside Chapel inside of twenty minutes.

"I'll get your clothes," he said, popping the trunk as they got out of the car.

"There's really no need to change, is there?" Macy asked, standing at the curb. "I mean, no one's even here to see us. If I don't wear it, I can take the dress back and save Lisa some money."

"Come on. We should get a good picture for Haley. She deserves a souvenir. And I'm sure Lisa wanted you to wear the dress, or she wouldn't have bought it."

"I don't think Lisa understands what's really going on here, even though I've tried to explain it to her," she muttered, but she dutifully took her hang-up bag and small suitcase into the changing room with her when they went inside.

Thad used another small room to change into his best suit and tie, then waited alone in what served as one of the actual "chapels." A small room with about ten fold-up chairs, it also had an abundance of dusty silk-flower arrangements and some candles arranged symmetrically in front of a sort of altar.

A noise drew Thad's attention to the doorway, where he

found Macy, looking as though she might bolt at any moment.

"You look…nice," he said, knowing it was a tremendous understatement, but trying to keep them on safe ground. She'd piled her dark hair loosely on top of her head, which revealed the delicate hairs that curled at her nape and accentuated the size and shape of her green eyes. Her dress was sleeveless and sort of bone-colored with a tailored bodice and a flared skirt that fell to midcalf. Nylons and strappy sandals finished off the ensemble, along with a touch of glossy, pink lipstick. She looked…well, stunning, and sexy as hell. But if he told her that, he might just pull her into his arms.

Hoping his expression didn't betray him, Thad motioned for her to come on into the room.

"Where's the minister?" she asked, hanging back.

"The girl out front said it's a woman. She should be here soon."

Macy nodded, sighed, then wrung her hands.

He smiled and handed her the bouquet he'd bought her. "You seem nervous."

Her chin came up, but when she answered, her voice was a little higher than normal. "I'm not nervous. Why would I be nervous?"

"Who knows what's going on inside that pretty head of yours? Why don't you tell me?"

She tugged at her lip with her teeth and moved closer to him, then looked over her shoulder once and lowered her voice. "I've just been wondering if…if you're going to kiss me. I mean, I think it might embarrass me if you let the minister know you don't want to. But—" she swallowed "—I understand if you don't…want to."

Thad watched her in amazement. She didn't know how appealing she was. That if he were any other man…

"This is just a business deal and all that," she was saying. "You don't really like me, I mean, in that way, but it wouldn't have to be a big kiss. Just a peck, so the minister doesn't know." Tears started to well in her eyes, but she blinked furiously and managed to hold them back. "I didn't think any of this would bother me, but now that I have this dress on and I'm holding this bouquet, I feel kind of like a real bride, you know?"

"I was going to kiss you," he said.

"Right." Her cheeks went pink and she nodded. "Okay."

MACY CRINGED INSIDE. Her and her big mouth. She'd already made a fool of herself once today, when she'd started that scene with her mother. She just didn't know when to quit, did she?

Avoiding Thad's curious gaze, she stared down at the perfect white roses in her bouquet, then smoothed the skirt of her dress, wishing the minister would hurry. She wanted to put this day behind her, get back to Salt Lake and what was real—soon. But another wedding party had arrived, a large and boisterous one, judging by the commotion in the lobby, and Macy guessed the entire staff was outside with them, trying to sell upgrades to the ceremony.

At last an attractive older woman of color breezed into the room. "Here's our happy couple," she said. Wearing a long black robe and introducing herself as Reverend Gilray, she promptly took her place at the front of the room. "Are we all set? Who's going to be our witnesses?"

Macy looked around the empty room. She hadn't thought of witnesses, apart from her mother....

"I paid for that service to be performed for us," Thad said.

"Fine." The minister's robes rustled as she went to the

door, spoke to someone in the lobby and returned with a stocky man and a petite dark-skinned woman, presumably chapel employees.

"Now we're ready. George and Amy will be our witnesses. Shall we get started?"

Thad motioned Macy closer. She took a deep breath and stood next to him.

George and Amy seated themselves and the minister cleared her throat.

"We are gathered here today…"

It was the customary ceremony, the one almost anyone could recite from heart, and yet the words stood out, having more clarity, more meaning to Macy than ever before. She was making a vow to love, honor and cherish Thad Winters for the rest of her life, and he was making a vow to do the same to her. Yet they didn't mean any of it. They were planning to divorce in nine months.

Macy's stomach knotted. Had they thought this through carefully enough? What if he left the cap off the toothpaste? What if he expected her to do his laundry? What if he stayed out late and came home reeking of another woman's perfume? Wouldn't that bother her even though it wasn't supposed to?

The minister was looking at her, waiting for her to respond, but when Macy opened her mouth, nothing came out. Thad didn't want her. He wanted a baby, and he had a way of getting one that didn't involve the intimacy most people shared in marriage. For a moment, she had a hard time remembering why she'd ever agreed to take this vow in the first place. Haley would get better. She wouldn't, couldn't die….

Thad touched her elbow. She could feel the force of his will, compelling her to respond, and finally the words came. "I do."

"You may now place the ring on your bride's finger."

Macy felt a circle of cool metal slide onto her finger and looked down, expecting the slim gold band she'd seen at Mateland's Jewelers. Instead, she saw the rock-size, pear-shaped diamond.

Her gaze flew to Thad's face. The smile she saw there shot warmth through her whole body. She'd told him he couldn't come to the birth, but he'd bought her the ring, anyway.

Oh, God. She was going to be hurt, completely devastated when he walked away....

"Why did you do it?" she asked, amazed.

He shrugged. "It looks good on you."

"You may kiss the bride," the minister said.

Time seemed to stand still as Thad pulled her into the circle of his arms and bent his head toward hers. She could smell wintergreen on his breath and felt the most incredible thrill of anticipation, as if she'd been waiting for this since the first moment they'd met.

But with Haley so sick, she couldn't afford to love Thad, too.

Ignoring the ripple of his powerful shoulders beneath her hands, and how badly she hungered for a real kiss, she went for the safe thing instead. Closing the last inch of distance between them, she brushed her lips quickly across his and jerked away.

He stiffened in surprise, and for a moment, Macy thought he was going to pull her back and kiss her right. But then the minister said, "I now pronounce you husband and wife," and the moment was gone.

"WHAT WOULD YOU LIKE?" Thad stared across the table at Macy, who appeared to be having trouble concentrating on her menu. Her gaze kept straying to the ring he'd given her, then to his face, then back to what she was supposed to be looking at in the first place, the words in front of her.

"Um—" she glanced at her ring again "—I'll have the salad."

He cocked an eyebrow at her. In his peripheral vision he could see the waitress approaching. "Which one?"

"The Cobb salad."

"We're in Vegas at a steak and seafood place. You sure you don't want scampi or lobster or something?"

She sighed. "I'm not very hungry. I just want to get back."

"Our plane doesn't leave for another two hours."

"I know."

"You might as well eat something and try to enjoy yourself."

"Okay." She glanced up at the waitress, who was already waiting, pad in hand. "I'll have the filet mignon."

"How would you like that cooked?"

"Medium well."

They went through the usual questions, soup or salad, choice of dressing, choice of drink. Then Thad ordered steak and lobster, relinquished their menus and turned his attention to Macy. "My partner, Kevin, and I went in to be tested as a marrow donor for Haley yesterday morning," he said. "Did they tell you?"

"No. Have you received the results?"

"Yes. I called the hospital while you were changing, hoping to be able to give you good news, but I'm afraid neither of us are a match. I'm sorry."

Her eyes grew bleak. After everything the nurse had told him yesterday about how difficult it was to find a donor, Thad knew why.

"That's okay," she said. "Unless it's a blood relation,

chances are pretty slim of it being someone I know. Thanks for being tested.''

She played with the rim of her water glass, and the diamond on her finger twinkled in the sunlight filtering in through the window. "Why did you buy me this ring?" she asked suddenly. "It's not very practical, considering we're only going to be married nine months."

Why had he bought the ring? Because she'd decided to go through with the pregnancy even though she didn't have to. Because of the sacrifices she was willing to make for her child. Because Haley might not make it despite the operation. And most of all because it was all he could give her. He was in love with his dead wife and couldn't plug the emotional holes in Macy's life, even though there were times he wished he could. Like when he visited Haley. Or when he saw Macy trembling with hurt and disappointment in her mother's living room. Or when she stood before him in her wedding dress, ready to trust him enough to marry him, looking more beautiful than he could have imagined.

Only, he didn't want to talk about any of those reasons. So he chose to rile her temper, instead.

"Maybe I was hoping it would make you relent and include me in the birth," he said.

Her eyes narrowed. "That's what I was wondering."

"So, will it work? What are my chances?"

"Next to nil. Does that mean you want the ring back?"

"No."

"And after the nine months are over?"

"It's yours. You can have the diamond reset, if you want."

"Are you giving me this so I'll have something to remember you by?"

He shrugged, wishing he was more impervious to the earnest look on her face. She really was beautiful, in an uncommon, elegant way. "I don't know. The money went for Haley. I felt like you deserved something, too. You can sell it if you want."

She looked out the window toward the casinos across the street. "I'm sorry I didn't get *you* a ring. But I don't have any money, and you'll have plenty to remember me by, anyway, right?"

He knew she meant the baby, but he didn't want her to think about that. Not today. He grinned. "You mean the bill?"

She smiled faintly. "Are you still planning to move in?"

"Yeah."

"When?"

"Tomorrow."

Their food came. Macy didn't say anything until the waitress had delivered their plates, asked if they needed anything else and walked away. "There's no hurry, right?" she said then. "I mean, why don't you wait until after finals to move in. I'll be under a lot of pressure until then and—"

"Chicken," he accused. "That's an excuse."

Her eyes widened. "What do you mean?"

"You're scared."

"Of what?"

"If that sorry excuse for a kiss you gave me at the chapel means anything, you're scared of me."

Her jaw dropped. "No, I'm not! It's just that I put you under a lot of pressure about that kiss, and I didn't want to make you feel like...I don't know...like it had to be a bigger deal than it was. It was nothing to worry about, just a quick peck—"

"Any quicker and I would have missed it altogether. But I wasn't the one who was worried about it in the first place."

"Well, it's over with now. There's no use even talking about it." She went back to her food.

He waited until she glanced up at him, then grinned. "I'd probably never mention it again if I could still move in tomorrow."

She paused. "And if you can't?"

"You might never hear the end of it."

Stabbing a bite of steak with her fork, she shoved it in her mouth. "Have it your way," she grumbled, and Thad nearly laughed out loud.

"THANKS FOR THE…the wedding and everything," Macy said, hopping out of Thad's car almost as soon as he pulled into her driveway. He wondered if she thought he was going to try to force his way in and convince her to let him stay the night or something. But that was too inconsistent with the other things she'd said and done that day, such as how she'd behaved about the kiss. She didn't know she stirred anything in him. And it was better that way.

She probably just wanted to be alone. They'd already stopped by the hospital and presented Haley with a bunch of balloons and the Polaroid pictures, taken by one of the witnesses at the chapel. The poor little girl had gotten up so early she could hardly keep her eyes open, despite the excitement. Another round of chemotherapy and radiation had taken their toll, as well, and when she fell asleep only minutes after they arrived, Thad was able to convince Macy to let him take her home. It had been a big day for everyone.

Well, it wouldn't take long to see Macy safely inside. He put the car in Park and cut the engine. "At least let me walk you to the door."

"That's okay. I'm sure I can make it," she replied. Exactly what most people told the bagger at the grocery store when faced with the question of whether or not they wanted help out. He thought it would be nice if sometimes they didn't ask and just loaded the damn things in the car.

Ignoring her, he popped the trunk, retrieved her luggage and carried it to the house. She unlocked the door, and they both went inside. He delivered her suitcases to her room, noting the neatly made bed with the thick goose-down comforter and the orderly dresser top, on which sat a jewelry box and pictures of Haley. Curious to know what Richard looked like, he glanced through all the photographs and poked his head into the other rooms looking for pictures of Macy's ex, but couldn't find any.

He came down the hall wondering how Macy had managed to erase him from her life so completely. Had she ever really been in love with Richard? "There's no boogeymen hiding in the closets," he said when he saw her. "I checked."

"Thanks. I'll rest a lot easier knowing that."

He grinned at her sarcasm, aiming to soften her up and almost yelled "Bingo" when a slight smile curled her lips. She really was too responsive for her own good, which made it very difficult to keep people at an arm's distance.

"It's only ten o'clock," she said. "I guess we may as well finish off our wedding day with a few minutes of conversation and a cup of coffee. I have a particularly good blend that one of my professors gave me as part of a gift basket when he heard about Haley. Any interest?"

He opened his mouth to accept, but she cut in before he could respond. "I'm warning you, though, if you say anything about caffeine being bad for the baby, you'll go home right away and you won't be allowed back here for weeks, maybe months."

Chuckling, he raised his hand like a pledge. "I won't say a word about caffeine."

"Good, then I won't have to kill you and plant you in my backyard."

She really had a sexy smile, he thought, not quite a dimple, but close, and lots of teeth. Even and white.

"I'm not pregnant yet," she was saying. "I may as well enjoy my last cup."

"So you are going to give it up?"

Macy growled at him, but he just laughed and followed her into the kitchen.

He took a seat at the table while she changed the filter in the coffee machine and set it to brewing a fresh pot. Thanks to the food he'd purchased, she had some poppy-seed muffins in her cupboard. He was about to suggest they have one when she reached up to get them down herself. Her sweater lifted to reveal a section of creamy skin on her midriff; her narrow skirt hugged her trim behind.

Shaking his head, Thad let his breath glide silently through his teeth and pulled his gaze away. It had been a long time since he'd looked at a woman like that. Must be something to do with the wedding. A preacher pronounces them man and wife and suddenly he feels he has a right. But they weren't serious when they took those vows. He had to remember that.

"Hardly what you'd expect on your wedding night," she mused, setting a plate in front of him, "but it's the best I can do."

Not if she set her mind on giving him something better, he thought, shifting uncomfortably in his seat. He shouldn't have come in. He'd been enjoying her quick wit, admiring her beauty, taking in the musky scent of her all day, but his libido had definitely shifted into high gear since they made it home. It had to be the expectations associated with a wedding night. The sudden and complete privacy. The frustration of missing her lips as they passed quickly over his during the ceremony. She'd been so close he could almost taste her, and then she was gone.

"You're awfully quiet," she said. "What are you thinking about?"

He rubbed a hand behind his neck and drew a deep breath. *About eighteen months of celibacy and how long that can seem.* "Nothing."

Putting one slender hand on her hip, she faced him more fully. The coffee perked and bubbled in the background. "I think you're getting tired."

He wished he was. "Did you really love Richard when you married him?" he asked.

She laughed. "Of course."

"Where are all of his pictures?"

"Right after he left, I gouged out the eyes, then burned them. The ones of us, anyway. I saved all the ones with Haley, for her, despite my anger. Someday she might forgive him for abandoning her and want them."

"But you won't. Forgive him, I mean."

"Maybe I will. When life gets easier. I don't feel ready to tackle that right now. And I don't think he cares much either way."

"Tell me how you met him."

She leaned against the cabinets. "Richard is the last thing I want to talk about. Besides, you know my whole life history, remember? Even the skeletons in my closet. Which gives you a distinct advantage."

"Why? Because you don't have any dirt on me?" He stretched his legs out in front of him and crossed his arms, enjoying the smell of the coffee as it brewed. He knew she felt embarrassed about the night she'd slept with that stranger, but it was nothing compared to some of his exploits. "What would you like to hear about? The drinking? The fights? The women?"

The coffee machine finally clicked, turning itself off, and Macy poured them each a cup. "Definitely not your sexual escapades."

"Don't worry. I was never like Richard. I had my share of women, but they liked it just as light and easy as I did. I never made promises I didn't keep, and I never left anyone in the lurch."

"Okay, then, tell me about the fights. Were any of them very serious?"

"Not really. My older brother was small for his age and had to wear thick glasses to see the blackboard. The other guys used to pick on him. I thought it was my duty to make the harassment stop."

"So you fought older boys?"

He ran a hand through his hair, chuckling. "Probably once a week. I was always getting suspended from school. And not only were the guys I fought a couple years older, they were a whole hell of a lot meaner. They usually kicked my ass."

"How did it stop?"

"I finally learned how to fight."

A smile curled her lips. "Any scars?"

"A few."

"Where?"

He lifted his shirt to show her where some drunk had cut him with a beer bottle on his left pectoral.

She surprised him by blushing, as though the sight of his bare chest embarrassed her.

"Ow!" she muttered. "You got that when you were just a boy?"

"No. I got this when I was twenty, in a bar fight, but it didn't hurt much at the time. I was too angry to feel anything. The asshole had just sideswiped my car and was trying to drive away."

She arched her delicate eyebrows. "I take it he regretted his decision."

"I hope so," Thad said, touching the raised flesh. "I know I regretted mine."

She laughed, her eyes lingering on his chest. "You don't seem so reckless now. What reformed you?"

"I met Valerie."

"Oh." She looked away. "That's testimony to the power of a good woman, I guess."

"Yeah."

She brought the sugar and cream to the table and a couple of spoons, then their cups and saucers. "Tell me about your brother. Does he live in Salt Lake?"

Evidently she didn't want to talk about Valerie any more than he did. Except that it helped build a barrier between them, stopped his body and the chemistry between them from taking over. "He's married now. Lives in Murray. I have an older sister who lives in Sugarhouse. I get to see them occasionally, but my parents are snowbirds now, ever since my dad retired."

Her spoon clinked against the sides of her cup as she added enough sugar and cream to make ice cream, if she wanted to freeze it, but her eyes slanted up at him as she listened.

"They go back and forth between here and Phoenix," he said, taking his coffee almost black.

"Are they coming home for the summer?"

"Yeah. Right now they're visiting the Grand Canyon. They should be home next week, just in time to hear the news that we eloped. I'm going to tell my whole family at the same time, get it over with all at once."

"And what are you going to say about the baby?"

He set his spoon on the table, wanting to choose his

words carefully. "As you know, our marriage solves a lot of problems."

"And that's one of them, because it puts the horse before the carriage."

"Right. They've been bugging me to move on with my life, get married again."

She licked her lips. "So you're going to let them think you tried. What, are you planning to tell them that I ran off and left you with our baby or something?"

Thad didn't answer.

"Well?"

He felt what could only be guilt stomp through his heart like a construction worker with muddy boots. "Something like that."

She frowned, staring down into her cup, and he had the urge to lift her chin and tell her everything would be okay. But he couldn't make that promise. He wasn't feeling too sure of it himself, so he kept his distance.

"That'll make me look good," she muttered.

He studied her reflection in the light that bounced off the window and the darkness beyond. "I'm sorry, Macy, but the truth would be worse, especially for the baby, right? We've already talked about all of this, or most of it." He hadn't specifically mentioned his parents before. Maybe that was one ramification she hadn't considered. He guessed there'd be aspects of their deal that would surprise him, too. His desire to slip his hands up under Macy's sweater was one of them.

"I know." She sighed and finished stirring her coffee, then twirled a finger in the wisps of hair that had fallen down from the mass of curls on top of her head. "Haley will have her operation. That's what matters. I can't forget that."

She spoke more to herself, so he didn't answer. Toying

with the sugar, he took the conversation in a different direction altogether. "What made you go home with him?" he asked.

"Who?"

"That guy from Studio 9."

Macy grimaced. "I don't know. I was drunk, but I can't really use that excuse. I'd gone there planning to go home with someone. I think I was trying to convince myself that I wasn't so unappealing, you know? My husband had just left me for a girl more than ten years my junior, someone not even out of high school yet. I wanted to make sure I could attract a man."

Attract a man! If he wasn't still in love with Valerie... If he had any less restraint... "You could have had them standing in line," he said. "Why did you choose him?"

She shrugged. "He'd come on to me a lot. He was convenient. And I wasn't about to risk rejection." She took a sip of coffee. "I never knew how badly I'd regret it, though. I realized that night that I'm not cut out for meaningless sex. I just didn't want to be alone. You probably know as well as anyone, but after you've been married—even if it's not a great marriage, like mine—it's hard to be alone."

He focused on his own cup, finished his coffee and muffin, and crossed the room to set his dishes in the sink. He could make it so that she wasn't alone anymore, at least for tonight. There was nothing to stop him. Except his conscience. And probably, hopefully, her. "Loneliness makes people do crazy things."

"Yeah, like having a baby with a stranger." She gave him a weak smile.

Or taking more from another person than one has a right to take. She was already giving him his baby. He had no right to hope for more.

Marshaling his self-control, he turned and smiled. "Thanks for the coffee. I'll see you tomorrow."

She finished her own cup, set it on the counter and followed him out. "Good night."

He reached for the doorknob, hating the thought of going home to his empty bed and cold sheets, when a knock sounded on the opposite side. Surprised, he glanced at his watch, wondering who would be showing up on Macy's doorstep at nearly eleven o'clock.

The voice that came through the panel explained everything. "Macy, it's your mother. I know this probably isn't a good time to barge in, but I haven't been able to stop crying since you left. I'm sorry I missed the wedding. I think we should talk, honey, don't you?"

CHAPTER ELEVEN

MACY'S HEART LODGED in her throat. She stared at Thad. He was leaving and it wasn't even midnight *on their wedding night!* How would that look? He couldn't go. Her mother would know something was wrong right away.

"Go get in my bed," she whispered. "And take off your shirt or pull the blankets up to your neck or something."

He paused. "What about you? If this were a real marriage, you wouldn't be dressed, either."

She glanced down. She was wearing the same outfit she'd had on when they'd visited her mother in Vegas. That would definitely appear strange. "Hurry," she said as they both dashed down the hall.

Thad peeled off his shirt. His shoes thumped on her bedroom floor almost the same time he landed on the bed with a *wump*. Macy ducked into the privacy of her closet, stripped and pulled on her thigh-length summer bathrobe.

The pounding outside continued. "Please, Macy. I know it's your wedding night, but I have to talk to you."

"Coming," she hollered, forgetting to sound the least bit tired. "Damn!" she upbraided herself. "She's going to know. She *can't* know."

She headed out of the room, but Thad called her back. Meeting her halfway, he pulled the pins from her hair and ran his fingers through it, purposely messing it up. "That's more like it," he said with a wicked grin. "I'm not so tame that your fancy hairdo would have survived."

Macy didn't have time to respond. She darted down the hall just about the time her mother found the key she'd replaced under the mat and started letting herself in. Slowing to a walk, she tried to look sleep-tousled, which was difficult with so much caffeine and adrenaline pumping through her veins.

"Mom?" she asked as if she hadn't known it was Edna from the first knock.

Her mother entered the living room carrying a suitcase that was almost bigger than she was. How long did she plan to stay?

"I had to come," she said simply, setting her luggage down in the middle of the floor. "I'm sorry, Macy. I've done a lot of thinking today, and…and you're right. I haven't been there for you like I should have been. I was hiding from reality, closing my eyes and hoping Haley's cancer would go away." Her voice quivered with tears. "I'm getting old, Macy, and I just can't face another tragedy—not when it means we might lose Haley."

"Oh, Mom." Macy embraced her. "I'm sorry, too. You were probably doing the best you could. I just don't have any reserves right now. And you *have* helped me a great deal, in many ways."

Edna sniffed and passed a hand over her wet eyes. "Don't worry about the money I paid for your rent. That's not the issue here. I'm your mother, and that's what family is for. I'm just glad I had it to send. Besides, now that you have a husband to help you, we don't have to worry about that anymore."

Another ramification of her bogus marriage. Macy couldn't help wondering how many more there would be. But she didn't want her mother's help anymore, anyway. Almost since the day she'd turned eighteen, she'd taken care of herself, and she liked it that way. After school was out, she'd be able to continue with her medical transcription, in Haley's hospital room if necessary, and make enough to squeak by. Several of her old clients were already calling to see when she'd be able to start again. Her med school work made her particularly good at deciphering the names of drugs and details of treatment.

"Where's Thad?" her mother asked. "I feel terrible dropping in on you like this."

"He doesn't mind. He's already asleep."

"Mom, is that you?" Thad came padding down the hall, wearing one of Macy's robes, which was stretched taut across his shoulders. The ends couldn't meet until it reached his waist, and judging from the muscled calves extending below the pink, fuzzy fabric, he had little or nothing else on.

Macy blinked at him in surprise. "I was just telling my mother that you were asleep. There's no need to wake up, *dear*. You can talk to her in the morning."

"Wouldn't want her to think I'm antisocial," he said, giving Edna a hug. "I'm glad you came, Mom. Is this your luggage? Do you want me to take it into the guest room?"

"If you don't mind my staying a few days."

Only Macy would have noticed the slight hesitation before Thad's response. "Of course not. We don't mind, do we, honey?"

Macy forced a smile. "Of course not."

"Did you hear that?" Edna whispered, fresh tears starting down her face as Thad picked up the suitcase and moved away from them. "He called me Mom, twice!"

"That's what you asked him to call you," she mumbled. "Don't take it personally."

"What?" Her mother's forehead wrinkled.

"I said he's very personable."

"Oh." The puzzled look cleared. "I'm so glad you've

found him. He seems wonderful, Macy, just perfect for you.''

That's unfortunate, Macy thought, *because he might not make it till morning. At least not if I'm strong enough to strangle him.*

"Who's looking after Champ?" she asked, to change the subject as much as to satisfy her curiosity.

"My neighbor. He's not much for animals, but he'll watch Champ occasionally, and he's conscientious about seeing to his needs.''

"That's good. Well, you've got to be exhausted, Mom. It's late. Why don't you turn in? We can talk in the morning.''

"I am tired," Edna admitted. "And I want to get up early to see Haley.''

Macy gave her another quick hug. "Thanks for coming. It means a lot to me.''

Her mother followed Thad into the guest room. Their voices were too low for Macy to hear what they were saying, but she didn't move any closer. She didn't *want* to know. She stood in the living room, staring at nothing, waiting for the house to fall quiet. Then she crept back down the hall to find Thad sitting on the corner of her bed.

"What now?" he whispered when she'd closed the door.

"What now?" she echoed, propping her hands on her hips so she could glare at him properly. "What do you think you were doing calling her Mom?"

"She told me to. I was just trying to play the part, make it believable.''

"There wasn't any need for you to say anything. I had it all under control.''

"I didn't want her to think I resented her coming here. She'd think you married a jerk.''

"So what? You're leaving in nine months!''

"Why make enemies if I don't have to?"

"Why not? You're going to tell your family that I ran out on you and our baby. Nothing could make me look worse!"

"But you'll be gone by then, and you'll never have to see them again."

"That's supposed to make me feel better?"

He scowled. "Yes…no. I don't know. I didn't really take the time to analyze it. I just think it's worth the extra effort to make things pleasant while we're together. Is there anything wrong with that?"

"No." Macy closed her eyes and took a calming breath. It wasn't as though Thad had committed the unpardonable sin. He'd been a little overzealous, that's all. She just had a hard time with the deception, especially where her mother was concerned. By nature, she was honest and forthright, an open book.

But if she divulged what they were really doing, her mother would try to talk her out of it, or worse, give her the go-ahead and then feel partially responsible for the decision. The lie spared Edna that. It was actually a kindness. And, like Thad had said, there wasn't any reason things had to be unpleasant.

"I guess I'm just tired," she said. She looked at the fuzzy, pink bathrobe he was wearing and started to laugh.

He followed her gaze. "It was all I could find," he said defensively.

"Which was probably your first clue that you should have stayed in bed."

"I think we've already established that. The question is, what do we do now? I mean, your mother is going to find it strange if I go home tonight."

"Which is exactly why you're not going anywhere."

He eyed the bed. "Are you suggesting what I think you're suggesting?"

"I'm not suggesting anything. This sham of a marriage was your idea, and now we're stuck, so play your part, as you put it, and get into bed, *hubby*."

He rubbed his lip with one finger. "I don't know if that's a good idea. I might…forget myself."

"Oh, no, you won't. Because then I'd call the whole thing off." Macy went into the closet to change. She thought of donning the frumpy old nightgown he'd seen before. It was hanging on a hook only inches away from her and would probably go far toward keeping him from "forgetting himself," but she couldn't bear to wear that tonight. It was a matter of feminine pride.

Grabbing the ivory-colored silk pajamas she'd gotten at her bridal shower when she'd married Richard, she pulled them on, instead, came out and flipped off the light. "What are you wearing under that robe?" she asked. "Anything?"

He was still sitting on the bed, his arms on his knees. "A pair of boxers."

"That's close to a pair of shorts, anyway. You can sleep in those. Or in your pants." She shrugged. "Heck, you can even sleep in that gorgeous robe, if you want."

She climbed in on the right side of the bed, leaving plenty of room for him on the other side. Burrowing beneath the blankets, she adjusted her pillows, rolled onto her side and closed her eyes.

"You're going to trust me that easily?" he asked.

She kept her eyes closed. "You can sleep on the floor if you want."

He hesitated, and Macy finally leaned up on one elbow. "Look, I know you won't try anything. If you were interested in sex, you wouldn't have cooked up this whole artificial insemination scheme."

A muscle in his cheek tightened. "I think you're assuming too much."

"You still want the baby, right?"

"Of course."

"Then you won't do anything to jeopardize our agreement."

His eyes ran over her, then moved quickly away. She imagined it was because she looked a mess after what he'd done to her hair. "Right."

"Fine. Good night." She lay back and closed her eyes again.

After a few minutes, she heard Thad strip. Then the bed creaked and he stretched out beside her, lying on top of the covers.

Suit yourself, she thought, begging sleep to come and carry her away. But something told her it was going to be a very long night.

MACY COULDN'T turn over. At least she couldn't turn over and take the blankets with her. Something was tangled in them. Refusing to open her eyes for fear she wouldn't be able to go back to sleep if she did, she fisted her hands in the blankets and pulled. Hard.

Damn! They wouldn't give an inch, and she was cold!

Reaching out to get a better grip, she encountered something big and warm and... She quickly pulled her hands away as memory flooded her, bringing her instantly awake. Thad was in her bed. The covers wouldn't budge because he was sleeping on them, and taking up far more than his share of room.

Pressed to the very edge of the mattress, she made a noise of impatience, but he didn't stir. She leaned up to see if there was possibly more room on the other side of him, but he seemed to have settled himself right in the middle.

"Of course," she muttered, lying on her back and staring up at the ceiling. At least he didn't snore. Richard had made enough racket to rattle the walls, and used to keep her awake for hours. She'd try to race him to sleep, hoping to slip into oblivion before the snoring started. But at least with Richard she hadn't had to worry about moving for fear she'd touch him. Feeling like she couldn't move made her fidget all the more.

Rolling onto her side, she noticed how the moonlight peeked through the partially closed shades, highlighting Thad's silhouette as he slept, facing her. She could see his stubbled jaw, the contour of his cheek, the thick, dark lashes of one eye.

He had beautiful eyes, she thought, the sexiest pair she'd ever seen. She remembered how they'd lowered to her mouth as he'd bent his head to kiss her at the chapel and wondered what that kiss would have been like had she not taken matters into her own hands.

Would it have been tentative, experimental? No. He was too confident for anything that weak. Possessive? If she were Valerie, maybe. No, she'd guess Thad Winters's kiss would be gentle yet demanding. His lips would meet and mesh with hers, molding her mouth to his. He'd palm the back of her head and his fingers would delve into her hair as he parted her lips with his tongue to thrust inside. And she'd...oh, God, she'd melt. Her heart was racing just thinking about it.

"You're staring at my mouth."

Macy's gaze flew up and encountered Thad's eyes, now looking at her with something akin to amusement or curiosity or both. She couldn't tell. It was too dark.

"You were snoring," she accused, hoping he couldn't see her blush.

"It's pretty tough to snore when you're not asleep."

"You were asleep."

"Not once you starting wiggling around."

"Well, you were hogging the bed. What was I supposed to do?"

He lifted his head and looked around. "Oh. Sorry." He slid over, but didn't turn away.

"Where's all that bravado you went to bed with?" he asked.

"I don't know what you mean."

"You're hugging that foot of space like you think its home base."

"I just think you should stay on your own side."

"Or what?"

"Or nothing. That's the polite thing to do."

"But I'm beginning to think you don't really want me to stay on my side. When a woman looks at a man's mouth like that, it usually means—"

"Nothing. It meant nothing. I was just wondering how I was going to get all two hundred pounds of you off my blankets."

"Because you want me beneath them?" His teeth glinted against the darkness as he rolled off the bed and climbed under the covers. "All you had to do was ask."

And play by the light and easy rules he reserved for all women besides Valerie? "I don't think I want to be having this conversation." Not when they were completely alone, with his bare chest gleaming in the silvery light, its muscular contours more tempting to her hands than chocolate.

She started to flounce over, but he caught her arm. Pausing at the contact, she looked up at his face, trying to see through the shadows, then sucked her breath through her teeth when he let his fingers slide ever so lightly all the way down to her hand.

Macy told her flesh not to tingle, but that was a lost cause. The butterflies in her stomach mutinied, as well.

"We could amend our little deal, if you want," he suggested, drawing back. "I've been thinking about it all night. Forget the artificial insemination. We could do it the old-fashioned way. We're married, after all, and it would be a lot more fun. As long as we both went into it with the understanding that—"

"No." She didn't want to hear the understanding. Somehow she knew it would be something quick and temporary. "Our original deal has already changed into something much bigger than I ever dreamed. I think we'd be crazy to complicate the issue further by…by having sex. I know it's probably been a long time for you, and I'm sorry. A healthy man your age has a strong drive and you probably miss it a great deal, but—"

"Don't you miss it?" he asked, his eyes glinting in the moonlight.

"I…that's not the point. I have other things to worry about."

He didn't say anything.

"Good night." Macy turned away from him and curled up, feeling miserable and alone. He'd struck a nerve. She didn't miss Richard, or sex for the sake of physical gratification. She missed intimacy, unity, sharing her life with someone she loved. The first time, she'd made the mistake of marrying a man who couldn't think of anything beyond feeding his own ego. But they'd had Haley, and she'd tried to make the most of it. Now that Richard was gone, she wasn't going to sell herself short again. She wanted to fall in love, raise Haley, have other children. She didn't want a few nights' roll in the hay, didn't want the memory of it when the time came for Thad to move on.

The bed squeaked as Thad rolled away from her.

"Do you have enough covers?" he asked.

"Yeah, thanks."

"No problem."

"Did you ever get your sperm count?"

"Yeah. Lots of great swimmers."

Macy would have expected nothing less. For a moment, she was tempted to change her mind about letting him get her pregnant the old-fashioned way. What did it matter? She was going to have his baby one way or another. And she suspected that Thad was an incredible lover. If she gave in to the attraction she felt for him, perhaps she could let down the incredible load she was shouldering and lose herself in something tangible and real and exciting. Even if it was only temporary.

But she knew, with morning, reality would intrude. And her self-respect demanded she be able to look it squarely in the face.

THAD LOOKED TIRED and disagreeable. Wearing the same clothes he'd worn yesterday, he sat at the kitchen table, drinking a cup of coffee. He hadn't yet showered or shaved, and his hair stood up on one side.

If they were really in love, Macy would have hugged him from behind or planted a kiss on his cheek. Instead, she accepted a glass of orange juice from her mother, who was making scrambled eggs, gave him a polite smile and sat across from him at the table. "Good morning."

"Morning," he muttered.

"How did you sleep?" Edna asked from where she stood at the stove.

Had she slept? She and Thad had tossed and turned, waking each other up every few minutes. They'd kept as far apart as they could without actually falling off the bed, but somehow it wasn't far enough to allow either of them to fully relax. Macy had spent the night smelling his after-shave, sensing the heat of his large body only a foot or two away and dreaming of the kiss she'd denied herself at the wedding.

"Like a log," she mumbled.

Thad cocked an eyebrow at her, and Macy nearly made a face at him, but she was afraid her mother would see it.

"Will you eat some breakfast?" Edna asked.

"Sure." With her mother and Thad in the same room, Macy knew better than to refuse anything good for her health.

"Thad, Macy said you want children right away." Edna spoke with her back to them. She was still wearing the hair net she slept in every night and what she called a housecoat, a cotton print smock that snapped up the front. "Do you want a big family?"

"I'll take as many children as Macy will give me," he replied, a smile slanting one side of his mouth.

Macy ignored him.

Edna stirred the eggs, scraping the pan across the burner. "I'm so glad the two of you met. After Richard left, I was afraid Macy would marry on the rebound. That's what I feared had happened when she first told me about you. But now that I've met you, I think the two of you are perfect for each other."

Great. Her mother finally approved. She'd brought home at least a dozen men before she married Richard, but Edna had to like Thad.

The toast popped up, so Macy got out of her seat to butter it.

"With Haley so sick," her mother went on, "a new baby might be just the thing to…ease the pain."

Macy winced. A new baby she would never hold.

Thad didn't say anything. Looking a trifle guilty, he

downed the rest of his coffee and shoved his mug out of the way when her mother placed a plate of eggs in front of him.

"You're awfully quiet this morning, Macy. Must be all the excitement about the wedding," her mother said.

Macy carried the toast to the table. "Oh, yes. I'm so excited I can hardly see straight."

Her mother smiled. "I love seeing you so happy."

CHAPTER TWELVE

MACY SET her glasses aside and rubbed her eyes. It wasn't sinking in. She'd been trying to study since arriving at the hospital at eight, but the words were blurring together and seemed to bounce off her brain. *Superinfections: the overgrowth of Staphylococci, Pseudomonas or fungi...* The overgrowth of what?

Her mother and Haley were just a few feet away, talking and giggling as they worked the puzzle of a large Saint Bernard. It felt good to see Haley enjoying her grandmother. Macy wanted to close her pharmacology book and join them. She was too stressed, too tired, too worried to absorb anything remotely difficult. But time was so short. If she could just hold on long enough to pass her finals, just ten more days...

Putting her glasses back on, she took a deep breath and forced herself to keep reading. *The basic human T cell is a—*

"Ms. McKinney?" Dr. Forte stuck his head into the room, causing them all to look up.

"It's Mrs. Winters now," Edna volunteered. "Macy got married yesterday."

Forte raised his eyebrows. "That's wonderful news. Congratulations!"

Macy willed herself not to blush to the roots of her hair. "Thank you."

"Can I speak with you for a moment alone, please?" he asked.

A chill swept through Macy as she caught her mother's eye. What now? Every new hope the doctors had held out for her over the past year had been crushed in its turn. When they'd first found the tumors in Haley's abdomen, they thought surgery would take care of the problem. The cancer spread to her spleen. They tried chemotherapy, hoping for a remission, but the disease only paused before marching on to her pancreas. Next came radiation and the discovery of more tumors, these ones in her liver. Another operation, more chemotherapy, more radiation. The result? Cancerous cells in her spinal fluid. Now they were facing a bone marrow transplant. If that didn't work, Macy knew they were at the end of the line.

Edna drew Haley's attention back to their puzzle. Macy followed Dr. Forte out of the room and down the wide hall to a small cubicle that served as his office.

Perching on a hard plastic chair, Macy clamped her hands together to keep them from shaking.

"I've got good news," he said, smiling as he took his own seat behind a small cluttered desk.

Macy relaxed, but only fractionally. With a child as sick as Haley, *good news* was always a relative term.

"We've found a donor."

A donor! Fresh hope, too strong for the scars of past experience to temper or jade, charged through Macy like a lightning bolt. They had a donor. At last. "That's wonderful!" she breathed. "How? Through the National Marrow Donor Program?"

"Actually, he's local."

"I've been posting notices at school, begging people to come over and be tested. It's probably a student at the U."

"His age is about right. He's twenty-three."

"What's his name?"

"John Taylor."

A total stranger was going to help her save her child. His generosity awed her. "I'm grateful to him," she said, knowing the words were barely adequate. "When do you want to do the transplant?"

Footsteps padded down the hall outside. A man and woman glanced in as they passed, and Dr. Forte stood and closed the door. "First we've got to up the chemotherapy and radiation treatments to kill all the cells in Haley's blood. That will take a few days."

Macy nodded. She knew about this. The treatments would destroy Haley's own marrow, but that couldn't be helped. Haley's body had to start over using the healthy stem cells—the blood cells that have matured in the bone marrow—she would receive from Mr. Taylor. "Are you thinking of doing it next week?"

"Or shortly thereafter."

"And this donor, Mr. Taylor, he matches all six antigens?"

The doctor looked faintly uncomfortable. "Actually he matches five out of six, but it's a minor mismatch."

"A *minor* mismatch?"

"A technical term. It means there's hope for—"

"It means he's not a perfect match." Macy's heart sank. "It won't work," she said, shaking her head. "We have to put as many odds in Haley's favor as we possibly can. We have to keep looking for a donor."

"As you know, that's a lengthy process. We've narrowed the search to a handful of potential donors, but they still have to be contacted and scheduled to come in for further compatibility testing. Then we have to receive and evaluate the laboratory results and, if we find a better match, fly the donor in from out of state. The preliminary search found no matches in Utah.'' He frowned. ''And we're running out of time.''

Ice-cold fear blasted through Macy's veins. ''The cancer is moving that fast?''

''I'm afraid so. Her recent blood tests and X rays have me concerned.''

Macy squeezed her eyes shut. Her little girl. What she wouldn't do to save her little girl. If only there was something she could do!

''I need your permission to proceed,'' Forte was saying. He shoved a piece of paper full of fine print toward her. ''You've already paid for the transplant, so that's no longer an issue.'' He consulted his day-planner. ''Why don't we schedule it for a week from Tuesday?''

Macy stared at the paragraphs of legalese and the signature line below it. In order for the transplanted marrow to feel at home in Haley's body, the donor's and patient's human leukocyte antigens had to match as closely as possible. The closer the match, the less trouble Haley would have with ''graft-versus-host-disease,'' a complication that could arise after the marrow engrafts.

She could die from those complications. She could die while waiting for a better match. It was a decision no mother should have to make. ''Can I have tonight to think about it?'' she asked. Before med school, she would have taken the doctor's advice and signed on the dotted line immediately. But she'd learned a lot in the past two years; she'd learned just how human and fallible doctors really were.

Even though he was probably frustrated that she wouldn't simply sign the release, the lines of Dr. Forte's face creased into a long-suffering smile. ''Of course. Just let me know in the morning.''

"I LOVE YOU, Haley," Macy said, staring down at her beautiful daughter.

Haley smiled sleepily. "I know, Mommy."

"Don't leave me, baby."

"Huh? I won't."

"Promise?"

Haley made a quiet murmur of assent before her lids closed.

Macy rubbed the back of her daughter's hand and let the tears gathering behind her eyes slide down her cheeks. They were alone, and it was late. Edna had gone back to the house for the night. Macy guessed Thad was there, too, by now. He'd called earlier to say his parents had arrived home a week early. He was going to go see them and his siblings, but she hadn't heard from him since.

She should probably call to keep up the charade of their new marriage, for Edna's sake, but after she'd talked to Dr. Forte, Macy didn't have it in her to do any acting. She was too busy trying to decide which of the options open to her would provide her child with the best chance at life. She'd asked her mother and Lisa what they thought, but neither had been able to give her an answer. She was on her own with this. And all she wanted to do was sit and stare at her daughter, memorize every detail of her face so she'd never forget, just in case she guessed wrong...

Richard. For a moment, Macy's ex-husband crossed her mind, and she almost called him. He was Macy's father. He should be helping her make these kinds of decisions. But he wouldn't know what to tell her, anyway. She was grasping at straws, looking for an easier path.

"I thought I'd find you here."

At the sound of Thad's voice, Macy wiped her cheeks on the sleeve of her cotton-knit top and turned to see him standing in the doorway, dressed casually in a pair of blue jeans and a T-shirt from some Mexican *tacqueria*. Fortunately the lights were off, the room lit only by the glowing dials on the medical equipment along one side of the bed and a small night-light on the far wall. She doubted he'd be able to tell she'd been crying.

"How are your folks?" she managed to say, keeping her voice low so she wouldn't wake Haley.

"Fine. They had a great time in Arizona. They want to meet you, by the way. I told the whole family we eloped this weekend."

She kept her face averted, just in case he could see more than she thought. "I bet they loved that."

"They were more than a little surprised, but it was my brother and sister who were the most shocked." He chuckled. "They couldn't figure out why I never mentioned you when I had dinner with them a little over a week ago."

"I'm sure they're certain you've made a terrible mistake."

"I assured them that I haven't."

Macy had her own opinion about that, but she held her tongue. "Where did you tell them I was today?"

He settled himself in the seat on the other side of the bed. "Here. I explained about Haley. Otherwise, it would have seemed too odd that you weren't with me. Besides, the closer we stay to the truth, the better off we'll be." He nodded toward Haley. "How is she?"

Macy had to clear her throat before she could answer. Then she said, "Fine," so he'd tell her whatever he'd come to say and go. Or maybe this visit was strictly about impressing her mother. Well, Edna had left the hospital. He could go home, too, and get some sleep. Macy didn't have the energy to be civil to anyone, to deny the ache inside her that longed for someone to hold her. That longed for Thad to hold her.

Forget it. Don't want. Don't feel. He loves the beautiful woman in the photograph.

"It's getting late," she said to stop his focused regard. "Aren't you tired?"

"Probably not as tired as you are. Are you going to tell me what's wrong?"

"No. Did you move in today?"

"I didn't have time. I'll do it tomorrow. I did swing by my house to get my razor and clothes, so I can get ready for work in the morning, though."

"What are you going to do with your house while you're living with me?"

"Just lock it up. I don't want renters in there."

Macy glanced at her pile of books. She had class in the morning and lab in the afternoon, but she had no plans to attend either. She should have withdrawn from school when she had the chance. Now that she'd missed the deadline, she could only plead with her professors to give her an incomplete. But even if she managed to get them all to agree, an "I" would revert to an "F" if she couldn't finish her courses in three months. If she fell behind, she feared she'd never catch up. She was struggling as it was.

"Did you get some studying done?" he asked.

"No."

"Did you and your mother have another problem?"

"No."

He leaned forward, elbows on his knees. "Come on, Macy. Work with me here."

Twisting the ring he'd given her, she watched the shadows play across his handsome face. "Just go home, Thad," she said quietly.

"Here's your rollaway, Mrs. Winters." The nurse pushed a fold-up cot into the room.

Macy stood and Thad moved her chair to make room alongside Haley's bed.

"Is this your new husband?" the nurse asked. "Will you be staying here together?"

"This is Thad, Nurse Galloway, but he was just on his way out."

"So you're all set for the night, then?"

Macy nodded.

"Nice to meet you," Thad interjected, shaking her hand.

"It's a real pleasure to meet you," she replied. "We've been so excited here at the hospital about your good news."

"Thank you."

Macy didn't say anything until after she left. "Everyone's so happy for us," she echoed sarcastically. "My life is suddenly bright because you're part of it."

Thad's manner cooled. "So you want me to go?"

Yes…no. What Macy really wanted was to fling herself into his arms. He seemed so strong, so capable, and she was drowning. *Just hold me,* she thought. *Let me feel your heart beating near mine, reassure me that I can survive this nightmare.*

But she refused to be such a coward. She could face the tragedy in her life. She had no choice. Besides, his strength was an illusion. Men didn't stick when the going got tough. How many times had her mother told her that?

"Please," she said softly. She wasn't sure if it was a plea for him to go or to stay, but when he walked out the door, she wept.

THAD WENT BACK to his own house that night. To hell with what Macy's mother thought. To hell with Macy, for that matter. The past eighteen months had been difficult enough. He didn't need to complicate his life by inserting himself into her problems. He just wanted a baby. That was all.

After a quick trip to the bathroom to brush his teeth, Thad stripped down to his boxers, flipped on the television in his bedroom and climbed into bed. Tonight there'd be no sharing the covers, no tossing and turning, no sexual frustration. He'd watch the sports news, as he did every night. Then he'd go to sleep so he'd be rested for tomorrow. He had to pitch an ad campaign for a local restaurant chain that wanted a whole new image. They were looking at print, television and radio ads. It was an important account, and he'd already wasted too much time thinking about Macy and Haley this weekend, not to mention putting on a show for Edna.

The sportscaster came on and Thad turned up the volume. "Another home run for Mark McGuire put the St. Louis Cardinals on top five to four—"

The telephone rang. He glanced at it, hoping it was Macy, then tried to squelch the thought. Why would he want to hear from her? What did it matter if she'd treated him rudely at the hospital? That she wouldn't really kiss him at the ceremony or let him touch her last night? Theirs was a business arrangement.

It was probably his parents or maybe his sister calling.

Not likely at eleven o'clock.

Muting the television, Thad snatched the phone off its cradle. "Hello?"

"Finally. Where have you been?"

Thad turned the volume back up, telling himself he wasn't disappointed that it was only Kevin. "My parents got back today."

"Sam and June made it home safe and sound, huh?"

"Yeah, they're settling in for another summer."

"You ready for Rustler's Roost tomorrow? You got the storyboard done?"

"Not yet."

"...struck out for the third consecutive time at bat..."

"What? We're supposed to be at Martin's office at eleven!"

Martin Slinkerhoff owned the Rustler's Roost. Whether or not they got the account rested in his hands. "I'll be there."

"Man, we work too hard to piss away opportunities like this one. Ever since you got that baby idea—"

"I said I'll be there. And I'll be ready."

"Tell me what you got."

Nothing. He had nothing. And instead of coming home and working tonight, as he should have done, he'd driven all the way up to Primary Care Hospital to see Macy.

"I said I'll be ready. I'm coming in early tomorrow."

"Shit. You don't even have the creative."

"It's been a busy weekend." *And a lousy night.*

"Right. You've been too busy marrying a woman you plan to divorce."

"Anything else?" Thad asked, cutting him off before he could go anywhere with the Macy issue.

"...elsewhere in Major League Baseball, the Giants racked up their fourth straight win against the Dodgers last night..."

"Yes. I'm glad they found a donor for Macy's little girl."

"Run that by me again?"

"I called the hospital today to see if I was a match. I've been wondering about the results ever since you dragged me down there."

Thad felt a moment's guilt for not passing on the news. "And?"

"They said I'm not, but they think they've found someone who is."

He hit the mute button again and sat up. They'd found

a donor? Why hadn't Macy told him? "Who is it?" he asked incredulously.

"They didn't give me a name. I'm sure there's confidentiality issues involved. You didn't know?"

Thad didn't say anything. He was thinking about Macy and how she'd behaved tonight. If they'd found a donor, she should have been happy, hopeful. Something was wrong.

"Thad?"

"I gotta go."

"What?"

"I said I gotta go. I'll see you at eleven."

"You're not coming into the office before that? You said you were coming in early. What about Rustler's Roost?"

"I'll be there."

"Shit!" Kevin cursed. "Thad—"

Thad paid him no attention. He hung up and hopped out of bed.

STANDING IN THE DOORWAY of Haley's hospital room, Thad could see Macy sitting in a chair, leaning on Haley's bed, her chin on her hands. She was watching her daughter, but at the sound of his entrance she turned, and despite the dim light, now that he knew what he was looking for, he could see she'd been crying.

His chest tightened as he witnessed the evidence of her pain and worry, and he nearly turned around and walked right out again. She deserved her privacy. He had no right to intrude.

But he couldn't leave. He'd married her, hadn't he? And deep down, he wanted to stay, to help, if he could. Macy and Haley needed him, and the connection made him feel human again.

Unfortunately, being human meant he felt pain, as well as pleasure.

Macy dashed a hand across her face and sat up straight. "What are you doing back here?" she whispered. "It's nearly midnight."

He shoved his hands in the pockets of his jeans and leaned against the doorjamb. "Why didn't you tell me?"

"Tell you what?"

"That they've found a donor."

She studied his face for a moment. "Because it's not your problem. It has nothing to do with the artificial insemination. Nothing to do with our deal." A ghost of a smile flitted across her delicate features. "And things have already gotten complicated enough," she added.

He knew she was talking about last night, when they'd shared her bed. It had been complicated. He'd wanted to feel her beneath him, feel himself thrusting deep inside her. And there were moments when he could have sworn she wanted the same thing.

But she was only lonely, he told himself. Her feelings had nothing to do with him in particular. And his own desire stemmed from the need to appease his body after eighteen months of celibacy. He still loved Valerie, could never betray her by offering his heart, along with his body, to someone else. That would somehow lessen what they'd had, maybe make it disappear entirely, and too much of himself was still wrapped up in those years.

"If they've found a donor, what's the problem?" he asked.

She pinched her lip. "I have to make a decision."

"Do you want to talk about it?"

"Do you know anything about HLA typing?"

He moved into the room, sitting on the end of the cot

the nurse had brought in earlier. "No, but I know a med student who could probably explain it to me."

She leaned her head on one hand while drawing designs on the blanket with the finger of the other. "Well, transplant recipients and donors are matched by comparing human leukocyte antigens, or HLA typing."

He leaned back and stretched his legs in front of him, crossing them at the ankle and supporting his weight on his hands. "What's an antigen?"

"It's a protein molecule that exists on most cells of the body. They mark the cells as being 'of self.'"

"Okay. So the body's defense uses these protein molecules to recognize cells that should belong."

"Right. There are six HLA antigens that are considered important for marrow matching—two A antigens, two B antigens and two DR antigens. A perfect match is a donor who matches all six antigens as the patient. The donor they've found for Haley matches only five out of six."

"So it's not a perfect fit. But isn't six out of six hard to find?"

"Hard, yes, but not impossible. In order for the new immune system to work, it is important the HLA antigens match as closely as possible. The closer they match, the less problem Haley will have with graft-versus-host disease, or GVHD."

"GVHD, huh? That doesn't sound good."

Macy stared down at her sleeping daughter. Haley's profile was just visible in the dim light. "It's not. GVHD happens when the immune system from the new marrow attacks what it feels is foreign. What it's really attacking, though, is the cells of various organs. These attacks can cause rashes, diarrhea or jaundice. Or they can be far more severe."

"Then certainly we can find a better match. The nurse

who drew my blood last week said there's a registry of over three million volunteers who are willing to donate bone marrow."

"She was probably talking about the National Marrow Donor Program. They do have a lot of registered donors, but only about thirty percent of them have been DR typed. An initial search of their registry has shown several possible candidates for Haley, but they're all out of state, and it takes about two weeks to receive the DR-typing results once the donor has been contacted and agrees to participate. Even if the DR typing matches, the donor has to have counseling and a physical before the transplant can be scheduled."

He looked over at Haley, wishing, somehow, he could trade places with her. "And Haley can't wait?"

"Dr. Forte feels it's too big of a risk to wait any longer. The mismatch is 'minor,' meaning the mismatched antigens look alike and are crossreactive, which is better than a mismatch between two antigens that are not at all similar to each other. But..."

"But it's not a six for six."

"Right." Macy cleared her throat, probably fighting the same despair he felt. "I have to decide whether to let them go ahead with the imperfect match or wait for a better one."

"When do they want to do the transplant?"

"A week from Tuesday."

Thad rubbed his chin without speaking. Macy watched him, looking small and vulnerable, as though she was staggering under the weight she shouldered.

"What would you do if she were your daughter?" she asked at last.

Closing his eyes, Thad pinched the bridge of his nose, remembering the night he'd had to make the toughest de-

cision of his life. When Valerie was in the hospital after
the accident, the doctors had told him they could save his
wife or their baby, but probably not both. He'd chosen Valerie, of course, but the guilt of having turned his back on
his own child had never gone away. Probably never would.
Some decisions just left an indelible mark on a person's
life, like that Robert Frost poem said he'd read in college:
"Two roads diverged in a wood, and I—/I took the one
less travelled by,/And that has made all the difference."

Unfortunately for him, choosing Valerie hadn't made the
difference he'd wanted. He'd lost his wife and child
both....

"I'd probably go ahead with the transplant," he said at
last. He'd been tempted to take the easy way out, to tell
her he couldn't say, that it was a decision only she could
make. What if she took his advice and he was wrong—
again? But like the night of Valerie's accident, there were
no guarantees either way. And Macy looked so alone, so
lost and weary. He decided the only way to truly help her
was to have the guts to answer her honestly. To stand up
and help carry some of the responsibility, maybe even to
give her someone else to blame if things went wrong.
There'd been no one to do that for him. Just myriad faces
smiling sympathetically. *We're so sorry...such a tragedy...I know it's difficult, but you'll feel better with time....*

Now Macy was suffering the same kind of pain and confusion. Maybe he could give her something to cling to.

She nodded. "Okay. I think you're right."

"Come here." Thad stood and pulled the blankets back
so they could both climb into the cot and lie down. It was
the least he could do—to hold her and offer another soul
who was hurting, as he had hurt, the comfort of his body,
the support of his understanding.

He thought she might resist. She had so damn much

pride, was so busy trying to do it all on her own. But the day's events had taken the fight out of her. Still fully dressed, except for her shoes, she curled up in his arms as soon as he opened them to her and tucked her head into his shoulder.

"We'll get through this somehow, Macy," he whispered, kissing her forehead.

"We?" she whispered.

"You're a married woman now, remember?" he teased.

Silence settled over the room for several minutes, then, "Thad?"

"Hmm?" he responded, feeling warm and sleepy and comfortable with Macy curled around him.

"You can come to the birth," she whispered.

He smiled into the darkness. Macy had to have one of the softest hearts he'd ever known. How could she have gotten herself involved with him when she already had so much her plate? "We'll make that decision later," he said.

She didn't answer. Slowly her breathing evened out and, eventually, she slept.

CHAPTER THIRTEEN

"DADDY! DADDY!"

Macy blinked awake to see Haley sitting up in her bed, trying to gain Thad's attention. He was still asleep but was starting to stir as Macy reluctantly moved away from his big body.

"Haley, what's wrong?" Macy asked. Her daughter had another sore on her top lip, a side effect of the chemo, but she seemed to be in good spirits.

"My new daddy's here," she answered simply, as if Thad's presence was enough to start anyone's day off on the right foot.

Her daughter's easy acceptance of a relative stranger still bothered Macy, but she knew it wasn't in Haley's nature to approach anything with caution or reserve. What happy five-year-old did? It was her job as a mother to teach her those things, right?

"Haley, honey, you don't have to call Thad 'Daddy,' you know. You could call him Thad, just like I do."

"But I want to call him Daddy. He is my daddy, isn't he?"

"Well, um…yes, in a way, I guess that's true, but it's okay if you want to take a while to get to know him first. That's all I'm saying."

Haley's eyebrows knit above her swollen face, another side effect of the cancer drugs. She obviously didn't understand. But before Macy could explain more, Thad interrupted.

"She can call me Daddy," he said, sitting up and offering Haley a smile. "Hello, angel. How are you today?"

Haley's grin was like the sun coming out from behind a cloud. She reached her arms out to him. "Good," she said, even though Macy knew Haley no longer knew what feeling good was like.

Careful not to upset the IVs, Thad moved to her bed, took her in his lap and gently rubbed his large hand over her bald head.

"Where's my wig?" Haley asked, self-conscious, suddenly, about her lack of hair, which was something that bothered her occasionally.

"I think it's in the closet." Macy got up to retrieve the blond wig. Haley went through periods where it was very important to her to feel pretty. Or, at least, to look like a normal child. That she'd thought of the wig now testified to how much she wanted to impress Thad. Knowing that made Macy uncomfortable all over again. *Don't let him hurt her.*

But Haley was happy for now, she told herself. And now might be all they had.

Macy settled the long blond wig on Haley's head and adjusted it so the bang fell across her forehead, not above her ear. "Don't you look pretty, honey."

"Hmm, I don't know if I like it," Thad said. "I can't kiss your head with all this hair in the way." He kissed the wig in several places, always missing Haley's face, and soon Haley was giggling with abandon. Finally, she ripped the wig off of her own accord so he could kiss her.

The nurse who came in to administer Haley's medication smiled at the sight. "Someone's happy this morning."

"This is my new daddy," Haley announced.

Thad grinned up at the nurse. His hair was sticking up, but Macy resisted the urge to smooth it back. They'd slept with their bodies pressed close together, but she hadn't let her fingers seek the warm skin beneath his shirt, the toned muscles of his chest and arms, even though she'd awakened more than once and longed to do just that.

"What time is it?" he asked.

"Six-thirty," the nurse answered, bustling around the room.

He set Haley back on her bed while she replaced and adjusted the IVs that would deliver another round of chemicals into Haley's bloodstream. "I've got to go. I have an important appointment at eleven, and I'm not even close to ready. I'm going to give poor Kevin an ulcer."

"Kevin?" Macy echoed.

"My partner, remember?"

She nodded but felt a flicker of disappointment at the thought of his leaving.

It's just a reaction to the stress. I have to concentrate on my conference with Dr. Forte, she reminded herself. Somehow she'd hoped Thad would be with her when she met with the doctor. She wanted him to talk with Forte, get a feel for how much he thought she should trust his opinion. But that was silly. She was the one in med school. Haley was her daughter. And Thad knew nothing about non-Hodgkin's lymphoma or its treatments.

"Thanks for last night," she said, walking him partway down the hall. "It was nice not to be alone."

With a glance around them, he stopped and took her elbow, turning her to face him. "The insemination is scheduled for Thursday morning," he said, "but I've been thinking that we should wait until after the transplant—"

"We'd have to wait until I ovulate again. That would take another month."

"I realize that. But you're going through so much right now, it doesn't make sense to add to your stress level."

She grinned. "Aren't you afraid I'll back out?"

He watched her for a moment. "You have that right. I'm not going to try and railroad you."

"I know."

"Except that you did say I could go to the birth," he added, giving her the sweetest smile Macy had ever seen. "Did you mean it?"

The thought of having Thad's baby caused Macy's stomach to tingle, along with an area a little farther down. What was happening to her? she wondered.

She was falling for him, that was what, falling hard—and asking for a whole new world of heartache. "I meant it."

His eyes warmed. "I'll call and reschedule the appointment, then."

Macy caught Thad's arm before he could go. "No, let's go through with it this Thursday." *While I still have the courage.* "It should only take an hour or so."

Thad raised his eyebrows. "You're sure?"

"I'm sure," she said. And for the first time since she'd met him, Macy decided that maybe she wouldn't give him up without a fight, after all.

THAD SAT STARING at the results of his brainstorming session and frowned. It was still early. He was alone in the office, but he was getting nowhere. Fast.

Taking out the battery-powered razor he'd brought to work with him, he laid an old T-shirt across his desk to catch the whiskers and began to shave. What now? He'd considered trying to sell Rustler's Roost on adopting an animal mascot for their television commercial, but everything he thought of was too juvenile for the upscale steak and chicken restaurant. They'd hired one of the best chefs in the area to create some new pasta and salad entrées, but without a bold new advertising campaign, the same old clientele would frequent the restaurant and would order the same old things. And their normal clientele was aging, which made it easy to forecast a decline in sales in coming years. To grow the market the way they wanted, they needed to appeal to the younger crowd and the growing number of vegetarians in the populace. But how to reach the twenty-to-thirty-five-year-old cohort in an effective, innovative way...

"How's it going?" Kevin entered his office without knocking, carrying two cups of coffee, one of which he deposited on Thad's desk.

Thad glanced at the clock encased in a perpetual-motion device sitting on top of his credenza. Seven-forty. The secretaries would be in shortly, and his quiet think time would be gone. The phones would ring, employees would congregate at the coffee machine and talk and laugh, and Kevin would remind him every five minutes that the time of their meeting was speedily approaching.

"Pretty good," he lied, shutting off the hum of his razor and trying to look more optimistic than he felt as he rolled up the T-shirt. He'd been doodling, trying to free his mind up enough to do his favorite part of the job—the creative, or the idea for the ad. But thoughts of Macy and Haley kept intruding. He was worried about them both, excited by the upcoming insemination, confused by the desire that licked at his nerves whenever he and Macy were close enough to touch. It warred so completely with the loyalty he still felt toward Valerie, yet seemed so right in other ways.

He sensed he was losing...something. He'd hung on for eighteen months only to feel a part of himself slipping away, which caused a bit of panic, enough so that he was almost glad to be thrown into crisis mode on this job. Especially when, as a bonus, it kept Kevin too preoccupied to grill him about his new wife.

Sitting in the artsy black and silver chair across from Thad's desk, Kevin angled his long, thin, basketball player–type legs out in front of him. "We're in trouble, aren't we?" he said. "You don't have anything."

Thad shrugged and shoved his paper under his blotter so Kevin couldn't see just how much of nothing they really had. "I wouldn't say we have nothing. I've had a few ideas that might work."

Kevin took a drink of his coffee, then grimaced as though it was still too hot. "Okay, shoot. Let me hear what you've got."

Advertising agencies typically employed two distinctly different kinds of thinkers: creative minds and business minds. In Thad and Kevin's homegrown firm, they each did both, sales and marketing, and the creative. And they often did it as a team, which had its drawbacks. Thad wouldn't be able to bluff his way out of this the way he could if Kevin were some completely left-brained number cruncher.

"Well, I was thinking we could go with a Mafia theme," he said. "That always makes for a smile and ties into the distinctly Italian bent of some of the Roost's new entrées. We could have some guy sitting at the table wearing concrete shoes but eating with apparent gusto. Then the Godfather, who's sitting across from him can rasp, 'At Rustler's Roost, you'll get the best meal you've ever had, even if it's not your last.'"

Kevin raised his eyebrows.

Okay, so it was pretty weak. But there wasn't a lot to tie

the Western images evoked by the restaurant's name to pasta and salads.

"How about we use a cow wearing a big sign that says, 'Give cows a break. Try the new pasta entrées at Rustler's Roost,'" Kevin suggested.

Thad had thought of something similar, back when he was still considering animal mascots, but had discarded it. "I don't think they want to go that far. Beef is still their main business. We're not out to destroy that, only to bring in a sector of the populace that isn't interested in red meat."

Kevin tried his coffee again. "What about, 'Get a thief of a deal on pasta at Rustler's Roof.' You know, play into the rustler part."

"It's a pretty pricey menu. I don't think we want to go for the price angle." Thad slid his paper out and started doodling again. "Maybe I should quit fighting the cowboy theme. With a name like Rustler's Roost and the restaurant's saloon-style appearance, I think we're pretty much stuck with it, anyway. We could have an old cowboy do the commercial and say something like—" Thad lounged back to adopt the correct attitude and spoke in a drawl "—'Rustler's Roost has the best darn pasta and salads a body can rustle up, and that ain't no bull.'"

"That ain't no bull." Kevin thought for a moment, rubbing a finger over his upper lip. Finally he said, "I like that. We could even use it for the radio spots."

"Yeah. We'll get someone with a deep, distinctive voice—"

The telephone rang. Thad picked it up because none of the secretaries were in to answer it, secretly hoping it was Martin Slinkerhoff needing to reschedule their eleven o'clock.

No such luck. It was Thad's mother. "Hi, Mom. What's up?" he said, glancing at the clock again.

"Your father and I were hoping we could go to the hospital today and meet Macy and Haley."

"I don't think so. Not today. She, I mean *we,* just got some bad news. Haley's tests aren't coming back with the kind of results we were hoping for. They're going to have to do the bone marrow transplant next week, so they've upped Haley's chemo and radiation. And Macy's got finals in a week and is pretty stressed out. I think the family should give her some space—for a little while, anyway," he added, to soften his response.

"Give her some space?" His mother's tone sharpened. "She's losing her only daughter, and you want us to give her some space? We may never meet Haley if we give Macy space. And we're her family now, Thad. She needs us." His mother's voice cracked, causing Thad to realize the size of his blunder. June was the most empathetic woman in the world. Just the mention of Haley's sickness had caused tears to stream down her face when he'd told her yesterday, and he suspected she was crying again now. He wanted to caution her not to overreact, to admit to her that they weren't *really* family, but the truth was out of the question. His parents would never understand about the baby, not when they'd been after him for months to put Valerie's ghost to rest and start dating again.

"Her own mother's in town right now," he hedged. "And having a lot of visitors increases the risk of infection for Haley. They have her in a sterile room—"

"We can't scrub up?"

They could. Thad and Macy and anyone else who came to the hospital to see Haley did just that every time they visited.

Thad pinched the bridge of his nose, wishing Kevin wasn't sitting across from him, a mocking expression on his face as he sipped his coffee.

"Mom, I don't have time to argue about this. I have a really big appointment—"

"You're concerned about a business appointment at a time like this?" she interrupted, her voice rising another octave. "Where are your priorities, Thad? If your wife's at the hospital with your stepdaughter, that's where you should be, too."

Thad shook his head and rubbed his left eye, which was beginning to twitch. "Calm down, Mom. Macy's handling things quite well. She understands that this appointment is very important, not just to me, but to everyone who works here. And I'm heading back to the hospital as soon as it's over," he added for good measure.

She sniffed. "That's more like it. We'll meet you there. What time do you think that will be?"

Aw, hell. His mother had maneuvered him right where she'd wanted him in the first place. Thad would have laughed if he didn't want to strangle her so badly. "Just after noon, around one o'clock."

"And she's at Primary Care?"

"Yes, the one next to the University Hospital. It's on Medical Drive, just off South Temple."

"I know where it is. We'll see you there at one."

With a sigh he didn't bother to hide from Kevin, Thad hung up. His mother meant well, but once she got something in her head, there wasn't any telling her different. And she threw herself behind a worthy cause faster than anyone else he knew.

"June wants to meet Macy?" Kevin smiled like the Cheshire cat.

Thad nodded and took a bolstering sip of the coffee Kevin had brought him, only to grimace at the amount of sugar in it. "Jeez, do you drink your coffee this way?"

"What?" Kevin blinked at him innocently. "There's got

to be some redeeming feature to this bitter brew besides the caffeine.''

Thad chuckled. Heaven help him through this day! Somehow, when his parents were out of town, it was easy to picture them playing only a minor role in his and Macy's lives.

Not a very realistic expectation, at least not with June.

''Let's get working on the storyboard,'' he said. ''As long as we can pitch the idea, we don't have to have anything fancy. We can always do a more detailed workup if Martin wants it, but I'd like to have something simple to give him an idea of what we're suggesting.''

''You're trying to change the subject.''

Maybe he'd strangle Kevin, too. Or instead. At least his partner could defend himself. ''Of course, I'm trying to change the subject. Our meeting is in less than three hours.''

''Good morning!'' Luanne, his middle-aged battle-ax of a secretary, poked her head in the room, bringing her usual scent with her, which was two parts antique store and one part cedar storage. ''You missed a spot,'' she said, touching her chin, and Thad wondered how she could see so well from the doorway. Nothing got past her.

Turning his razor back on, he stroked the head of it across his face, then angled his chin up for her approval. ''Perfect,'' she said. ''I see you've got your morning coffee, but I'll go ahead and brew a pot for everyone else.''

Thad shoved the sickeningly sweet coffee away. ''No, bring me some, too. Black. And hold all my calls. I've got—''

''Rustler's Roost at eleven. I know,'' she said.

Thank goodness he had such an efficient secretary. Too bad his mother hadn't called just a few minutes later. Luanne would have been a good match even for June.

He turned his attention back to Kevin, only to find his friend watching him with one eyebrow cocked.

"What?" he asked, feeling more annoyed by the minute.

"Tell me what's going on with you and your new *wife*."

"Nothing. You know we have a deal. Nothing's changed."

"Deals like that *always* turn into much more than you bargained for, and usually something ugly. I tried to warn you. You're in over your head, aren't you?"

"No!" Thad growled, but then he remembered Macy's body snuggled up against his the night before and how badly he'd wanted to claim her as his wife in more than word alone, and knew the "deal" was getting away from him, after all.

"GRANDMA'S COMING to visit!" Haley announced just after Macy returned from grabbing a quick bite of lunch in the cafeteria.

"What?" she asked. Her mother had stopped by the hospital over an hour ago to say goodbye. When she'd come to Salt Lake, she'd left Vegas in a hurry and felt that she should go home and take Champ off her neighbor's hands, pick up her mail and water her plants. After making arrangements to be gone longer, she was planning to return next week, in time for the transplant. But she should have been well on her way back home by now. "Did she forget something?"

"Huh?" Haley had glanced at the Pokémon program that was playing on the television above her bed, and it had sucked her in that fast.

"Grandma. Why is she coming back? Did she forget something?" Macy prompted.

"No, silly." Haley giggled. "She's not coming back. It's my *new* grandma, Grandma June."

"You don't have a—" For a moment, Macy almost forgot she was married. Thad was never far from her thoughts. He was too large, too in charge, too sexy to forget. But she'd never considered his family when she'd consented to marry him. She'd thought only of how their arrangement would affect the crises at hand. "Do you mean Thad's mother is coming?" she asked in surprise.

Haley nodded. "She called me. She's bringing me some presents. She said I could have anything I want."

"Oh, really." Letting Haley go back to her television program, Macy grabbed the phone to dial Thad. If his mother was coming, she wanted him here with her to field the more difficult questions. She didn't know what he'd told his family so far and didn't want to contradict him. Besides, the marriage was his idea. Let him worry about what should or should not be said.

Which sounded good in theory, but the secretary on the other end of the line told her that Thad Winters was out until after three o'clock. She got only his voice mail when she tried his car phone.

Great. Now what should she do? For a moment, she thought of heading back to the cafeteria to hide. But she didn't want to leave Haley alone with a virtual stranger.

"Hi, Macy babe!"

Macy jumped, but it was only Lisa.

Thank God it was Lisa! "You can't leave here until they're gone," she blurted.

Lisa looked behind her as though she expected to see someone else. "I think you're finally cracking up, Macy. What happened to 'Hello, how are you? Don't you have to work today?'"

"Hello, how are you? Don't you have to work today?"

"Nope." She gave Macy her customary hug. "I traded shifts with someone who needed a day off next weekend."

"Great, then you can stay."

"Sounds like I don't have a choice. What's going on around here?" She turned to give Haley a squeeze before the little girl fell out of bed reaching for her.

"My new grandma's coming," Haley told her.

Lisa's eyes widened. "Thad's parents?"

Macy nodded. "What if I say something that gives us away?"

"I think we'll have a bigger problem if you don't."

"What's that supposed to mean?"

Lisa pulled Macy out into the hall and lowered her voice. "It means that it's not fair to these people to think they have a granddaughter when they don't."

"I know that. But what can I do about it now? It's Thad's family. The marriage, what he told them about it, was his decision."

"But what if they take this whole thing seriously and get close to Haley and—"

"If she lives, she'll be hurt even more by the divorce. And if she doesn't, they'll have to suffer right along with me." Macy groaned and dropped her head in her palm. "This whole thing was a mistake, wasn't it?"

"No, just the part where you married Thad Winters and agreed to let him move in. Having his baby was necessary to—"

"Macy?"

Macy whirled at the sound of Thad's voice, but her relief was short-lived. No less than six adults followed him, all of them beaming at her with a mixture of curiosity and warmth. "Oh, no, he brought an army," she whispered.

Lisa cleared her throat and smiled. "Don't look so stricken," she advised through her teeth.

Macy masked her nervousness, focused on Thad and tried to look a lot less tentative than she felt. "Hi, honey."

"Hi." He grinned and looped his arms around her waist, pulling her to him for a peck on the mouth. A show for his family, no doubt, but Macy would have enjoyed it all the same, if she hadn't been so concerned about their audience.

"My folks have been dying to meet you. I hope you don't mind the surprise. I was tied up all morning but tried to call a little while ago. No one answered."

"Haley must have been too intent on the television. I was downstairs eating lunch. How did your big meeting go?"

"We have an appointment next week. I have to finish the storyboard and talk to a couple of directors so I can get a better estimate of how much the commercial is going to cost, but Martin Slinkerhoff, the owner, likes the idea. We're moving ahead."

"That's great." She looked to the older woman, who was positively beaming at her. Short and plump, she had bluish hair and her arms were loaded with gifts. "This must be your mother, June," she said, offering a smile.

The woman shoved the gifts she'd been carrying into the hands of the young, slender woman next to her and hauled Macy into her arms. "Call me Mom," she insisted. "We're so happy to have you in our family. I can't tell you what a relief it is to see Thad married again. And we want you to know we're here for you. Haley belongs to us, too, now. We'll fight this thing together."

The last thing Macy had expected was the unquestioning support of Thad's mother. She started to back away, feeling guilty for the lies she and Thad were perpetuating and the assumptions others drew from them. But June wasn't finished with her yet. She held her for several minutes, rocking her like a child, crying in empathy for her and Haley's struggle.

While the others looked on, their faces earnest and kind,

Thad's mother's motion and her touch soothed something so deep inside Macy she never dreamed anyone could ever reach it. Tears started to fill her eyes, but she struggled valiantly to hold them back, telling herself the whole thing wasn't real. It was an illusion, built on a falsehood.

Yet the love June offered seemed real. Macy felt as if she'd been running a long, hard race, and just when she couldn't go any farther, just when she was fighting for every painful inch on willpower alone, this woman came out of nowhere, gathered her in her arms and began to carry her with fresh energy and determination.

Caught in an awkward box of guilt and hope and need, she glanced at Thad, who shifted uncomfortably.

As soon as June let her go, Thad cleared his throat and introduced her to his father, Sam, who was almost as tall as he was, with short gray hair. Sam kissed and hugged her, then Debra, his slender, attractive sister, Gary, his brother, and their spouses, Steve and Melissa respectively, all hugged her in turn.

"Welcome to the family."

"We're so sorry about Haley's illness."

"We're glad Thad's found someone to love again."

You mean, Thad's found someone to give him something to love, Macy thought with a pang of envy. If only he wanted her as much as he wanted the child they had yet to conceive…

She risked another glance at his face. He'd just introduced Lisa to everyone and was talking to her and his brother-in-law about some movie they'd all seen recently. And it struck her then that his family, these people, were part of the reason he was such a fine man. He'd known nothing but love and generosity his whole life, a legacy their child would inherit. Even if he shut her out, she knew their child would never want for a warm embrace, a listening ear, a feeling of belonging. Somehow that made what they were going to do in less than three days easier. And somehow it made it harder, too.

"Well," Macy said, devastated and overwhelmed on the one hand and already completely enamored with Thad's family on the other, "I guess you'd like to meet Haley."

His mother shifted the gifts that were now back in her arms to squeeze Macy's hand. "We'd love it, dear," she said simply. "We have only three grandchildren. Haley will be our fourth."

Oh, no. Macy couldn't take any more. She felt like a thief, robbing these people of love she had no right to accept. "I'm sorry," she started, "but before we go any farther, Thad and I need to tell you something."

Before she could say more, she felt Thad's long fingers close on her elbow. He gave her a warning squeeze, but she looked up at him and shook her head.

"I have to tell them the truth," she whispered.

"What truth, dear?" his mother asked. "You can tell us anything."

"We're going to have a baby," Thad blurted.

CHAPTER FOURTEEN

"WHAT ARE YOU DOING?" Macy whispered harshly, now alone in the hospital corridor with Thad. "You told your family we're having a baby! Now they're talking about throwing me a baby shower and knitting baby booties!"

"We are having a baby," he said. "You told me this morning that you'd keep the appointment this Thursday. Have you changed your mind?"

She hesitated, and his stomach knotted. "Have you changed your mind?" he asked again.

"No." She sighed. "I just can't be the fraud you want me to be. I think we should tell everyone the truth."

"Including your mother?"

"No, not her! She'd never understand. Our relationship would never be the same if she learned—"

"So you just want to tell *my* family. Is that it?"

"You don't know how guilty it makes me feel when they hug me and say all those nice things," she argued.

Thad glanced behind him. The nurse sat at her station, talking on the phone. Two doctors conferred outside room 2. His family's voices could be heard inside Haley's room just down the hall.

"You're taking it too seriously," he insisted, even though, since his family had met Macy and Haley, he'd had to stretch his collar a few times, too. He'd never dreamed they'd be so passionate about embracing the situation. He'd pictured himself easily in charge, filtering the bits of information he wanted them to receive. But they'd grabbed the ball and run with it, and now he had to figure out a way to wrest it back. "Everything's fine."

"Fine? Your parents are planning to stay at the hospital in shifts. You call that fine?"

He shrugged. "I'll talk them out of it, tell them the doctor won't allow any more extra visitors."

"More lies?"

"Wait a second." Thad propped an arm against the wall, near the side of Macy's head. "It's okay to tell your mother whatever story will smooth the way for a healthy relationship between you, but when it comes to my family, what we're doing is wrong? It's our lives. What we do is none of their business."

"I think they plan to make it their business. Have you any idea how much they love you?"

Thad ran a hand over his face. He did know they loved him. And he owed them more than the concocted story he was feeding them. But he and Macy were already this far into the deal. They couldn't turn back now, not when he was so close to achieving what he wanted. "I love them, too, but in nine months this will all be over. And for now..."

He pushed away from the wall and took a step back because the scent of Macy's perfume brought back memories of the night and its temptations. She hadn't changed her clothes since sleeping in them, had cried away any trace of makeup and had pulled her hair back in a ponytail to compensate for the fact that she had bigger things to worry about than curling her hair. And still he thought she was one of the loveliest women he'd ever seen. And every day she seemed lovelier.

It was her need that attracted him, he reminded himself. He was a sucker for a woman in distress, anyone in distress, really. It came from being his mother's son. The fact that he was creative on top of softhearted is what had landed him in this mess to begin with.

"For now it will be good for Haley to have my family behind her," he said. "It might help her through this difficult time."

"And tomorrow will take care of itself?" Macy asked dubiously.

"Let's just say we'll handle first things first. Don't you think we have enough going on for one week?"

"Artificial insemination for me this Thursday, Haley's transplant on Tuesday, then my finals." She smiled for the first time since he'd pulled her out of Haley's room. "I'm nuts."

"You're beautiful," he said before he could stop himself.

Macy blinked up at him in surprise, and he noticed her eyes, their incredibly clear green. He wanted to kiss her. She wouldn't stop him, judging by the way she was looking at him.

Forgetting that they were standing in the middle of the hospital corridor where anyone might see them, Thad started to lower his head, his gaze intent on Macy's moist warm mouth, intent on how good it was going to feel to let himself melt into her.

"Give me more than a millisecond this time," he murmured, and she seemed to know exactly what he was talking about because she smiled even as her lips parted slightly in anticipation.

He could feel her sweet breath on his chin, could almost taste her. Then his sister's voice shattered the moment. "Here they are!"

Thad drew away to stare at Debra, at last remembering Valerie and all their promises and plans for the future. Valerie had been gone only eighteen months, and already the physical part of him was ready to move on. He'd justified his willingness to make love to Macy on the night of their wedding as a means to an end. He wanted to get her pregnant. He couldn't develop a more direct approach. But there wasn't any reason he should want to kiss her here in the middle of the damn hospital. Maybe he wasn't the man he thought he was.

Macy's needy right now, that's all.

He shoved a hand through his hair. *Hell, maybe I'm needy, too.*

"Haley wants you to watch her open her other presents," his sister said, obviously embarrassed at having interrupted them.

Hauling in a deep breath, Thad managed a smile, took Macy by the elbow and led her back into the room.

THE NEXT TWO DAYS passed quickly. The chemo was making Haley sick again, so Macy lived at the hospital, studying and sleeping when she could, holding and loving her daughter when she couldn't. Thad's family came three or four times a day but never stayed long. They didn't want to tire Haley and seemed to know just how much support to give and when.

Macy was beginning to believe Thad's mother was clairvoyant—although she hadn't yet divined the falsehood of their marriage. She understood the pain and worry of others without them having to say a word, and she had the most generous heart Macy had ever known.

But as warm as Macy's feelings toward the Winterses were, they fell far short of Haley's. Macy's daughter lit up at the sight of anyone or anything remotely connected to Thad, and to her new daddy, most of all. She talked incessantly about him, showed Macy again and again whatever new toy or bracelet or book he'd brought her, colored picture after picture just for him and proudly announced that he was her daddy when any of the nurses or doctors were present.

Macy was beginning to suspect it was Haley that put that special sparkle in Thad's eye, too. He came as often as his family, but stayed longer each time. Last night he'd even shared a cot with Macy again and helped with Haley when she got sick during the night. But besides giving Macy the comfort of his arms around her, he hadn't touched her in any more intimate way.

"All set?" Thad stood at the door, waiting for her.

Macy glanced once more at Haley, who was busy with a new stamping set, before nodding. It was Thursday, time for the artificial insemination, and she had just returned from home where she'd showered and dressed in a sleeveless sundress that flowed almost to her ankles, and a pair of sandals.

She and Thad had agreed to meet at the hospital so they could check on Haley right before they left, but if they didn't leave soon, they might miss their appointment. And strangely enough, Macy didn't want to do that. At least she didn't *think* she wanted to miss the insemination. Her feelings were too mixed to sort out in the middle of everything else going on in her life. Thad had given her the money to save her daughter. For that she was overwhelmingly grateful and felt a certain obligation; but combined with it was a not-so-easily explained hesitancy to disappoint him and a secret thrill at the prospect of carrying his child.

"You going to be okay if we leave for an hour or so, angel?" Thad asked Haley.

They'd talked about asking Thad's mother to come sit with her while they were gone, but had decided against involving June so they wouldn't have to lie to her about where they were going. The deception was bothering them both enough already.

Haley reached out to give Thad a hug, and he lifted her into his arms. "I'm tired," she admitted.

Clearing away her paper and stamps, Thad tucked her in bed. "Why don't you lie down and rest, then? I'll turn on that tape of Disney songs I brought you yesterday, and you can listen to it while we're gone."

"Okay."

Macy's jaw dropped. She'd tried not more than two minutes earlier to talk her daughter into a nap, but Haley wouldn't have any of it. Then Thad suggested the same thing, and her daughter was suddenly fine with it.

Hiding a smile, Macy stepped out of the room. Thad could walk on water while she had to swim, upstream evidently, but Macy didn't mind. The joy Thad brought Haley had certainly been an unexpected bonus to their bargain. Her only concern was how her daughter would react in nine months, when he left.

Thad joined her in a few minutes, the theme song from *Beauty and the Beast* trailing out of Haley's room behind him. "Are you ready for our big day?"

Macy nodded. "Do you have enough ammunition?"

"What?"

"Are you armed to the teeth with *Playboy* magazines?"

He scowled. "I'm sure they provide all that."

Macy grinned, but the thought of Thad extracting semen in any way was more arousing than funny. Her own starved body started making its long hibernation felt, and she passed a cool hand over her hot neck, looking away from him as they waited for the elevator.

"You're blushing," he said.

"No. I'm not."

"What are you thinking about?"

"The Rustler's Roost account."

"Oh, yeah? I didn't know the thought of a good steak could do that to a woman."

Macy's blush deepened when she realized he wasn't buying her story, but she persisted in trying to change the subject. "Do you really think Martin will sign your contract next week?"

The elevator doors *whooshed* open and Thad waved her in ahead of him. "Once I have all the numbers together, I don't know why not. He's already called me several times with questions, so he's keeping in close touch."

There was that slightly weightless feeling as they descended, then, "What about you?" he asked. "You've been studying, I know that. Is anything sinking in amidst all of this?"

That I suddenly have a greater interest in biology than I do in pharmacology, perhaps, not much more. "A little," she hedged.

"Are you going to be able to pass your finals?"

"One week will tell."

"You'll do it."

Macy nodded, trying to think positively as they made their way through the lobby and out to Thad's car.

They drove to the fertility clinic in silence. Thad seemed to be deep in his thoughts, whatever they were, and Macy couldn't believe that in a matter of minutes Dr. Biden was going to place Thad's semen in her womb and, hopefully, help them create a baby. It was incredible, incredible that it could happen, incredible that she could actually want it to.

After Thad parked, he took Macy's hand. "Before we go in, I just want to tell you—" his gaze lowered to her mouth as it had that day in the hospital corridor, then stubbornly returned to her eyes "—that I'm grateful to you for doing this for me, and…."

"And?" Macy prompted.

"And, damn, you look great in that dress."

Macy laughed and raised his hand to her lips for a quick kiss. As much as she wanted to prolong the moment, hoping for a better indication of how he felt toward her, there wasn't time. "Let's go."

THAD STARED at the plastic cup the nurse had given him, then eyed the magazines in a rack along the wall of the closetlike cubicle.

Talk about putting a guy on the spot, he thought, smiling ruefully to himself. If he came out with his sample too soon, Macy, the doctor and those in the reception area would think he was a premature ejaculator. If he took too long, well, God knows what they would think.

Good thing he was comfortable with his masculinity. Good thing he wasn't worried about what anyone else thought. He'd just focus on why he was here in the first place, because he wanted a son or a daughter.

No, on second thought, a centerfold model was definitely a better focus for his purposes today.

Glancing through a few magazines, he admired the beautiful women. Then memories of Valerie paraded through his mind, wonderful memories, all of them. He loved her; he missed her. Sex with her had been very different from the blatant carnality represented in the magazines. Because his mind, his heart and his body were equally committed. But the past didn't have the same impact on his emotions as the present, and somehow those days seemed to be slipping away like sand through his fingers.

He closed his eyes as, unbidden, a picture of Macy lying beneath him came to mind, instead, and almost instantly his heart started to pound and he felt heat in his loins. She was beautiful and responsive and demonstrative, and so very sexy with that sultry voice and those big green eyes....

And he knew from that moment on that he definitely wasn't going to err on the side of taking too long.

MACY WAITED nervously for Thad's sample to be treated. Flipping through *Woman's Day* magazine, she repeatedly glanced at the clock, careful not to let her arm brush against Thad's, who was now sitting next to her. She'd just called to check on Haley and found that his mother was at the hospital. The nurse had said Mrs. Winters was reading in the lobby while Haley napped.

At least Haley wasn't alone anymore. That brought Macy a measure of comfort, along with the news that her daughter was getting some of the rest she so desperately needed. But her mind wasn't on Thad's mother, or Primary Care Hospital, or even Haley's bone marrow transplant. It was on the door through which she would pass to become pregnant with Thad's child. The one that would open any minute to reveal a nurse dressed in a white smock, pants and rubber-soled shoes, who would invite her past the point of no return. Was she doing the right thing? Or was she simply asking for more heartache?

Accurately reading her last-minute jitters, Thad reached over and took her hand. He didn't meet her eyes, but he threaded his fingers through hers and kept both their hands in his lap.

Macy took heart from the contact, but bravely broke away when the nurse called her name.

"Do you want me to come with you?" Thad asked, wearing a teasing grin that told her he already knew her answer would be no.

Macy shook her head. "This diamond isn't *that* big,"

she said. Then, more seriously, "There's nothing to it, right?"

"That's what they say."

She wiped her sweaty palms on her thighs. "Okay."

"Don't be scared. It's not going to hurt."

"No, but it's not going to feel anything like your contribution to this event did, either."

He grinned, and the blue of his eyes darkened. "I know a way that it could."

Macy's mouth went dry, and she had to clear her throat before she could speak. "Is that an invitation?"

His eyes never wavered from hers. "It could be."

She glanced back at the nurse, who wasn't close enough to hear them but was frowning at the delay. "I think that would require an addendum to our agreement."

"Why? We're married."

"We're not committed."

He sighed and shifted in his seat. "I'm sorry, Macy. I can't promise you anything more than what we've got already."

"Because of Valerie?"

He nodded.

So his first wife was still alive and well, at least in Thad's heart. Macy tried not to feel the inevitable sting of disappointment. She'd expected as much. "But a physical relationship is okay?"

"Yes...maybe. I don't know." He glanced self-consciously at the handful of people sitting and reading elsewhere in the waiting area. None of them seemed to be paying any attention, but Macy knew it was a strange thing to discuss in a doctor's office. "I'd be lying if I said I've never thought about it," he admitted.

"Well, I don't need you to do me that sort of favor."

"I wasn't thinking of it as a favor."

Macy lowered her voice even further. ''Still, three's a bit of a crowd in the bedroom, don't you think?'' Without waiting for an answer, she got to her feet, slung her purse over her shoulder and followed the nurse through the doorway, down a short hall and into an examination room.

At first she'd agreed to have Thad's baby because of what it would mean for Haley. Then, when he'd released her from her part, she'd decided to go ahead with the insemination because of her sense of obligation, gratitude, empathy, even admiration.

Now she feared she'd fallen in love with him.

She should have walked away while she still could.

WHITE WALLS, white ceiling, white floor, the smell of antibacterial soap and plenty of light. Miserable, Macy sat on a padded table in the middle of the small examination room, staring around her and taking deep breaths in an effort to slow the pounding of her heart.

I'm an idiot. Thad had just told her he was still in love with Valerie. His heart was sealed tighter than a drum, yet she was being artificially inseminated with his child. Why was she doing this to herself? Why was she asking for more trouble?

The stiff paper beneath her bare bottom crinkled as she shifted to get a better look at the underwear folded neatly atop her sandals on the chair in the corner. She should dress and go. She felt doomed, as if she couldn't turn back. But it wasn't too late. She could still—

The door opened just as Macy was about to stand, causing her to jerk back and adjust the blue paper lap covering the nurse had given her when she'd told her to strip from the waist down. Macy hadn't actually removed her dress, but it was bunched up around her hips, leaving her feeling vulnerable and unprotected. In just a few moments, a Dr.

Howes—Dr. Biden was delivering a baby—would deposit Thad's semen into her body. Aided by medical science, the little sperm cells would swim like there was no tomorrow, and they wouldn't have far to go to reach the egg that was just sitting there, waiting to be fertilized. Then it would all be over. No backing out allowed. And nine months from now…

Macy didn't even want to think about nine months from now. Her world revolved around next week. Haley's transplant, her finals. That was it.

"I'm Dr. Howes," the doctor was saying. A short, balding man with thick glasses, he shook her cold hand before stretching on a pair of surgical gloves. Then he sank onto a rolling chair and took a moment to study her chart. "Let me see here," he murmured.

The nurse came in carrying a tray of medical instruments and a large syringe.

"I-I'm sorry, but I think there's been some mistake," Macy stuttered as soon as she saw the syringe, fighting an impulse to shout to be heard over the thudding of her heart.

"A mistake?" The bespectacled doctor scowled at her. The thickness of his lenses magnified his eyes to something much bigger than their normal size, and Macy had the fleeting impression that she was about to be impregnated by a giant praying mantis.

She nearly scrambled off the table and ran for her life, and would have had the nurse not taken her hand. "There's nothing to be frightened of, dear. This isn't going to hurt a bit."

Perhaps not now, Macy wanted to say. It was nine months from now that worried her, and her concern had nothing to do with labor and delivery. The physical pain she could handle. Watching Thad take their baby, load it into his car and drive away was another story.

But could she walk out there now and tell him she wouldn't go through with their agreement? He'd given her the chance she needed to keep her little girl alive. He'd thrown her a line when she thought she would drown in despair.

"Are you having second thoughts?" the doctor asked, the tone of his voice a subtle rebuke for wasting his time. "Would you like to postpone the procedure until you and your husband can be sure?"

Macy clenched her fists so tightly she could feel her nails cutting into her palms. "No, I—it's fine. Let's go ahead."

"You are sure?"

"Yes," she said, sounding far more convinced than she felt.

The doctor pulled the rolling tray toward him and scooted closer, and Macy willed herself to calm down. But when he touched her leg, she nearly jumped off the table.

"Relax," he said, slightly impatient now. "I just need you to scoot up, bend your knees more…that's it…and lie back."

Closing her eyes and focusing on Haley and the transplant Thad had made possible, she did as directed. A very personal, intimate part of him was about to fuse with a very personal, intimate part of her.

The most amazing thing about it was that, despite all her fears and the fact that what she was doing contradicted every ounce of common sense she possessed, something about it felt incredibly, wonderfully right. And something else—her heart?—whispered that a lot could happen in nine months.

CHAPTER FIFTEEN

MACY SEEMED REMOTE when she came out of the fertility clinic. Thad followed her all the way to his car without speaking, but when he'd opened her door for her and climbed behind the wheel himself, he let the keys dangle in the ignition and turned to face her.

"You okay?"

She nodded.

"They said it wouldn't hurt."

"It didn't."

"Do you feel any different?"

"Physically? Not yet. That will take a while."

"And emotionally?"

"I guess I'm as well as one could expect, considering."

Considering the fact that her daughter was dying. "Okay. Do you want to talk?"

While she stared straight ahead, Thad admired her profile, the small straight nose, the full lips, the gentle swell of her breasts, the soft skin that was everywhere the dress wasn't. He almost ran a hand down her arm, but he knew, if he touched her, he wouldn't be able to stop at a friendly pat. The fantasy he'd let himself indulge in, the one where he'd made mad passionate love to her, was still too fresh in his mind.

"About?" she asked.

"About how we're going to handle the next few months.

I mean, the way I see it, things have changed a bit. I'm thinking we should reassess.''

She plucked a piece of lint off her dress, her nails neat and well shaped but short. Folding her arms in what appeared to be a bolstering or defensive move, she finally met his eye. "Why? What are our options?"

"Well, I was planning to live with you for the next nine months, but I'm not sure that's such a good idea anymore." *Not if you want me to keep my hands to myself.* He almost added the words but was afraid she'd get the wrong idea and think he might force himself on her sometime, when in reality, she'd probably only drive him mad. He'd prowl at night, hoping she'd admit him to her bed, and then, if she did, he'd wake up feeling guilty for having taken advantage of a single mom.

Except that she wasn't single. She was his wife. That entitled him to something, didn't it?

No, not in their case. A baby was the end of their agreement. Anything more wasn't fair to Macy. Not if she couldn't enjoy the physical intimacy while it lasted and then walk away. And how could he ask that?

"Moving in was your idea," she said. "There's certainly no need to do it if you've changed your mind."

Thad knew he should feel relieved, but he never felt the way he should anymore. For a few moments in the doctor's office, he'd thought she was hoping for a real relationship, but if that was the case, she wouldn't have let him off so easily.

"So you're okay with the way things are?" he asked.

"I'm fine. As far as I'm concerned, we're right on track. You gave me the money, which I paid to the hospital. Haley is getting her transplant next week. And I've taken the first steps toward fulfilling my part of the bargain. After today, I should be pregnant. What's the problem?"

She nearly blinded him with a huge smile, but it didn't have the reassuring properties one might have thought. Thad stiffened beneath a surprising wave of disappointment. Evidently he'd misread the signals she'd been sending him. Spending their nights together in a platonic embrace didn't wreak the same kind of havoc with her body that it did with his.

"No problem," he said.

"Your parents and my mother see us as newlyweds. If we don't keep up the charade now, they're going to know something isn't right."

"True."

"So what's changed?"

He laughed, and hoped it didn't sound as nervous to Macy as it did to him. If she could go on the way things were between them, then he could, too, right? After all, he was the one who wasn't interested in a more permanent relationship. "Nothing. Forget I said anything. I've already moved a lot of my clothes. I'll bring the rest to your place after work."

"Fine."

And then I'll spend another sleepless night with you in my arms, caught between the misery of telling myself no and the fresh wave of yearning I feel every time your firm little backside presses against me.

MACY GRABBED her towel, clutching it to the front of her as she dashed out of the shower to answer the telephone. Her own mother hadn't returned from Vegas yet, but Haley's newfound interest in her grandma Winters had freed Macy up enough to study at home this weekend, where it was quiet. She'd spent a good number of hours preparing for her final exams and was just beginning to believe she might pass a few of them, God willing, but after two days of intense reading and note taking, her eyes were burning and her back ached from sitting so long. She deserved a long hot shower, but she couldn't let the phone ring without answering it. Not when it could be the hospital.

"Hello?"

"Macy? You sound like I caught you running the forty-yard dash. Are you okay?"

Lisa. Macy smiled and dried her naked body, then propped the phone against her ear with her shoulder so she could wrap the towel around her wet hair to keep it from dripping on the carpet. With everything going on in her life, she and her friend hadn't had a chance to talk privately for several days. "I'm fine. I was just in the shower."

"Alone?"

Macy rolled her eyes. "Of course alone."

"Then you're not making much progress."

"It's a little difficult to take a shower with someone who's not even here. And Thad all but told me he's not over his dead wife yet, which isn't anything new. I think he's got a few years of mourning left in him."

"Not to be disrespectful, but like I've said before, Valerie's dead, and you're wonderfully alive. His practical side will win out eventually."

"I don't want to be some kind of consolation prize. I want him to fall head over heels in love with me." Macy almost gasped at her own admission. That certainly wasn't what she'd meant to say. "Wait, I didn't mean that."

"Yes, you did. And I can't blame you. Where is he, by the way?"

"At the hospital, I think."

"I was there yesterday, with him and his parents."

"Was Haley okay with my not being there?"

"Are you kidding? With all that attention? She was at

the height of her glory. But the doctors seemed a little uptight about all the visitors.''

"I've talked to them about that. Everyone's being very careful about scrubbing up, and I think the positive energy they're infusing into Haley's life is doing incredible good. Haley's been happier this week than she's been in a long time, despite her poor health.''

"I agree. She's a tough kid. She sure thinks Thad's pretty great.''

Thad was great, but Macy was trying not to think like that. It made the nights when they were sleeping together unbearable, the days when they weren't together longer. "He's been good to her.''

"The question is, is he being good to you?''

"He bought me a diamond ring.''

"That's not what you want.''

"I know. But I don't think things are going to work out the way I want.''

"And you think this because…''

"He's slept with me a number of nights already and hasn't made any kind of move. Surely if he had interest in me, he'd want to touch me, or kiss me, at least, don't you think?'' She chewed her lip, considering Thad's circumspect behavior. "He offered to once, but I'm not sure that really counts. We were in the waiting room of the doctor's office, so he was pretty safe.''

"Then maybe you should help things along. Have you ever thought of that?''

"No.''

"Seduce him. Remind him what it's like to have a wife.''

"But I don't want him to sleep with me if he doesn't love me. I'd feel like sloppy seconds. How much fun could that be?''

"Have some confidence, kiddo. There aren't many women more attractive than you are."

"I lost my husband to a—"

"I know, to a seventeen-year-old. But that says more about Richard than it does you."

Everyone said that, and it made sense—to Macy's head. Her heart, however, was more difficult to convince. "Still, sometimes I'm afraid I'm not, I don't know, woman enough to hold a man, I guess," she said, voicing her worst fears. She stretched the phone cord and began to pace, then crossed to the window to gaze out at the backyard, which was completely concealed by the tall shrubs lining the fence.

"Thad's not like Richard. There's a maturity about him that Richard never possessed," Lisa pointed out.

"But he's in love with another woman. A dead woman, granted, but…"

"At least his being so devoted and loyal says a lot."

Macy had to concede that point, but it didn't change anything, at least for her. "He doesn't want me, Lisa."

Tucking a dripping tendril up into her towel, she turned and started to pace back toward the telephone table, then froze. Thad was standing in the living room, staring at her, his keys still in his hand, his jaw sagging. "Who doesn't want you?" he asked.

"Macy? Macy? Are you there?" Lisa's tinny voice came through the receiver, calling her several times before Macy had the presence of mind to whip the towel off her head and drape it around her body.

"Um, I have to go," Macy murmured.

"Are you okay?"

"Fine." She set the phone on its cradle, careful to keep her new shield from revealing a healthy dose of what Thad had already seen.

"That was Lisa," she said to him, trying to act normal, as though it was the most natural thing in the world for him to walk in on her while she was naked. "I was in the shower when the phone rang, and I was afraid it was the hospital...I didn't hear you come in...."

She let her words drift away when she realized he wasn't listening. His focus was farther down, on her bare legs.

"Who doesn't want you?" he repeated.

Macy's throat constricted until she could scarcely swallow. "No one you know," she managed to say. Then she skirted past him and dashed for the safety of the bathroom.

THIS JUST ISN'T GOING TO WORK. With a curse, Thad stabbed a hand through his hair and stared blankly at Macy's now-empty living room. When he'd made his deal with her, he hadn't counted on his body's complete rebellion. He'd thought her lovely, mysterious, but how could he have guessed she'd affect him so completely? Since Valerie's death, he'd dated a few times, and every single one of those women had left him stone cold. He'd told himself that Macy's vulnerability, her need, her obvious love for her daughter, was what drew him, but the raging desire that coursed through his veins at the sight of her pacing in the buff had nothing to do with anyone's needs but his own.

I can have her. She's my wife.

He started down the hall, then stopped.

No, sex wasn't part of the deal.

But if she agreed...

Dropping his head into his hands, he rubbed his temples. He should move out and tell her to lock her doors against him.

Instead, he covered the rest of the distance to the bathroom door and knocked. "Macy?"

"Yes?"

"Mom's doing great with Haley."

"That's good."

"And you've been studying for two days straight. It might be good for you to take a break."

"I think you're right. I'm seeing double my eyes are so strained. I thought I might run over to Lisa's for a little bit, you know, get away."

"What about letting me take you to dinner?"

A long pause.

Thad held his breath, hoping…for what? That she'd tell him to go fly a kite? That she'd agree? Damn, he didn't know what he wanted anymore. Except for one thing: he wanted at least one night with Macy, maybe, probably, more. And the thought that she might be carrying his child only made his desire for her stronger.

"Where do you want to go?" she asked, hesitant.

Thad recalled the most romantic restaurant he knew. It had been a long time since he'd tried to impress a woman, but he hoped he hadn't forgotten how. "Leave the restaurant to me. I know the perfect place."

THE CANDLE on the table flickered, throwing subtle shadows against Thad's face as Macy sat across from him in the quaint Italian restaurant he'd chosen. She gazed at the wall of windows overlooking Salt Lake, the loaves of crusty bread along the bar, the hanging meats overhead and thought she'd never been anywhere quite so wonderful. Richard's idea of a night on the town had included burgers or ribs and possibly a movie, but never anything with so much atmosphere.

Dressed in a pair of black silk pants and the sleeveless jade sweater her mother had given her for Christmas, Macy felt more attractive than she had in a long time. She wasn't sure if it was the elegant setting, her dressy clothes or what she read in Thad's eyes when he looked at her that made the difference, but she did know that Thad was incredibly handsome in his starched shirt, slacks and loafers. She loved his square jaw and the slight cleft in his chin, his solid build, his crooked grin.

Macy focused on her fruity, nonalcoholic drink, knowing she'd have to be very careful how she handled herself tonight, or they'd both wake up to some significant regret in the morning.

"Do you like this place?" he asked.

Macy breathed in the smell of garlic and fresh-baked bread and smiled. "I haven't been out in so long you could have taken me to a soup kitchen and I would have been grateful. But this is especially nice."

"Well, it won't be hard for them to outdo the hospital cafeteria, I'm sure. Are you all ready for your exams?"

"In my current frame of mind, I don't know if a year of studying would make me ready. But at least I have a fighting chance now. I'm certainly not going to ace them, but I may pass, if I'm lucky."

"I think it's your turn to be lucky."

Macy had to admit, at least to herself, that her thoughts were beginning to revolve more around *getting* lucky than *being* lucky. But she was trying not to let her mind go there. Thad wasn't ready to make a commitment, and she wasn't ready to have sex with him without one. She'd learned too much from Richard, wasn't willing to set herself up for the hurt such premature intimacy would entail.

"Are you feeling okay about going ahead with the transplant?" he asked.

Since the decision was made, Macy had felt a measure of peace, but the worry that she'd made the wrong choice was always there in the back of her mind. "I think so."

Thad leaned back and hooked one arm over his chair. "Who's going to do it? Dr. Forte?"

"Dr. Vincent. He's the hematologist."

"Can you explain how it works?"

"They take the marrow of the donor from the posterior iliac crest—"

"In English, please, Student Doctor."

She chuckled. "Okay, the marrow is harvested from the donor's hip joint, usually from a series of small incisions in the back. It looks like blood, but it's thicker and contains the beginning of all the blood-cell lines. Through a process called hematopoesis, immature white blood cells, red blood cells and platelets are produced and mature to a certain level in the marrow—at this point they're called stem cells—before they enter the bloodstream.

"And these are part of the body's immune system?"

"They perform many different functions. Besides fighting infections, they deliver oxygen to the body and control bleeding. Before a bone marrow transplant, the patient's marrow is destroyed through a series of high-dose chemotherapy and radiation treatments. That's what they're doing to Haley now. The transplant will provide her with new marrow containing stem cells that will grow, divide and mature into all the blood-cell lines the body needs."

"That's amazing," Thad said, obviously impressed. "They'll basically give her a new immune system. But marrow is in the hollow part of bones, right? How do they get at it through small incisions?

"They use a needle-syringe technique."

"Does it hurt?"

"The donors are under anesthesia so they don't feel anything, but I've heard some say that afterward, it feels like they took a hard fall on ice and landed on their butt. They're stiff and sore in the hips and back for a couple of days, but they usually stay in the hospital only one night. Most donors are back to work in a couple of days."

"So how does Haley get these new stem cells?"

"The marrow from the donor is filtered, then injected into one of her veins."

"Through her catheter? So it won't be painful for her?"

"No, it won't hurt her."

Thad sighed and shifted forward, leaning his elbows on the table. "That's good news. She seems so fragile. I've been worried the procedure would be hard on her."

"You've been very good to her, Thad. I've been meaning to tell you that I appreciate the attention you've given her. It's made a big difference in her life."

"It's nothing." He cleared his throat and changed the subject as though her praise embarrassed him. "When's your mother coming back?"

"She called yesterday. I guess she's nervous about leaving Champ with the neighbor again. He and Mr. Purdy don't get along too well, but he's too big to bring with her and she won't leave him at a kennel. She says Champ hates it. I think she just hates spending the money. Anyway, she's not coming until Monday night."

The waitress brought their food, and they nodded when she offered them fresh-ground pepper and Parmesan on their pastas. Thad had ordered a small, wood-oven-baked pizza, in addition to his pasta. He offered Macy a piece as the waitress left, and she accepted. Topped with red onion, goat cheese, artichoke hearts and pancetta, it smelled delicious.

"Mmm, that's good," she murmured around her first bite. "You have excellent taste."

He quirked an eyebrow at her. "I chose you to be the mother of my child, didn't I?"

Macy felt a warmth start in the pit of her stomach that she couldn't credit entirely to the excellent food. "What were some of your other candidates like?"

Thad entertained her the rest of the meal with stories of the other applicants and their interviews, gifts and persistence. By the time he paid the bill and escorted her out of the restaurant with one hand on the small of her back, she was wondering why on earth he'd made the concessions he'd made for her. Certainly the other women who'd applied sounded much more eager and far less demanding. But probably none of them had a sick daughter. He really was a soft-hearted guy.

"Thad!" A male voice boomed his name out over the crowd of people still standing by the entryway, waiting to be seated, and Thad turned. Macy followed his gaze to the man she'd met that first day in Thad's office.

"Kevin, what are you doing here?" Thad asked, clapping his partner on the back.

"Celebrating the Rustler's Roost account, same as you, probably." A young, leggy blonde stood next to Kevin, one arm looped through his while she nuzzled his shoulder.

Kevin introduced her as Rhonda, and Macy took her long-fingered hand. "Nice to meet you."

"Same here," she said.

"Thad's the *man* this week," Kevin announced. "We almost lost the Rustler's Roost account on Friday, but he talked to Martin and got him to agree to sign the contract next Thursday, after all, providing the costs fall within our estimates."

Macy glanced up at Thad, wondering why he hadn't told her about the close call. "What happened?"

"Martin had decided to meet with some other firms, just to see what else is out there," he told her. "I convinced him there wasn't any need to do so, that if he didn't end up liking the ads I'm putting together, we'd come up with something else."

"And he agreed to stick with you?"

"Fortunately."

"That's great," Macy said.

"It's better than great," Kevin added. "Once Rustler's

Roost signs up, we'll be able to get other restaurants to follow.''

Thad shrugged. "I don't know if it was as much of a close call as we thought. I think Martin didn't really want to go through the hassle of meeting with different firms. He just wanted to be reassured he was doing the right thing."

"Well, he certainly wasn't letting me assure him of that. He didn't change his mind until after you called him." Kevin grinned at Macy. "But enough of business. We have even bigger things to celebrate than the Rustler's Roost account. Thad tells me you're expecting."

Macy cleared her throat. Thad certainly wasn't wasting any time letting everyone know about the baby, if there *was* a baby. "Well, we're not absolutely positive yet, but we're hopeful."

"Congratulations," Rhonda murmured.

Kevin winked at Macy. "Thad's a very lucky man, Mrs. Winters."

Thad cocked an eyebrow at his friend, and Kevin put his thumb and finger in the shape of a gun he pretended to fire at Thad. "There it is again. There's no hope for you, pal," Kevin said, laughing as he steered his date inside.

"What was all *that* about?" Macy asked as Thad opened the car door for her.

"Nothing."

She fastened her seat belt and waited for Thad to come around and get in. "Those knowing glances between you and Kevin meant nothing? I felt like you two had some sort of private joke going between you."

Thad started the car and eased onto the road. "He wants to date you after we divorce." He glanced at her. "But you're not interested, right?"

She wasn't. From their brief encounter, she could tell Kevin played fast and loose, which wasn't her type at all, but she wasn't about to let Thad dictate whom she could see once he tossed her back. "I take it *you're* the one who's not interested in having us date. Is it because of the baby? Are you afraid we might run into each other sometime? That could happen anyway, you know. It's not like one of us will be moving out of state."

He took the next turn a little too fast, and Macy grabbed on to her door handle to keep from leaning into him. "He wouldn't be good for you," he said. "Kevin doesn't want to get married."

"And what makes you think I can't go out with a guy just for fun?"

She could feel Thad studying her in the darkened car. "Is that what you want, Macy? Some fun? Because *I* could show you that. And you can't be surprised I'd offer. I know you're aware of…whatever it is that's going on between us. I couldn't be feeling it so strongly if you were oblivious."

Macy's breath caught in her throat. "What are you telling me?"

"That I'm frustrated!"

Frustration wasn't exactly what Macy had been hoping for. She crossed her arms and pretended to be interested in the 7-Eleven on the corner as Thad slowed to turn up into the Avenues. "And you're taking your frustration out on me?"

"I'm not taking it out on you. I'm telling you that you're the reason."

"You don't think eighteen months without a sex life has anything to do with it?"

"I think seeing you nude has everything to do with it."

Macy swallowed. "I told you, I didn't hear you come in—"

He scowled. "I'm not blaming you. It's my own fault. I thought you might be resting, so I let myself in as quietly as possible, but what I saw hasn't left me, and I don't think it's going to until…"

"Until?" Macy raised her eyebrows in challenge.

He pulled into her driveway and shut off the engine. "Until I see you naked again," he said softly. "Until I hold you, and mold you to my own body, and hear you cry out my name when I—"

"Stop!" Macy put up a hand to combat the dark intensity of his eyes, the huskiness of his voice. He wasn't touching her, but his words and the need behind them was enough to raise goose bumps all along her spine, especially when she wanted what he wanted, only worse. If not for that experience at Studio 9, where she'd learned how unsatisfying sex without commitment could be, she probably would have dragged his head to hers and silenced him with a kiss of assent. Instead, she forced herself to open the door and made her trembling limbs support her as she got out.

"I think maybe you should stay at your place tonight," she said, leaning back into the car.

A muscle clenched in his jaw and his hands tightened around the steering wheel. "You're not interested?"

"Not interested?" She chuckled incredulously. She'd never wanted a man more. So she told him only a portion of the truth. "Let's just say I'm not interested in making another mistake," she said. Then, closing the door, she made her way to the front porch and into the house before she collapsed on the couch and chanted, "I did the right thing. I did the right thing. I did the right thing."

But no matter how hard she tried to convince herself, her heart always tagged a small question onto the end: "Didn't I?"

CHAPTER SIXTEEN

THAD LET HIS breath go all at once, feeling as if someone had just knocked the wind out of him. She'd shut him down cold, walked away, told him to go home. She thought making love with him would be a mistake. And he was fairly certain she was right.

Starting the car, he pulled out of the driveway, then paused in reverse for a moment while he struggled with the temptation to go back and bang on the door. He and Macy hadn't known each other long, but there was definitely a powerful attraction between them. Part of him wanted to act on that attraction in the most literal sense, to confirm he'd been right about the signals she'd been sending him lately, signals that indicated she was every bit as tempted to take their relationship into the physical realm as he was. But she was hurting and looking for an anchor, so he couldn't put his trust in those signals. No man with a conscience would take advantage of a woman going through what Macy was going through—and he wanted to believe he had a conscience.

Throwing the transmission into drive, he peeled off, hoping to put as much distance between him and her house as possible before he changed his mind. He was going mad with wanting her, but he'd committed himself to support her through the pregnancy, in any way necessary, and he intended to do just that. She was giving him the child he'd wanted. That would have to be enough.

Unfortunately, at the moment, it didn't *feel* like enough.

For a fleeting moment, he wondered what might have happened in their relationship if he'd never met Valerie. Maybe he and Macy would have had a chance. There was certainly that spark. He always felt excited at the prospect of seeing her, being with her, and he respected her a great deal.

But he had met Valerie. He'd married her; he'd loved her. And now he couldn't go on as if she'd never existed. What would that make of his promises? What would it say about his level of commitment?

His cell phone rang, and Thad answered, trying to mask his frustration with the Macy situation. There was no way to win here. He couldn't have her, and he couldn't leave her alone. Perhaps, if she wasn't already pregnant, they should call the whole thing off...

It was his mother. "Hi, Mom. How's Haley?" he asked.

"She's tired. Debra is sitting with her while she sleeps. Are you and Macy back from dinner?"

"Yeah."

"Is she studying, then?"

"No, I think she's studied all she can for one day. She's taking a break."

"Perfect. I have a surprise for her I'd like to bring over."

Thad pictured Macy's stiff carriage as she let herself into her house. "Um, we're kind of tired, Mom—"

"We didn't get to be part of the wedding," June said, accusation ringing loud and clear in her voice.

"I know. I'm sorry. Considering the situation, we thought it best to elope."

"You didn't want your family to share in your happiness?"

"It wasn't that."

"Well, you could have told us, at least. We would have liked to give Macy a bridal shower or something."

Thad's hold on his temper was tenuous at best. He was hurting and angry and frustrated all at once, and the tension had been mounting from the moment he'd married Macy. Struggling to keep his voice neutral, he said, "The truth is, Mom, Macy and I have had a little disagreement. I'm heading home tonight. Alone."

"Oh!" Silence, then, "What did you say to her?"

"Nothing." How did he tell his mother that it was what he couldn't say to her that was the problem? He wanted to give Macy his heart, but he'd already promised forever to Valerie. He could only offer his body.

"Then what happened?"

"Mom, I don't want to talk about it. Don't worry. We're newlyweds, just getting used to each other. It'll be okay in the morning."

"Your father and I have been married thirty-five years and have never gone to bed angry at each other. It's not right. If you want a marriage to last, you have to swallow your pride on a regular basis. Now turn yourself around and go back to her. It doesn't matter who was at fault. She needs you."

"I'm the last thing she needs right now."

"Then you're not thinking of her and that poor child," she argued. "It's no wonder Macy's having a hard time. There's nothing worse than watching your own child suffer—"

"She's mine now, too," Thad said, then wondered where the hell that had come from. Haley wasn't his. She never would be. Apparently he was taking his part as Macy's husband a little too seriously.

"I know, dear, but it's not quite the same. Macy's been

going through this for almost a year. It's a wonder she's managing as well as she is.''

The guilt pressing down on Thad's chest grew heavier. *Thanks, Mom.*

"Go back and tell her you love her," June continued. "Then put your house up for sale. It's not good for you to have somewhere like that to hide out.''

"We're keeping the house, Mom, for when Macy graduates from school. We won't need to stay so close to the university anymore." Which sounded good. He only hoped his mother would buy it.

"Then keep it," she said, "but don't stay there alone.''

Thad sighed. Seeing the situation from his mother's perspective, he had to admit it was good advice. He'd already learned from Valerie that the classic male response of retreating into silence and waiting for the argument to blow over wasn't half as effective as talking it out. But June didn't know the whole story this time, that Macy was actually safer without him, and Thad wasn't about to enlighten her.

"Are you turning back?" she asked.

Torn, Thad gave his mother a noncommittal reply, then drove slowly on home.

WHEN THE DOORBELL rang, Macy looked through her peephole and groaned. It was her in-laws. Her *temporary* in-laws. And she was at her worst. Dressed in a shabby knee-length robe, she felt frustrated, tired, worried, and she missed Thad.

Tightening her belt, she ran her fingers through her hair to tame it and took a deep breath. She wasn't sure she wanted company, but she certainly couldn't leave June and Sam standing on the porch.

"Hi, there!" she said, throwing the door back and smiling with as much enthusiasm as she could muster.

"Hi, dear." June hugged her instantly and Sam did the same. "How are you?"

You mean other than the fact that I'm head over heels in love with your son, who has no room in his heart for me, and my daughter is in the hospital?

"Fine." Fortunately, the automatic response easily overrode her thoughts. Stepping back, Macy beckoned them in. "What a pleasant surprise."

June and her husband stepped inside and looked around, nodding their heads in satisfaction. "Oh, this is beautiful."

Macy knew Thad's house was twice as nice, but June seemed sincere. "Thanks. Please, make yourselves comfortable."

She indicated the couch, and they positioned a purple gift bag between them before sitting down.

"I just talked to Thad," June said, looking sympathetic. "He told me about your little disagreement."

Macy blinked. "He did?"

"Yes, he said it was just a lovers' quarrel, but I wanted to let you know not to worry about it. Disagreements are bound to happen in any marriage. But he's a good boy. He'll come around."

"I think we were both tired," Macy hedged, smoothing the fabric of her robe so she wouldn't have to look June in the eye.

"And with what you're going through, it's no wonder."

Macy was searching for a polite response when keys jingled in the lock and the front door swung open to reveal a cross-looking Thad.

"What are you doing here?" Macy asked, standing. "I thought—"

He scowled. "My mother reminded me that my place is

here with you. It took me until I opened the door to my empty house to realize that she's right.''

Macy wasn't sure how to take his words. What did he mean, his place was with her? Instinctively, her hand went to her belly. The baby, of course. She'd never seen a man so dedicated to one goal.

''I told him the only way to keep a marriage intact is to put things right before going to sleep,'' June added, beaming now that she felt her son was finally behaving himself. ''Always kiss and make up. That's what I say. And we'll get out of your way and let you do just that, but first I wanted to bring you a little something I had made.'' She extended the gift bag to Macy, and Macy took it, wondering at its slight weight.

''What's this for?'' she asked. ''My birthday isn't for six months yet.''

''It's just a little surprise I thought you'd like.''

Curious, Macy dug through the tissue paper and pulled June's gift out into the light. Her stomach did a little flip when she realized it was a picture of Thad and Haley, smiling, cheek to cheek, encased in a piece of clear plastic that was cut around their two shapes and made to stand on its own. She loved it, knew, despite whatever happened with her and Thad, she'd treasure it always.

''Thank you,'' she murmured softly. ''It's wonderful.'' She glanced up at Thad and saw his scowl darken and wondered if he'd come back to appease his mother, or for some other reason. The look on his face certainly indicated that he wasn't entirely happy about being where he was.

''We saw them at the mall and thought it was a perfect way to enjoy a good picture,'' June was saying as she and Sam stood to go. ''You can set it out wherever you want it, on a shelf or table, so you can see it all the time.''

Macy knew she'd need no reminder of Thad. If Haley survived the operation, she'd owe her daughter's life to him.

"Thank you," she repeated. "It was very thoughtful of you."

June hugged her again. "We're happy you're part of the family," she said simply, and she and Sam left.

Part of the family. Macy stood at the door, closing her eyes and listening to the sudden silence. She hated feeling like a fraud, hated knowing that Thad's parents were lavishing love on her under false pretenses. Yet a small part of her desperately wanted to believe that the love was real, that they would be part of her life forever.

God, what was she going to do when it all unraveled?

FROM WHERE HE STOOD across the room, Thad watched Macy at the door and frowned at her bent head. He shouldn't have come back. After he'd spoken to his mother in the car, he'd decided that he really shouldn't leave Macy alone with his parents. Without him, the true nature of their relationship would come pouring out of Macy in a matter of minutes, he'd told himself, as it nearly had at the hospital. But deep down, he knew it was only an excuse to do what he wanted to do in the first place.

"What's wrong?" he asked.

"I really like your parents," she said. "I like your whole family."

"They like you, too. At first I wondered how well they'd accept you, considering all the surprises we've dropped on them, but they seem to like you just as much as—" He caught himself before Valerie's name slipped out, wondering at how easily it had come to his lips. "Never mind."

Macy turned and gazed at him with those unique, mesmerizing eyes. The delicate structure of her face, full of the classic beauty he'd admired from the start, was clearly visible in the halo of the lamp not far from her. "You can talk about her, you know," she said. "I've wondered why you rarely do. Obviously she's in your thoughts."

He shrugged. "We had a good marriage, but there's no need to bore you with the details." Details that used to be painful for him. But it seemed to be getting easier to think about Valerie, which meant he could talk about her, too. Only, he didn't want to discuss her with Macy.

Macy moved to the chair by the window and sat down, and Thad tried to ignore what the sight of her bare legs did to him. Was she naked under that silky robe? He felt his body respond instantly to that thought, and sat down himself, to hide his arousal and his surprise that he could react in such a way with thoughts of Valerie still lingering in his mind. Things were definitely changing, he realized, but he wasn't sure they were changing for the better. He felt guilty, which was something he hadn't experienced this strongly for a long time, and didn't particularly like.

"I'm sorry that you miss her so terribly," she said.

He ran a hand through his hair, telling himself not to be distracted anymore by the smooth, golden skin on her legs, not to imagine them wrapped around him. "Life doesn't always turn out the way we plan. No one knows that better than you."

"I guess pain is sometimes the price of loving so hard. But eventually, you have to let go of the side of the pool, so to speak."

Thad had never looked at love that way, but Macy was right. He'd always thought it was loyalty that kept him from letting go of Valerie, but maybe he was just hanging on to the edge of the pool. Maybe he was afraid to love again, to open himself up to the possibility of feeling such incredible loss a second time. If so, it made sense that he'd shy away from Macy. She and Haley weren't a very good gamble, not with Haley so ill. "What about you? Do you miss being married?" he asked her.

She flashed him her diamond. "Why would I? I *am* married, remember?"

He raised his eyebrows. "Take it from me, marriage is a lot more than we're making it."

A sad smile curved her lips. "Too bad Richard and I weren't a very good example of that." Bending, she picked up the picture Thad's mother had given her and stood. "I'm going to turn in. Feel free to use the guest room, if you like."

Thad watched her cross in front of him, hating the thought of letting her slip away and wishing there was something he could say to keep her, when she paused on her own. She studied the picture in her hands, arranged it on the table closest to her, then glanced back.

"Or you can sleep with me, if you still want to," she added in a rush, and hurried down the hall.

MACY SAT on the edge of her bed without moving, listening for any sound of Thad's movements. He hadn't left the living room yet. Was he going to take her up on her offer?

Was she out of her mind for making it?

Yes! Surely she'd thrown caution to the wind. She'd laid all her cards on the table and now felt more vulnerable than she'd ever felt in her life. Would he reject her the way she'd rejected him? Would he want to talk first, make some adjustments to their little agreement? Or would he come in and make love to her the way she wanted him to, with passion and abandon and complete absorption?

It was difficult to tell. Ever since he'd returned to the house, he seemed tense, almost angry. At her? Or himself? What was going on in his mind?

A soft knock and Thad's voice, calling her name, brought

Macy's heart into her throat. She jumped to her feet, glanced frantically at her closet, wondering if she should put on something more appealing than her summer robe, then decided it was too late. Crossing to the door, she opened it a crack.

"Are you going to let me in?" he asked when she didn't open it all the way. He sounded hopeful, unsure. "Or have you changed your mind?"

Macy hadn't changed her mind. She hadn't made it up to begin with. She was living minute to minute. "I was thinking about changing into something you might like better."

His gaze raked her from head to foot, his eyes full of appreciation, his jaw rigid with control. "I like you just the way you are."

Macy felt something flutter in her chest at the apparent need in his voice. She stepped back, opening the door wider, and he entered her room only a fraction of a second before his hands slipped inside her robe and closed around the bare skin of her waist. He sucked in a long breath and closed his eyes, then started running his fingers over the plane of her stomach, the valley of her spine, and finally, her breasts.

Bending her slightly back, over one arm, Thad pressed kisses up the column of her throat to her ear and across her cheek. "You're so sweet, Macy, so perfect."

Macy felt her body go boneless at the feel of him pressed against her, his breath rasping softly in her ear. Finally his mouth touched hers, lightly at first, gently, then his kiss went deep as he parted her lips and tasted her for the first time.

If not for Thad's arms around her, Macy feared her legs would give way completely. Never had she been kissed so expertly, so hungrily, so sincerely. It was enough to make the room shift and swirl.

She ran her hands over the hard ridges of his chest and back and began to tug at his shirttail. He helped her remove his shirt, then took her back in his arms. Macy gloried in the smooth feel of his skin and the clean, masculine scent of him as she delved into the thickness of his hair, letting the short, silky locks slide through her fingers.

"You have a wicked kiss," she whispered.

"I hope I've got more than that to interest you," he growled low in his throat, and the promise in his words made something clutch below Macy's stomach. He tightened his grip on her, letting her feel his arousal. Then his hands began moving again, exploring, as his tongue slid against hers.

Macy had lived for this moment. That was all there was to it. She was going to bear Thad's child. Whether they were in love when they'd married, he was her husband, and she was in love with him now. Certainly she could welcome him into her bed.

"Let me see you," he said, tugging on her robe.

Macy tensed, worried, suddenly, that Thad would not find her beautiful. But her moment of insecurity vanished when her robe fell away and Thad stood back to admire her. As his gaze scanned her body, a sensual smile curled his lips. "You're incredible, Macy," he whispered, his voice hoarse. Raising a palm to cup one breast, he bowed his head to lick the tip of the sensitive nipple, causing the muscles below Macy's belly to clutch again.

"You're everything a man could want," he murmured, suckling one breast while teasing the other.

She lifted his chin and kissed him again. She could feel his heart pounding in his chest, keeping time with her own. His spiraling excitement sent hers even higher. Cupping her bottom, he angled her hips into his own in a symbolic action that made Macy's breath catch.

"I want to feel you inside me," she gasped, wondering

if he knew he was tying the very core of her into a tight knot only he could unravel.

"Tell me that again," he breathed before his mouth closed over her other breast. "Tell me it again and again, and I'll make sure you're as pregnant as I hope you are."

Macy wanted him physically, but there was another dimension to her pleasure that was humming through every cell of her body, something she could no longer contain. "I love you," she whispered.

Suddenly he went still, except for his chest, which heaved in and out with his breathing. After a moment he stepped away, ran a hand through his tousled hair and picked up her robe, then belatedly tried to drape it back around her. "I'm sorry," he said, obviously shaken. "I shouldn't have let that happen. I know better."

Rubber-limbed, Macy struggled to rein in her raging hormones long enough to tie the belt to her robe. She wanted to act as though it was nothing, that she wasn't shaken to her very center, but she had no emotional strength or artifice left.

"I think we should talk," he said at last. "I'll be in the living room. Come out when...when you're ready."

Mortified by his unexpected and complete withdrawal, Macy slumped onto the bed, her face burning with embarrassment. She'd offered him her heart, her body, her future on a silver platter, and he'd turned her away. All because of three little words.

Tears stung Macy's eyes, but she pressed her fists against the sockets to block them. She wouldn't cry, dammit. She wouldn't cry over a man she already knew was still in love with his dead wife. She'd been a fool to risk what she had.

"Damn you," she whispered, but she wasn't sure if she was cursing Valerie, Thad or herself.

"Macy? Are you coming?" Thad stood just outside the partly opened door, but he advanced no farther.

"Can you give me a minute?" she asked, trying to keep the wobble out of her voice. "That kind of rejection packs a pretty big punch."

He hesitated for a minute, then, "I didn't reject you, Macy. I just...I just can't accept your terms for intimacy. And I know you wouldn't be happy with mine."

"So what do we have to talk about?" she asked dully.

"I want you to know how much I wish things could be different. I want you to know I never meant to take advantage of you or hurt you or... I..." Words seemed to fail him.

She sighed. "I know, Thad. You don't love me. Just go home to your empty house and your memories, okay?"

He stood there without speaking for a long moment. "Is that it, then?"

"I don't know what more to say. Are you worried about what our families will think?"

"I hadn't gotten that far."

"Well, when you get there, know this: the game is over. I can't pretend anymore."

"So you want to tell everyone we're divorcing?"

"I guess."

"What about Haley?"

"I'll explain to her we're all going to be friends, that you'll come see her sometimes. Your visits will be infrequent and get more infrequent until she forgets you." *At least I hope she forgets you. God knows I never will.*

"And the baby? If you're pregnant, I mean..."

Macy thought she heard tears in his voice but steeled herself against them. "I'll call you when it's born," she said, unable to think beyond that moment. The desire had fled and now she felt—what? Nothing. Numb.

He didn't say anything. He stared at her, a world of pain and confusion in his eyes. Then, after a moment, he left.

CHAPTER SEVENTEEN

HE'D KNOWN BETTER, dammit! When he'd spoken to his mother after he'd dropped Macy off, he'd known better than to return to her house. But he'd ignored his better judgment and gone back, and things had quickly gotten out of control, just as he'd known they would.

What the hell was wrong with him, anyway? Thad wondered. He used to believe himself a decent man. But that was when he was a loving husband, a father-to-be, proudly working and caring for his little family. Now he was just a lonely widower taking advantage of an even lonelier divorcée with a dying kid.

Haley. Thad's heart twisted at the thought of losing her. She called him Daddy and held her spindly arms out for him every time he crossed the threshold to her room, smiling like he was Santa Claus. A man would have to be made of stone not to love her instantly. Yet he'd tried to bail out, at least emotionally, several times. But it hadn't worked, and now it was too late. If she didn't survive her cancer, he was going to hurt, just as he had when Valerie and their son died. There was no avoiding it.

But he could avoid hurting Macy again, he decided, growing more and more resolute. If only he could remember, especially when he was around her, that to all intents and purposes, he was still devoted to Valerie. Macy was the only woman who could make him forget that, but the forgetting could never last long enough to let their marriage work. Which was the crux of the problem, wasn't it?

Good thing he'd left her house tonight before it was too late. Too bad he hadn't left even earlier. The more physical he let their relationship become, the more damage his leaving would cause. He'd see the next nine months through by respecting Macy's directive to keep his distance, and soon she'd realize that her love for him wasn't what she thought it was.

He must have been crazy to think he could watch her grow big with his child, take her to Lamaze classes and share in the birth. Kevin was right. All of that sucked him in too deep. If Macy was pregnant, the only way out was to take charge of the baby *after* she delivered—and to stay as far away from her as possible until then.

There was just one thing he had to do first. He had to see her through Haley's operation Tuesday morning. He couldn't leave her to face that on her own.

"YOU LOOK TIRED. Haven't you been sleeping?" Macy's mother asked.

Macy rubbed her eyes and pretended great interest in the last chapter of *The Science of Medicine*. She hadn't slept. She'd lain awake all night, calling Thad every name in the book and wondering how she could have been foolish enough to fall in love with a man who'd hired her to have his baby. And then she'd gotten up early to pick her mother up at the airport. Edna had flown in a day early to surprise the newlyweds, only to find they'd already broken up.

"I asked you if you're sleeping, Macy."

"Mm-hmm," Macy murmured, pushing her glasses farther up her nose.

"Come on, honey, he's not worth it," she said. "Don't

do this to yourself. You know what I've always said about men. Maybe now you'll believe me.''

"He's just in love with someone else. That doesn't make him a creep.'' Macy glanced at Haley to make sure she was as fully engrossed in her battery-operated keyboard as she sounded. "And I don't like you doing your male-bashing thing in front of Haley. She might meet Prince Charming someday. I don't want her to shoot him down before she gives him a chance.''

"She'd be wise to shoot and ask questions later.''

"Mom!''

"Oh, all right.'' Her eyes narrowed and dropped to Macy's stomach. "June told me you're pregnant already. Is that true?''

Macy frowned. "I don't know for sure yet. I haven't had a test, but I'm going to get one in the next few days.''

"Well, if you are pregnant, and you don't think it's a travesty that Thad would get you that way and then leave you, you haven't got a lick of sense.''

Her mother was probably right about her lack of sense. But she couldn't blame Thad for the baby. She'd done what she'd done knowing he didn't love her.

"Have you told Haley?''

Macy glanced at her daughter again. "You mean about the baby?''

Edna nodded.

"Thad told his parents so soon I had to tell her there was a good possibility.''

"Was she excited?''

The keyboard blared on a sour note, and Macy winced. "I think so, although it probably doesn't seem real to her yet. When I'm showing, she might talk about it more.'' She stood to turn the volume down on Haley's toy.

"Are you ready for your finals?" her mother asked, changing the subject.

"I'm going to school next year, Grandma," Haley interrupted, causing Macy an all-too-familiar pang in her chest. Would her daughter ever go to kindergarten?

"Yes, sweetheart, if you're well by then," Macy said, then looked up at her mother. "I'm as ready for my finals as I can be, under the circumstances."

"Good." Edna rounded Haley's bed and draped an arm across Macy's shoulders, giving her a little squeeze. "I'm proud of you, you know. I think I should have told you that more often."

Macy smiled. "Thanks, Mom."

THAD TOOK a deep breath before walking into Haley's hospital room. He hadn't talked to Macy since he'd left her house two nights ago and had no idea how she might receive him, but he had to see Haley again, before the transplant, before the big risk.

Except that every day contained risk for Haley, didn't it? They could lose her at any time.

Macy's mother, his mother, Lisa, and his sister were already there. Debra smiled and got up to give him a hug, but Edna wouldn't speak to him and neither would his own mother or Lisa. He'd told June on the phone yesterday that he and Macy were having problems and would probably divorce after the baby was born. She'd ranted that she couldn't believe he'd even talk about splitting up, with a baby on the way and Macy going through what she was. Then she'd planted her support firmly in Macy's camp and was making sure he felt it.

What Macy had told Edna and Lisa, he had no idea, but their hostility ran far deeper than June's. His own mother would forgive him eventually. Her heart was too soft to hold a grudge, but he had the sneaking suspicion Edna would slash his tires if given the chance.

What a mess, he thought, biting back a sigh. Apparently his creative side had finally gotten him into trouble, instead of out of it. Kevin had laughed at his morose mood all day yesterday, until Thad had packed up his briefcase and headed home to work. The last thing he wanted to hear was "I told you so," especially because his wasn't the only life he'd screwed up with his unconventional solution to obtaining a son or daughter. Macy was in it deeper than he was.

Or at least that was what he'd thought until her eyes flicked over him, containing none of the warmth he'd grown accustomed to seeing in their green depths. He couldn't blame her for being angry with him. What surprised him was the way his own heart sank at her coolness.

She's crossed you off her list, buddy, and that's good, he told himself. *She's a smart girl. Strong. She doesn't need you.*

Which should have made him feel better.

Instead, it made him feel worse.

"Daddy!" Haley finally spotted him through the bevy of doctors and nurses surrounding her bed, drawing blood, talking her through the procedure to come and checking her catheter.

Thad smiled. "Hi, angel." The crowd parted for him to be able to reach her and give her a hug. "You all set for this?"

She nodded. "It's going to make me better," she announced. "I had a dream last night. You and me were flying a kite. I was running. And I had hair," she added proudly.

The ache in Thad's gut turned into a sharp pain. Part of him wished he'd never met Macy, never learned of Haley's sickness, so he could have avoided this day. But the other part, the bigger part, believed the joy of knowing such a sweet child was worth the pain.

Just like knowing Valerie had been worth the loss. Maybe he needed to think a little more about letting go of the side of the pool....

"You get better, and we will fly that kite," he promised.

Standing, Macy nudged him out. She didn't look at him, but her body was so rigid he could tell his words had invoked her anger. He could almost hear her accusing, *How dare you tell her you'll do anything with her?*

"Mommy will be there with you, so you're not going to be scared, are you?" she said to Haley.

Haley shook her head. "Dr. Forte promised it wouldn't hurt."

Thad saw Macy bite her lip and knew she wasn't worried about the operation but what might happen afterward. He worried with her. "No, the operation won't hurt."

"Mrs. Winters?" The nurse who'd been sitting at the nurses' station when Thad was scrubbing up poked her head into the room. "I've spoken with John Taylor. He's agreed to let you see him before the transplant."

How DID a mother thank someone for giving her child a second chance at life?

Macy stood at the entrance to the hospital room, gazing in at the man named John Taylor. Tall and gangly, he had acne on his cheeks and chin and wore thick-rimmed glasses. Behind the glasses, his eyes were hazel, with pretty, gold-tipped lashes that matched his hair, but he wasn't much to look at, certainly not the kind of man to turn a woman's head. Still, to Macy he was beautiful, because he could be anywhere else, going about his life, going to school, seeing a movie, visiting his mother. Instead, he was here in the hospital with her, for Haley, willing to walk the proverbial extra mile to save a dying child.

Her child. *Thank God for this young man and his generous heart,* she thought.

A news channel blared on the television, but the moment he saw her, he flipped it off with the remote. "Hi," he said, looking shy and self-conscious.

Macy smiled and entered the room. "Thank you for letting me stop by before the transplant."

He shrugged and dropped his gaze to the blankets that covered his legs. "Sure, why not?"

"If we'd have found you through the Marrow Donor Program, we would have had to wait a year before making direct contact."

"Oh, yeah?"

"Yeah, it's supposed to protect both the donor and the recipient, but meeting you is making me feel a lot better about what's happening. I appreciate your willingness to take a risk on our behalf."

He cleared his throat. "No problem."

"What made you come in and be tested in the first place?" she asked.

"I saw the flyer posted in the library at school."

"You go to the U?"

He nodded. "I'm a business major. Actually, my brother Bill is a med student. He's mentioned you a time or two, and was tested himself, so when I saw you putting up that flyer in the library, I thought I'd be tested, too."

"Thanks," Macy said simply. "I can't tell you how grateful I am."

"You don't have to be grateful. I just hope everything works out for your little girl."

Macy hesitated, knowing she should leave but wanting

one last thing from this young man. "Can I hug you, John? Would that be okay?"

He looked slightly more uncomfortable than he had before, but he nodded, and Macy put her arms around him.

"Thank you," she whispered.

She felt his arms tighten around her for the briefest moment, then he pulled awkwardly away. But Macy thought it was the best hug she'd ever had.

"God bless you," she murmured, and left.

THE TRANSPLANT WENT smoothly. Macy stayed with Haley until it was over, then headed to the lobby where she knew Thad and his mother and sister were waiting, along with her own mother and Lisa.

When she arrived, she saw the women seated together on one side of the lobby and Thad by himself on the other, pacing near the far wall. His sister occasionally tossed him a sympathetic look, but his mother and Lisa refused to acknowledge his presence, and Edna looked as though she'd give him a good piece of her mind at the first opportunity.

Macy wondered if she should try to talk to them. How they were treating Thad wasn't really fair, but with everything else going on in her life right now, she couldn't face sorting through the reasons. Thad was a big boy. Certainly he could handle the consequences of their little business arrangement. He'd made Haley's operation possible, but she'd pay him in full measure with a baby, even if she wasn't pregnant now. Beyond that, she owed him nothing.

"How did it go?" her mother asked as soon as Edna saw her. Lisa stood, the others looked up expectantly, and Thad hovered closer.

"Fine. Everything went fine." She smiled, feeling the relief of it. So far, so good, she wanted to add. "They're taking Haley back to her room right now."

Lisa swallowed her in a hug. June followed suit. "I was praying for her, the poor thing. Thank God it went well."

Macy nodded, trying not to let her eyes dart to Thad, trying not to read the expression on his face or acknowledge the longing she felt in his presence. "Thanks for coming, everyone," she said.

"We're not going anywhere, honey," June said. "It's just about time for lunch. Why don't you go ahead and study for tomorrow's final, and your mother and I, or Lisa, will go sit with Haley. She'll nap most of the afternoon anyway, I'm sure. She's been pretty tired lately."

"Anyone who goes in has to wear a mask."

"We can do that," Lisa said.

One last opportunity to study.... "You'll beep me if anything goes wrong?" Macy asked.

"Immediately," Edna chimed in.

"Everything will be fine," Lisa reassured her.

Macy nodded. "Then I think I will study. No use failing my first exam, huh?" She gave them all a weak smile, forever conscious of Thad standing just a few feet away. He'd said she wouldn't be happy with intimacy on his terms, but sometimes her resolve felt so weak she thought she'd accept him on any terms.

She knew she was better off boarding up her heart and forcing it into cold storage, however, which was what she was trying to do now, but it wouldn't cooperate. It thumped against her rib cage at the merest thought of him. And her mind was in collusion with her heart, because every time she dropped her guard, it played back the memory of him touching her, kissing her. The hurt she'd gone through with Richard had been bad, but she'd been able to console herself with the fact that he hadn't turned out to be the type of man she wanted to share her whole life with, anyway. Occasionally she missed his smile and his practical jokes,

but his affairs had caused her to lose too much respect for
him. By the time he'd left, most of her love had died, too.
But getting over Thad was going to be infinitely more difficult, because he was so much more to lose.

"Thad, don't you have to go back to work or something?" his mother demanded, tossing him a cold glance.

Thad grimaced but finally caved in to the hostility surrounding him and stalked out. Macy would have felt sorry
for him except that she couldn't afford to soften where he
was concerned. She waited for the others to gather their
handbags, then went up to tell Haley goodbye before snag-
ging her backpack out of a chair and setting off to the
university library.

Her hopes of becoming a doctor hung on one more week.

HER FIRST FINAL was in hematopathology. At nine o'clock
Tuesday morning, Macy sat down in the testing center and
stared at the ten-page exam. Then she broke into a cold
sweat.

Taking a deep breath through her nose, Macy decided
she had to relax. She wouldn't be able to think if she didn't
calm down. The exam was going to be difficult enough
without heart palpitations and dizzy spells.

Flexing her fingers, she shook them out, then gripped her
pencil, careful not to raise her eyes to the level of the other
students for fear the testing monitor would think she was
trying to cheat. She could do this. She hadn't been able to
attend the lectures as much as she would have liked, but
hematopathology was her favorite class, and she'd read the
material several times.

Only problem was, she hadn't been able to concentrate
very well.

She wrote her name on the test and filled in the bubbles
that would enable the computer to score her work, then her

mind strayed to Haley and how well her daughter had survived her first day after the transplant. The doctors were saying that the marrow was already starting to engraft, and so far there hadn't been any hint of GVHD. Could it be possible that this less-than-perfect match was one Haley's body would accept?

It would be a miracle, a miracle made possible by a tall, skinny man named John Taylor. Macy pictured him lying in his hospital bed, and her heart swelled with gratitude.

Fortunately John hadn't developed any complications from the transplant, either, and had been released that morning. Macy had stopped by the hospital to wish him well, but he'd already gone without leaving any word for her and, apparently, without expecting any further thanks.

A testing monitor walked slowly past Macy's desk, drawing her attention back to the exam.

Focus, she ordered herself, and started on the first question. She'd managed to work her way through two pages before Thad stole into her thoughts. Then she set down her pencil and rubbed her eyes. She missed him. A full day hadn't passed since she'd seen him, but it felt like forever. Was he at work? Going on with his life as though they'd never met? Hoping she was pregnant? Hoping she wasn't?

Turning to page three, Macy picked up her pencil and got back to work. She was going to pass this exam, she promised herself, and all the others. She couldn't control Haley's illness and she couldn't control Thad's heart, but she could take charge of her personal success. She'd cram all week, give each subject her very best and get back to the original plan for her life—the one that didn't include a man.

And, God willing, Haley would get well and start kindergarten next fall, and she would go on to her third year of med school.

What if there was a baby?

Macy glanced at her watch. She had forty minutes left. After her exam, she'd go straight to the hospital and have them give her a pregnancy test. She'd been trying to allow enough time for her body to secrete the hormones associated with pregnancy so the reading would be accurate. But she couldn't wait any longer.

THAD SAT at his desk and stared down at a 3x5 glossy photograph of him and Macy standing side by side at their wedding, and let himself think of her for the first time in more than a week. He'd been so behind at the office that it hadn't been difficult to throw himself back into developing new ad campaigns, meeting with directors for various commercials, sitting through auditions for the actors, and wining and dining local radio execs. Since Valerie had died, he'd grown accustomed to ignoring his emotions and burying himself in work.

He was in charge. Things were back on track and going well. He'd visited Haley twice, both times while Macy was taking one of her final exams, and had finally made up with his mother. She still badgered him about trying to make his marriage work, but other than that, he hadn't let himself dwell on Macy. He hadn't even thought of her.

Okay, he'd had a couple of dreams where he finished what he'd started that night in her room. But he couldn't expect himself to be able to control his dreams. Dreams just happened. All he could do was forget her as soon as he awoke, and he did that right away.

Well, maybe not *right* away. It usually took him a good couple of hours to get her off his mind completely. But by lunchtime...or maybe it was closer to four o'clock, every thought of his new wife was well buried.

Except this afternoon. He'd forgotten he'd asked his secretary to have the roll of film he'd taken in Vegas developed. He'd returned from lunch with Kevin and Martin Slinkerhoff, where they'd spent two hours going over the revised budget for the new Rustler's Roost commercials, to find the Fast Photo envelope on his desk. And now he couldn't help smiling at the sight of Macy wearing that fabulous, formfitting dress.

"That's a sight I haven't seen for several days," Luanne observed, marching into his office to deposit a stack of mail on his desk.

"What sight?" he murmured, still mesmerized by Macy and the memories the pictures evoked. She'd been so nervous that day, so vulnerable and beautiful....

"You're smiling," Luanne said. "You've been scowling and growling for over a week now, and working harder than I've ever seen you work. And you were a far cry from lazy before."

Thad shoved the pictures away, feeling the scowl return. "I don't know what you're talking about," he said, going through the stack of envelopes she'd brought him.

"Oh, yeah? Well, everyone else around here does. Just ask them. We're all trying to decide exactly what's bothering you. We think Kevin knows, but he won't say."

Thad paused midway through the mail. At least Kevin had left him that one small dignity. Maybe he wasn't such a bad guy, after all. He'd quit laughing at him, too, but now he was starting to give him pitying, I'm-worried-about-you looks, and that was at least twice as annoying. "There's nothing wrong."

"I thought you'd say that." Luanne sighed loudly and headed back to her station out front of his office.

"Close the door behind you. I don't want to be disturbed."

"Heaven forbid," she muttered, but the door had barely

clicked shut when Thad came across an envelope from Primary Care Hospital. Was it a bill? Had there been additional charges for Haley's transplant that Macy couldn't afford?

Slipping his finger under the lip, he tore the envelope and pulled out something that looked like a lab report and bill combined. They wanted seventy dollars for something. He didn't understand the percentages and medical inscriptions on the report, but he recognized the name of the patient at the top: Macy Winters.

And the handwriting at the bottom was clear as crystal:

As you can see, the pregnancy test came back positive. Congratulations! The baby is due on Valentine's Day. I'll contact you closer to that time.

                                        Macy

CHAPTER EIGHTEEN

CALL HER.

Thad stared at the phone from where he sat on the couch and wished he'd stayed at work. He would have, had he not been too exhausted to think. He needed to relax and escape before he blew a gasket. His secretary and everyone else in the office had ordered him home. So here he was, at eight o'clock on a Friday night, trying to watch a movie. But even *Die Hard* wasn't enough to capture his attention tonight.

He eyed the phone again. What could one little conversation hurt? Macy was going to have his baby. He just wanted to talk to her, make sure she was doing okay, ask if she needed anything. But he was afraid if he called, he'd break down and ask to see her. And if she said yes, he'd head straight over there. And the moment she opened the door, he'd sweep her into his arms. And then he'd be right back where he was ten days ago.

No, he'd already let Macy down as easily as he could, and he'd set his family straight that everything was over between them. Haley was doing great, better every day, from what his mother said and from what he'd seen himself. If everything went as planned, she was getting out of the hospital on Wednesday. And Macy wasn't going to contact him until she was ready to deliver. She'd made that clear in the note she wrote on that lab report she'd forwarded to him. She'd let him go just that easily, and hadn't even called. She was probably over him already.

So everything was downhill from here.

Except that he was going out of his mind.

But better him than her.

Hauling himself to his feet, he crossed to the phone and dialed Kevin. "Hey, what are you doing tonight?"

"Thad? That you, buddy?"

Thad could hear a woman whispering something in the background and wondered if he'd called Kevin at a bad time. "Yeah, it's me. I didn't realize you had company, though. Why don't you call me back tomorrow?"

"No, uh, it's okay. Listen, remember Rhonda? You met her outside Bellini's a couple weeks ago?"

When he was with Macy. Thad remembered her, but he was surprised Kevin did. Most of his girlfriends didn't last two weeks. "Yeah."

"Well, she's here tonight, and she has this gorgeous friend, a real knockout. She's a friendly girl, if you know what I mean. Why don't you come over? We'll get the two of you together, have a little party."

Thad considered the kind of party Kevin meant and wondered why he couldn't muster any enthusiasm for it. Wasn't his excuse for wanting Macy that he hadn't had sex for eighteen months? So where was all that libido now?

"Actually I'm pretty tired," he said. "I think I'll go to bed."

"Man, what's up with you?" Kevin demanded. "How long are you going to mourn? You're turning into a freakin' hermit."

"I'm just not interested in getting it on with some girl I don't even know."

"Give her a chance. How do you know you don't want her until you've seen her? I'm telling you she's hot!"

"I'm married!"

"You're in love again, that's what you are. Only you're too stubborn to face it and too scared to let go of the old and bring in the new."

Anger flashed through Thad, causing his hand to tighten on the telephone until the muscles of his arm stood out in relief. If Kevin had said that to his face, he might have hit him. "What the hell would you know about it? You're so afraid of commitment that you won't take the same girl out more than three times in a row. Neither will you date anyone deep enough to tempt you to have a real relationship."

"Hey, I'm not the one with a thorn in my paw, buddy. And I'm not going to give you the target you want. You've been spoiling for a fight ever since you broke it off with Macy. Why don't you make it easy on both of us and call her?"

Thad opened his mouth to make a retort worthy of all the anger and frustration stewing inside him, but Kevin hung up, leaving him with nothing but a dial tone.

Slamming the phone down, he cursed aloud and dialed Macy. She answered on the fourth ring, just before he expected her machine to pick up.

"Hello?" She sounded as if she'd had to rush for the phone.

"It's me," he said, and held his breath, hoping for...something. What he got was silence. "I want to see you."

"Why?"

"What do you mean, why? I don't know. I'm...I just have to see you."

"Sorry," she said. "It's not in our agreement." And then she hung up.

"WHAT DO ALL the blood tests and X rays reveal?" Macy

sat across from Dr. Forte in his office at the hospital. It had been thirteen days since the transplant. She'd finished all her finals and felt fairly comfortable that she'd passed two, but the others? She couldn't say. They'd been difficult. She'd struggled through and done her best, but she didn't know if she'd succeeded or not. Grades hadn't been posted yet. There was a chance they'd be up today. If not, then later in the week. But Macy was more worried about Haley. The doctors had been running tests all week, checking for cancer cells. Macy dug her nails into her palms as she waited to hear the results.

Dr. Forte smiled. "Dr. Vincent and I agree that Haley's prognosis is very hopeful. I don't have to warn you that things can change," he said, raising a cautioning hand, "but for now, Haley's body seems to be accepting the new marrow with a minimum of problems."

"Does that mean she can come home as planned?"

"She's had a little jaundice. We'd like to keep her an extra two days so we can make sure her liver continues to function properly, but I don't see any reason why she can't go home on Friday. I think children recover much more quickly in their own environment. Just watch her closely for any sign of rash or fever."

Macy couldn't believe it. That was it? After spending nearly a year in and out of the hospital and nearly one hundred days straight during this last stretch, Haley might be well enough to come home on Friday? That was only three days away! She'd been hoping for it, telling herself to plan on it, but deep down, she'd feared something would happen to snatch that homecoming away.

"For good?" she asked.

"Unless something new crops up. Of course, we'll have to keep her on steroids and immunosuppressants for a while, just to make sure her body doesn't end up rejecting the graft, but I think you can handle that at home.''

Tears sprang to Macy's eyes, happy tears, the happiest she'd ever shed.

At long last, Haley's ordeal might be over.

Wiping her tears away, Macy stood. ''Thank you,'' she said. She would have hugged him, but there was still the desk between them, so she shook his hand, instead.

''Don't thank me,'' he replied. ''I won't take credit for those who survive just as I won't bear the blame for those who go the other way.''

COME ON, COME ON, Macy chanted silently, sitting in front of her personal computer in her guest room/office on Thursday and using her mouse to click on the test results for Pharmacology 6030. The cursor turned into an hourglass and grew and shrank until finally a list of names appeared on the screen.

Macy started scanning from the bottom, looking for ''Winters'' before realizing that she hadn't changed her name on any of her school stuff.

''McKinney...McKinney. Here it is.'' She clicked on it, and after another second with the hourglass, four words appeared on the screen. *McKinney, Macy Grade: B.*

Slowly, Macy let her breath go. She'd been right. She'd passed pharmacology without any problems. Combined with her other tests from earlier in the block, she could even end up with an A– for her final grade in the class. Amazing.

But Pharmacology had been the easiest exam. She had to pass all her exams in order to move on to her third year.

Still nervous, she backed out of Pharmacology and clicked on the test scores for Art of Medicine, then Science of Medicine, and finally Hematopathology. She'd received a C, a B– and a C–, respectively.

She could slip through by the skin of her teeth, if only she managed to do as well in Neuroanatomy.

Biting her lip, Macy waited for the score of her last final, the one she'd worried about most, but when the list of students appeared on the screen, her name wasn't there. Had something gone wrong? Had the computer been unable to score her exam?

Her stomach knotted. Oh, no! Had she forgotten to put her name on her score sheet? Surely not!

Grabbing her purse, she ran out of the house, jumped into the Pinto and thanked heaven when it started right up. She wasn't sure what kind of office hours her professor kept now that school was out, but it was barely three o'clock in the afternoon. Maybe she'd be able to catch him.

The campus was almost empty. Macy had no problem finding a parking space or making her way to Professor Lumkin's office, where she found him hunched over his desk. An older man with snowy white hair and piercing blue eyes, he looked up when she knocked on his open door.

"Ms. McKinney. I thought I might hear from you." He smiled.

Macy prayed it was a good smile. "Hi, Professor. I just tried to check the score for my final exam on the Web site, but…"

"It's not there," he finished. "Come in. I'd like to talk to you." Setting down his pen, he pulled a folder from beneath an avalanche of paper and began thumbing through it. When he reached Macy's exam, he pulled it out of the stack and set it in front of him, then motioned for her to pull up a seat.

"Neuroanatomy can be a difficult subject," he began,

but Macy couldn't concentrate on what he was saying. Her mind had shut out everything around her—everything except the 59 percent scrawled across her paper.

She'd failed.

THE SMALL MEXICAN restaurant on State Street in Murray smelled of the chili verde Macy liked so well. She stood at the entrance, close to the clatter coming from the kitchen, and searched the dining room for her mother and Lisa. They'd insisted she meet them for supper tonight, while Edna was in town for Haley's homecoming, to celebrate if she'd passed her finals, or to commiserate if she hadn't.

Spotting them sitting not far away, waving to her, she told the approaching hostess that she'd already found her party and made her way through the crowd.

"Haley's what's important," Edna said, watching her face as she approached. "She's coming home tomorrow."

"Right," Lisa echoed. "And if you didn't pass your exams, there are plenty of other things you can do with your life."

"Well, it's kind of mixed news," Macy admitted, sliding into the booth next to her mother, across from Lisa. "I passed all my finals except neuroanatomy."

Lisa arched a worried eyebrow. "Which means…"

"Normally it would lower my grade point average and get me kicked out of the college. But my professor knows what's been going on with Haley's illness and says in order to give me a fair shake, he's going to let me retry the exam in three weeks."

"You're kidding!" Lisa said.

"No."

"So you have more studying to do?" her mother asked.

"Yes, but I've got three weeks to do it in, and now that Haley's better, I can finally concentrate. Professor Lumkin even said he'd tutor me. I'm supposed to meet him at his office weekdays at three o'clock.''

Lisa gaped at her. ''That's great!''

Macy smiled and sat back so the waitress could deliver three glasses of ice water. Another stab at passing neuroanatomy was great, she thought, but not nearly as incredible as Haley coming home in the morning.

''So, are you going to call and tell Thad?'' Lisa asked.

Macy had just taken a drink of her water and nearly choked on it.

Her mother, who'd turned her attention to the menu, quickly lowered it. ''Why would she do that?'' she demanded.

''Because he called yesterday to talk to Haley and asked how things were going. I told him Macy would find out about her finals today. He sounded like he really wanted to know the results.''

''Then he could have stood by her, like he should have,'' Edna snapped.

''Let's not start that again, Mom,'' Macy said. ''Although it might be a bit premature, this is supposed to be a celebration, remember?''

''Well, Haley was really happy to talk to him,'' Lisa said, a defensive note creeping into her voice. ''You should probably know that she told him she's getting out of the hospital tomorrow and begged him to come see her off.''

A trickle of unease crept down Macy's spine. She'd boxed up Thad's toothbrush and hairbrush, his aftershave and cologne, and the few clothes he'd left at her place and delivered them to his back door almost two weeks ago while he'd been at work. But she hadn't seen him since the transplant and wasn't sure she was ready to face him again. ''Did he say if he was coming?'' she asked hesitantly.

Lisa shook her head. ''I doubt he'll show without some

indication from you that it's all right. But you could call him.''

''He doesn't deserve to be included,'' Edna said.

Macy wasn't so sure. He'd been good to Haley. And she *was* carrying his child. Part of her wished they could at least be friends. For Haley's sake, she thought maybe they should try. ''Haley really misses him,'' she pointed out. ''If she's expecting him tomorrow, she'll feel terrible if he doesn't come. She's been begging to see him for days.''

''But what about *your* feelings?'' Edna demanded. ''It might be a disappointment for Haley, but sooner or later she has to learn that he's out of the picture. He can't be trusted to—''

''Mom, don't,'' Macy interrupted. ''Thad's not like that.''

''Why are you always defending him? After what he's done?'' Her mother glared pointedly at her stomach.

After what he'd done? He'd given them Haley. If her mother only knew, Macy thought, and for her, it went even deeper than that. ''Because I love him,'' she said simply.

HE WASN'T GOING to come.

The following morning, Macy smiled and thanked the doctors and hospital staff that had stopped in to say good-bye to Haley, but she couldn't concentrate on the chaos in her daughter's room. She was too busy listening for Thad's tread in the hall, keeping one eye trained on the door just in case, and hoping—hoping to see him, hoping it wouldn't hurt too badly when she did, hoping her daughter wouldn't be disappointed.

But if Thad had received the message she'd left on his answering machine last night, inviting him to the hospital to help take Haley home, he hadn't responded. She'd told him to come at ten o'clock. It was nearly eleven.

Lisa and Edna stood on the other side of the room, out of the doctors' way, holding balloons and cards and stuffed toys they'd gathered from the tables and chairs. Haley sat on the bed, center stage, dressed in the matching shorts and T-shirt set Edna had bought her and looking healthier than Macy had seen her in almost a year. What a relief! What a tremendous blessing! The moment was *almost* perfect. If only Thad was here…

What was *wrong* with her? Macy chastised herself harshly. Wasn't the miracle of Haley's life more than she had a right to expect from God or the world or anyone else? That she might also pass her second year of med school was a bonus. She had no right to feel sorry for herself because she couldn't have Thad, too. That was asking too much.

"The nurse will be here with your wheelchair soon. You all set?" she asked her daughter when the last of the staff had wished them well and filed out.

Haley frowned. "We can't go yet," she said. "Daddy isn't here."

Macy glanced at Lisa, who looked almost as disappointed as she felt, then noted the you-should-have-listened-to-me arch to her mother's eyebrow. "I bet Thad had to work, honey," she said. "He would have come if he could have."

"He'll be here," Haley insisted. "He wouldn't want me to go home without him."

Macy tucked her hair behind her ears and zipped up the suitcase that held the last of Haley's things. "You know Thad and Mommy are only friends now, honey. I've explained that to you already. He might act differently than he once did, but you can still be friends, okay?"

Haley stuck out a pouty lip, telling Macy what she thought of her "friends" idea, but the nurse they'd been waiting for appeared at the door with Haley's wheelchair just then, distracting them all. Haley could walk short distances, but it was the hospital's policy to see she made it safely to the car via wheelchair.

"Are we ready for our little princess to take a ride downstairs?" the nurse asked.

"No," Haley responded. "I can't leave until my daddy gets here."

"I'll let you call Thad once we get home," Macy told her. "But we have to go now. We can't make everyone at the hospital wait. They may need this room for another sick little girl. Besides, I have a surprise waiting for you."

"What is it?"

"If I tell you, it won't be a surprise."

Evidently, that wasn't good enough. "I don't want to go without Daddy."

Macy sighed. "Okay, it's that new art set you saw in the toy magazine, remember? The one you wanted so badly?"

"With those special chalks?"

"Yeah."

"Can I play with it when I get home?"

"You bet."

The art set finally won Haley's cooperation, but her reluctance was still apparent when they loaded her up and headed out. "What if Daddy comes and we're not here?" she asked as they got on the elevator.

"He knows where you live, honey," Lisa responded. Macy was too busy watching the elevator doors close on the place she'd grown to know so well. It was difficult to believe she wouldn't be frequenting the hospital anymore, that she and Haley would be living a normal life. Excitement bubbled up inside her at the thought of having a future that was now bright because her daughter would be part of it.

"What are you going to do this summer?" the nurse asked Haley.

"I'm going to fly a kite with my daddy," she announced, and Macy almost groaned out loud, especially when her mother pinched her arm. Her poor daughter was as stuck on Thad as she was, and Edna thought she should burst her bubble once and for all. But Macy couldn't insist her daughter stop loving him, wouldn't tarnish his memory in the attempt. Thad was something they'd have to get over together.

The elevator settled on the first floor, and its doors parted with a mechanical *clug*. The nurse pushed Haley out and around the corner while Macy untangled the balloons her mother held so they wouldn't get smashed in the elevator.

"Daddy! You're here. I knew you'd come!"

The sound of her daughter's excited cries carried through the whole lobby, making Macy's heart nearly leap out of her chest. She rounded the corner just as Thad was entering the hospital, another bouquet of balloons and a stuffed friend for Bruiser in his arms. He bent and hugged Haley and gave her his gifts, telling her how beautiful she looked and how happy he was she was coming home. Then he straightened, and his eye caught Macy's.

The sound and movement in the lobby seemed to fall away in one instant. "Hi," she managed to say.

"Hi." Thad's Adam's apple bobbed. "How are you?"

Macy pasted a bright smile on her face. "Great. Good. I passed all my finals except one, but I get to retake it in a few weeks. I should be able to pull it off without too much trouble."

"That's good."

"How's the Rustler's Roost account? Did they sign?"

"Signed, sealed and delivered." He stepped toward her,

then paused and shoved his hands in his pockets. "Thanks for inviting me to come."

"No problem. Haley was dying to see you. She's really missed you."

Something in his eyes seemed to ask if Haley was the only one who'd missed him, but Macy thought she had to be imagining things.

"If you want, Haley can ride in your car," she offered.

"I'd like that." He took his hands out of his pockets long enough to loosen his tie. "Would you like to come with us?"

Dimly, Macy was becoming aware of her mother's scowl and Lisa's rapt attention. Clearing her throat, she forced her gaze to them. "No. I'll ride with Mom and Lisa. We'll meet you."

"Okay," he said, but he didn't turn to go. He just stood there, looking at her as if one sign of any kind would bring his arms around her.

"See you there, then," she said, amazed that she could even *think* he might be feeling any of the same emotions that were slamming into her like a tidal wave. *You're kidding yourself. He loves Valerie.* She purposely gave him a wide berth as they went outside to load Haley into his car.

HALEY'S FIRST WEEK at home was hard. Now that Macy was on her own, without the constant support and supervision of the doctors and nurses at the hospital, she felt frightened and alone. What if Haley was getting jaundice and she didn't see it in time? What if she missed something else? Some days she stared at her daughter so hard her eyes went blurry as she tried to decide whether or not Haley's skin was turning yellow, hoping to detect the signs of GVHD before it could damage her liver. And the nights were worse. Macy would often wake in a cold sweat, fear-ing Haley had died in her sleep. She'd creep to her daughter's room and hover over her bed until she saw the slight rise and fall of her chest. Then she'd breathe a sigh of relief and tiptoe back to her own room, and believe, just a little more strongly, that her daughter was really getting well.

Thad called a couple of times the first week, only once the second. Macy longed to talk to him, to voice her worries about Haley, to celebrate the vast improvement in her health, to see how he was doing. But he never asked to speak to her. He was quick and to the point if she answered, then talked to Haley and hung up, and she refused to open old wounds by pressing for more.

"Why won't you break down and call him?" Lisa demanded the night before Macy had to take her neuroanatomy final. She was lying on the couch above Haley, who was sitting on the floor watching *Tarzan*. They'd all been bingeing on the nachos Lisa had brought over, along with some soda, candy bars, ice cream and a cake from Smith's bakery that said, Congratulations on a Job Almost Done.

"Because breaking down won't fix anything," Macy insisted.

"It might help you get through this transition period of having Haley home."

"She's been home three weeks. The transition is nearly over, and Haley's doing great. She's almost back to normal, and my own fear is receding. I'm finally starting to relax and believe everything is going to be okay. So, you see? There's no reason to call him."

"Yes, there is." The ice in Lisa's glass clinked as she took a sip of her Coke. "You're pregnant with his baby, for crying out loud. And Thad loves you. He just doesn't know it yet. I saw the way he looked at you the day Haley got out of the hospital. That was naked longing, babe. An idiot could have spotted it."

"Who was naked?" Haley asked, pulling herself out of the movie for the first time since it started.

In the old recliner, Macy frowned at Lisa and repositioned the pillow she'd brought from her bedroom. "No one's naked, honey. Do you want some popcorn?"

Haley had already stuffed herself with pizza and root beer. She shook her head.

"Well, it's nearly nine o'clock, kiddo. Time for you to be in bed. Should we turn this off and finish it in the morning?"

"Mo-om, I want to watch the rest," Haley protested. "Can't I stay up a little longer?"

It was summer and Macy's final wasn't until tomorrow afternoon. There wasn't any reason either of them had to be up early. Macy had started working again, but she hadn't yet rebuilt her transcription business to include the number of medical practices she'd had previously. "Okay," she relented.

Haley went eagerly back to her movie, and Macy lowered her voice. "If he cares about me, why doesn't he talk to me when he calls Haley?" she asked Lisa.

"Because you gave him nothing to hope for at the hospital when he came to take her home. Every time the two of you got anywhere close to touching, you backed away as though he had the plague."

"I don't want to talk about it."

"Come on, Macy, give him a chance to get over Valerie."

"He's not asking for a chance."

"But you love him."

"I have Haley. I have school. I'm happy the way I am. Why are you pushing this, anyway?"

Lisa shrugged, opened an ice-cream sandwich and licked the sides. "I like the way he treats Haley. She talks about him all the time, misses him. I think you two are meant for each other.''

''He doesn't want *me*.''

''I think you're wrong. Anyway, I've met someone myself.''

Macy nearly dumped the bowl of popcorn she'd been holding in her lap. ''What?''

''I've met someone. We're going out this Friday.''

''Where did you meet him? Who is he?''

''He came through the checkout stand with a couple of cracked eggs. I sent the bagger back to get him a new carton, and he asked me out.''

Twisting in her seat, Macy tried to get a better look at Lisa's face in the dim glow of the television. All the other lights were off. ''Who is he?''

''Name's Robert Myers. He's a little older than I am. He's taking me out to eat on Friday, then he wants me to come out and watch him play baseball. He's on a summer league.''

''Sounds fun.'' Thrilled that Lisa, who rarely dated, might have found someone willing to look beyond her weight to the heart of gold underneath, Macy felt her smile spread across her whole face.

''He's divorced. Got a couple of kids,'' she volunteered.

''You're great with kids.''

''Yeah. That's what I thought.''

Macy laughed. ''Maybe we'll be shopping for your wedding dress next.''

Lisa pushed the junk food aside and settled back. ''It's just a first date, Macy. Don't go renting the chapel yet,'' she said, but Macy could tell she was happier than she'd been in a long time.

CHAPTER NINETEEN

"HOW'S SHE DOING?" Thad sat behind his desk, staring at his perpetual-motion clock as he talked to his mother on the telephone. It was November, almost five months since the day he'd taken Haley home. The leaves were turning on the trees, the days growing cooler. Macy would be well into her second trimester now.

God, he wanted to see her. He'd thought what he'd felt for her and Haley would fade, but it seemed to be growing stronger.

"You call me all the time and ask the same thing," his mother complained. "Why don't you call and ask her?"

He couldn't. It was too hard. He'd quit calling because every time he talked to Haley, it got harder and harder to hang up without begging to speak to Macy. "It's better this way."

"Better for whom?"

Not wanting to fall into that old argument, Thad ignored the question. "Are you going to tell me how they're doing or not?"

"Macy's morning sickness is gone, and school's going well. Dr. Biden thinks the pregnancy is progressing normally. And Haley is just like every other kid in her kindergarten now," his mother responded. "I think it's safe to say she's cured."

See? Haley was fine, and Macy was back on top again.

They didn't need him. He was just about to hang up when his mother said, "But Haley still asks for you, you know."

Thad closed his eyes. At first he'd tried to keep a relationship with Haley, but he'd soon realized that he couldn't do that and keep his distance from Macy at the same time. And if he couldn't keep his distance, he'd never be able to walk away when the baby came. And if he couldn't walk away, they'd need to work out some way of sharing both children, which sounded a lot like creating a real family. No, Haley and Macy came as a package deal, and he couldn't have anything to do with them, not as long as Valerie was still hovering in the background of every thought, every action.

"Are you ever going to tell me why you and Macy broke up, Thad? I've gotten to know her quite well over the past five months, and she's a lovely, bright young woman."

His mother had asked what had gone wrong in their marriage before, several times, and Thad had always said they'd simply jumped the gun and married too soon, only to realize they weren't compatible. But June hadn't bought it before, and he knew she wouldn't buy it now. So he told her the truth.

"I'm still in love with Valerie. It's almost like she's alive, watching me. Sometimes I turn around and expect to see her."

"You have to let go of her sooner or later."

"I know. It's just hard to turn my back on the years we spent together."

"You and Macy have only known each other a short time. If given the chance, maybe you could build something every bit as wonderful."

"That wouldn't be fair to Valerie." How did he explain that moving on, making the same promises to someone else somehow invalidated everything they'd shared?

"Do you believe Valerie loved you, Thad?"

"I know she did."

"Then how can you think she'd want you to live the rest of your life alone?"

"How can I believe she'd want me to love someone else as much I loved her? Yet it's not right to involve myself with another woman while holding back, to relegate someone to second place."

"That's true. That's why you let yourself love again and don't worry about places. It will never be the same as it was with Valerie. Macy and Valerie are two very different people. But it can be just as good. There's no betrayal in that."

Then why did he feel as if there was?

"If you couldn't be with Valerie, would you want her to be lonely and miserable for the rest of her life?" June asked.

"Of course not."

"Do you think you're a more generous person than she was?"

His mother certainly had her moments. Thad thought she was having one now. "No."

"Then you have your answer."

THE FOLLOWING SATURDAY Thad stood staring at the pile of objects he'd amassed, then bent to tape the bottom of one of the cardboard boxes he'd bought from the local U-Haul. He was packing up Valerie's things. His mother had volunteered to help him, but he'd chosen to face the experience alone.

And it was about time. Other than the items her family had wanted as keepsakes, he'd stowed her personal things in boxes in the basement just after the funeral, but that wasn't enough. He had to remove the cross-stitches, the

photographs, the painting she'd given him for their last an-
niversary and the lap blanket she'd covered herself with
when they watched television. There were books and trin-
kets everywhere, even certain pieces of furniture that reminded him of her constantly. Before he could even think
about moving forward, he had to put his feelings for Valerie
to rest. And to do that, he had to let go of the physical
objects that kept her so close. Maybe he'd even sell the
house.

"Hey, you moving without telling anybody?" Kevin
asked, coming through the front door Thad had left standing open since his last trip to the car for boxes. When he
saw what Thad was doing, he nodded approvingly. "This
is good, buddy. Way to go."

Thad chuckled. In his own way, Kevin had been telling
him to do this for months. He just hadn't been ready to
listen. "How 'bout you give me a hand?"

Kevin helped Thad heft one of the heavier boxes out to
the trunk of his car. "Where are you taking all of this?"

"Everything's going to Deseret Industries, except the
photos and the picture."

"And those?"

"I'm storing them in the basement with the other stuff.
I'll decide what to do with it all when I sell the house."

Kevin slammed the trunk closed. "Why the sudden
change of heart?"

Thad shrugged, knowing his change of heart had been
anything but sudden. "I guess it's true what they say about
time."

"Does this have something to do with Macy? Has she
called?"

"No. I'm sure she's forgotten all about me."

Kevin looked doubtful. "She's your wife and she's having your baby. That makes you pretty difficult to forget."

Picturing Macy big with his child did funny things to Thad. It made him warm and possessive, fiercely protective, and hungry to see her rounded middle. He wanted to touch it with his own hands, pull her back against his front while he kissed her neck and cradled her belly.

He wanted the baby. He'd wanted one for a long time. But this child was extra special because it came from Macy. Did that mean he wanted her, too?

"She was just particularly vulnerable when Haley was sick, and I was there, at least for a short time," he said to stem the excitement his thoughts engendered. "We both got a little confused for a while. That's all."

Kevin propped his hands on his hips. "If things are over, then you won't mind if I call her, right?"

Thad gave Kevin a look that promised violence if he so much as picked up the phone.

Kevin laughed. "For a bright guy, this thing with Macy is taking you a while," he said. "But I have faith that you'll get there eventually."

Deep down, Thad knew he was closer than Kevin realized. He just hoped he wasn't too late.

MACY GLANCED at the clock in the kitchen and drained her orange juice. "Thanks for coming to watch Haley. I'd better get moving, or I'm going to be late."

"What time is your appointment?" Lisa asked, helping Haley pour a bowl of Raisin Bran.

"Eight-thirty. Did I tell you I'm having an ultrasound?"

"You are? Is something wrong?"

"No. It's just routine. I'm twenty-four weeks along now, and Dr. Biden wants to be sure the baby's developing normally."

"Are you going to ask them to tell you the gender?"

Macy thought about attaching a "he" or "she" to the

child growing inside her and decided against it. She needed to keep as much emotional distance between her and the fetus as possible. She already doubted she'd be able to live up to her promises to give Thad the baby.

"I think I'll let that be a surprise." She dug in her purse for her keys. "I'm sure I'll be back, but if not, Haley has kindergarten at five to twelve."

"I know where the school is. I picked her up a couple of weeks ago, remember?"

Macy did remember. Lisa had been her mainstay, despite her preoccupation with one Robert Myers, who took her out almost every weekend.

"Where are you going, Mommy?" Haley demanded when Macy dropped a kiss on the top of her head.

"To the doctor's."

"Are you going to get the baby out?"

Macy smiled. "Not yet, sweetie." She'd tried to prepare her daughter for the fact that the baby would live with Thad by using the rationale that they had each other and wouldn't want him to be alone. But Haley didn't think much of that idea. She wanted the baby *and* Thad.

Unfortunately, so did Macy.

"Do you have class today?" Lisa asked.

"I only have lab on Fridays, at one. I'll be out in time to pick Haley up." Macy gave her friend a quick hug. "If Mom calls, ask her if she's coming up for Thanksgiving. It's only a couple of weeks away."

"You got it."

"I'm off. Wish me luck." Wearing a pair of black leggings with a large maternity shirt, Macy hurried into the living room and barreled through the front door, only to slam into someone coming up the walk. She stumbled and would have fallen, if not for the arms that reached out to catch her and pull her up against a broad chest.

"Thad! What are you doing here?" The sight and feel of him after so long made Macy want to fling her arms around his neck and pull him close. She ached to hold him and never let go.

But she wasn't foolish enough to put herself in the same position she'd been in six months ago. She stepped back, and his gaze fastened on her stomach, which had finally swollen enough to make her pregnancy obvious. Then his eyes slowly climbed to her face, holding some emotion Macy feared to name. "I just came to see how you are."

She braved a smile and recovered herself enough to pull the front door closed. The last thing she needed was for Haley to hear Thad's voice and come bounding out of the house to welcome him with open arms. She had to get rid of him before he upset the careful balance she'd achieved in their lives. "I'm fine. Haley's fine. Everyone's fine. And you?"

She wished she didn't sound so breathless, so panicked.

He reached out as though he would touch her stomach. When she backed up another step, he dropped his hand.

"I could be better," he admitted.

"I wish there was something I could do to help, but I'm really in a hurry. I've got to go."

As she tried to dart around him, he caught her by the arm and pulled her left hand up to look at her fingers. Then he frowned. "You're not wearing your wedding ring."

It wasn't an accusation. He spoke as though the absence of his ring indicated something important, but Macy wasn't about to guess what that could be or why he'd care at this late date.

"I don't know why you ever bought me that ring. We're not married, not really, right?" She smiled as though the ring meant nothing to her when, in reality, she'd hidden

Thad's diamond away because she couldn't stop gazing at it, wishing for him.

"I guess that's a matter of opinion," he said slowly. "The law says we're married. All that's left is the consummation."

Macy's heart skipped a beat, but she wouldn't meet his eyes. How many nights had she lain awake dreaming of that? "And we both know how well that went last time. I think all that's left is the divorce."

Desperate to escape him before she crumbled and admitted that she'd never craved a man the way she craved him, that a day hadn't gone by she hadn't longed for him, she wrenched her hand away and marched to her car, hoping he'd make things easy on her and just leave. Her life was finally her own again. She wouldn't risk her happiness another time, wouldn't be forced back into the position of having to explain to Haley why Thad didn't really want them.

"Macy, wait," he said, but she held up a hand to silence him. Whatever he was going to say, she didn't want to hear it. At least, that was what her head said. Her heart felt as though it might break.

"I'm really late," she mumbled. "I have to go."

THAD JAMMED his hands in the pockets of his jeans and watched Macy pull out of the driveway. Man, she looked great. With her shiny black hair pulled back in a short ponytail, her cheekbones seemed even more prominent, her lips fuller, her eyes greener. And Thad found her figure more appealing than ever, knowing he'd put that swell in her belly. He wished, not for the first time, that he'd done it the old-fashioned way and promised himself that someday he would. They'd make two, maybe three more babies and have a houseful. If Macy ever gave him the chance.

At this point, it wasn't looking too hopeful.

The door opened behind him, and he turned to see Haley standing in the doorway.

"I told Lisa I heard you," she said, but she didn't come running to him as she once would have. She regarded him almost as warily as her mother had.

He'd hurt them both. He prayed he'd have a lifetime to make it up to them. "I had to come see my angel, didn't I?"

"Where have you been?"

Lisa came to stand behind Haley. Thad acknowledged her with a nod, then turned his attention back to Macy's daughter. "I guess you could say I've been doing some reorganizing. But I think everything's all set now."

"Some what?"

He chuckled. "I've been putting some old things away, where they belong."

"Are you done?"

"Yep." He regretted Haley's mistrust, missed her easy acceptance and knew he'd have to earn back her love. But he had no doubt she'd be easier to convince than Macy. Remembering Macy's passion-filled voice when she'd declared her love for him, he wondered if he'd ever hear her say those words again.

"Does the fact that you're here mean anything?" Lisa asked.

Thad looked behind him to where Macy had disappeared down the avenue in her old Pinto, wishing he'd parked behind her, instead of on the street. "That remains to be seen."

"Now's the time to walk away if you're not sure."

He was sure. He'd spent the past six months making sure. "I'm not going anywhere. It's up to Macy now."

"In that case, she's on her way to the doctor's for an

ultrasound.'' Lisa grinned. ''If I were you, that's something I wouldn't want to miss.''

THAD DIDN'T BOTHER to go to Dr. Biden's office. He knew she scheduled her ultrasounds with the lab on the first floor of the same medical complex her office was in, because he'd been there before, with Valerie.

Pushing through the glass swinging doors with the lab's name painted across them in white, he scanned the lobby for Macy. She wasn't there, so he approached the front desk, where a form on the counter listed all the patients who'd checked in today. It was early yet, but Macy Winters was one of about eight names, second from the bottom.

Behind the desk, a copy machine hummed as the receptionist pressed its green Print button, then turned to smile at him. ''May I help you?''

''I'm Thad Winters. My wife is here getting an ultrasound. She's expecting me to join her.'' He smiled. ''Sorry I'm a little late.''

''No problem, Mr. Winters. I'll take you in.'' She came around to open the door leading to the offices in back, and Thad followed her through an area with temporary partitions and small workstations used for drawing blood to a darkened room where a screen hung on one wall. On that screen was the image of a baby. Thad could see its tiny hands and feet, the curve of its back, the roundness of its head. He could even see the flutter of its heart.

Spellbound, he watched his baby move inside Macy's womb. His baby. *Their* baby. The sight brought tears to his eyes.

Blinking rapidly, he swallowed against the sudden tightness of his throat, trying to temper his reaction. A man didn't cry, at least in public. Except for the night Valerie had died, he'd survived the past two years without breaking into tears. But this...this was something else.

"Mrs. Winters? Your husband is here," the receptionist murmured.

Macy's startled gaze fastened on him, and everything Thad had planned to say simply disappeared. He just looked at her, knowing his heart was on his sleeve but having no power to shield himself against the rejection he feared.

"Thad?"

His name held the question he'd thought she'd voice out loud: what was he doing here? But she hesitated, as if she could sense his vulnerability, or was reacting to a little of her own.

When she didn't insist he leave, he moved closer, to the head of the table where she was lying with her shirt up, the technician's wandlike instrument on her belly. "Hi," he said, touching her hair.

She closed her eyes and reached for his hand, not to push it away, but to press her cheek into his palm, and the lump in Thad's throat grew until it almost choked him.

"Do you want to know the sex of the child?" the technician asked, focused on her job and oblivious to the powerful emotions humming between him and Macy.

"Thad?" Macy questioned. "Do you want to know?"

Thad nodded because he couldn't speak, and the images on the screen changed as the technician examined the baby's various body parts. At first he couldn't tell what he was seeing. It was all shades of gray going to black. But then he got a clear look at the baby's buttocks, and the sack between his legs, and didn't need anyone to tell him.

He was having a son.

HE'D TAKE IT SLOW, give her time, he told himself as he walked Macy out of the doctor's office. She'd permitted him to be included in the ultrasound, which was a step in the right direction and, for him, surpassed almost everything he'd experienced in his life so far. He'd been excited about his and Valerie's baby, but he'd taken the pregnancy much more for granted. Now that he understood just how fleeting and precious life could be, he had a whole new respect for such momentous occasions.

"You're awfully quiet," Macy said.

Thad nodded. He didn't know what to say, how to adequately express what he was feeling, at least while his heart was still so tender. So he remained true to his sex and said nothing until they reached Macy's car.

"I don't like you driving this old jalopy," he said, because it was a lot easier than finding the words to tell her how grateful he was that he'd met her, how much she'd come to mean to him.

She raised her eyebrows in surprise. "You just found out you're going to have a son, and the first words out of your mouth are about my car?"

"It's not safe," he explained.

She laughed. "Well, until I make it as a successful pediatrician, I'm going to have to get by with it." She unlocked her door and put her purse inside.

"Where are you going?" he asked before she could get in.

"I've got lab today."

He reached into his pocket and pressed his keys into her hand. "Take my car. I'll feel better knowing you're driving it."

She frowned in confusion, making him shift uncomfortably. "What's going on, Thad?"

"Nothing." He cleared his throat. "I was just hoping you'd go out with me tonight. I mean, a man should be able to date his own wife, right?'' He offered her a hopeful grin.

A look of uncertainty crossed her face. "I don't think so, Thad. I don't think I can be friends with you just yet.''

"I'm not talking about being friends.''

She studied his face for a moment, then shook her head. "No, I'm not ready for any emotional entanglements, either. I just got Haley and me back on the right track. I need to move forward and not look behind, at least for a few years.''

"A few *years?* I understand why you'd say that, Macy, but it's different this time. I'm different. I—'' Ah, to hell with words. They were enormously inadequate, anyway. Bending, Thad pressed his mouth to Macy's. She shoved at him, but it was a feeble attempt at escape, and Thad couldn't take it seriously, not when he felt her soft lips give way beneath the pressure of his own until he could slide his tongue into her mouth. He was sinking and flying at the same time, and the next thing he knew, she was in his arms, their baby between them. What had started out as a gentle communication of emotion had turned into a passionate, all-consuming kiss. But as deeply as he tasted her, as tightly as he held her to him, he couldn't get his fill of Macy. He wanted to drown in her, feel her welcome him inside her for now and forever.

The heels of someone's shoes clicking on the pavement not far away brought Thad back to the fact that they were standing in the middle of a parking lot in broad daylight. He broke off the kiss, breathing hard, but he couldn't take his eyes off Macy's flushed face. Heaven and earth had just moved for him, and she'd felt what he'd felt. He knew she had.

"Come home with me,'' he whispered.

Macy looked dazed. She blinked up at him, then

squeezed her eyes shut. "Don't do this to me," she whispered, shoving his keys back in his hand.

"Just tell me if you still love me," he said.

She took a deep breath and shook her head, but when she spoke, he could tell the words were painful for her. "No. Go away. And don't come back."

Then she climbed into her car and rumbled out of the lot.

CHAPTER TWENTY

"I'M OUTTA HERE!" Kevin said that afternoon, poking his head into Thad's office.

Thad glanced up from where he stood behind his desk sorting files, trying to decide which ones he needed to take home with him. "See you Monday."

Kevin arched an eyebrow at the open briefcase on his desk. "Don't tell me you're actually leaving at a decent hour. You got plans tonight?"

Macy had refused to see him, but Thad wasn't going to let her get away so easily. Not after that kiss. Her voice might tell him no, but her body was sending entirely different signals. "I've got something in mind."

Kevin gave him a questioning look. "What's up with you? You've been smiling all afternoon."

"I'm going to have a son," Thad said simply. He knew he was probably beaming like a little boy with a shiny new truck, but was unable to curb his elation.

"A son?" Kevin came a few steps farther into the room to brace his hands on the back of one of Thad's chairs. "Macy called?"

"No. She had an ultrasound this morning, and I was there." Sitting down for a minute, Thad put his arms behind his head, crossed his legs at the ankles and closed his eyes to relive it. "I got to see the baby and everything."

"Give the man a cigar." Kevin smiled. "Any other news?"

"Such as?"

"What's happening with you and Macy?"

Thad grimaced and sat up straight. "That's going to take some work."

"But it's fixable, right?"

"I hope so."

"Come on, I'll walk you down to your car."

"No, you go ahead. I have a quick call to make." Picking up the phone, Thad dialed Macy's number. Kevin paused at the door as Haley answered.

"Hi, angel, this is Daddy."

"Hi, Daddy!"

"What are you doing?"

"Nothing."

"Where's your mommy?"

"In the kitchen. She's making me some macaroni and cheese. It's my favorite."

"That's great. But be sure and save room for popcorn afterward, okay? I want to take you to the movies tonight."

"Is Mommy going?"

"No, just me and you."

"Oh, I get it," Kevin said softly. "You're using the little girl to get close to Macy. You're playing dirty."

Thad smiled. "No, I'm playing for keeps."

"MOMMY, MOMMY! Daddy's on the phone! He wants to take me to the movies! Can I go? Please, Mommy? Can I, huh?"

"What?" Macy set the macaroni she'd just drained onto a cold burner and shucked the pot holders. "What are you talking about, sweetheart?"

"Daddy's on the phone."

"He is?" She'd heard the phone ring, but she'd expected it to be her mother or June or Lisa, all of whom called often and were just as happy to talk to Haley as Macy. She never dreamed it would be Thad. Not after this morning when she'd told him to leave her alone.

"Can I go?" Haley asked again.

Macy shook her head, wondering how to handle this new turn of events. "Let me talk to him."

Tucking the hair that had fallen out of her ponytail behind her ears, she snagged the phone off the far counter. "Thad?"

"Hi, Macy."

Macy's stomach did a triple somersault and dived, just at the sound of his voice. What was ever going to become of her? "Haley said you want to take her to the movies."

"If that's all right."

Haley was jumping up and down next to her, a look of desperation on her face. "Pl*eee*ase, Mommy."

"You didn't think to ask me first, Thad?"

"So you could tell me no?"

Macy sighed. She thought he'd understood that when she'd told him to stay away from her, she'd meant Haley, too. It appeared she should have been more specific. Turning away from her daughter, she lowered her voice. "You can't just keep waltzing in and out of our lives."

"I'm not going anywhere this time," he cheerfully informed her. "As a matter of fact, I'm not even going home tonight."

Surprise stiffened Macy's spine. "You're not? Where are you going?"

"I'm staying at your place. Just thought I'd give you some notice."

Macy's heart slammed against her rib cage and stopped. She resisted the urge to smack her chest to get it going again. "I'll prepare the guest room."

"Don't bother, I'll be sleeping with you," he said. Then the phone clicked and a dial tone hummed in her ear.

MACY DIDN'T CARE if Thad was spending the night or not. She wasn't going to sleep with him. After what had happened last time, he was the last man on earth she'd trust with her heart or her body.

But she showered, washed her hair and shaved her legs, twice. The makeup she applied was to make herself feel good. She wasn't trying to impress him. And the expensive, vanilla-scented lotion? She put that on after her shower almost every day. Or at least once a year.

When the doorbell rang, Haley rushed to answer it while Macy feigned interest in a novel. She'd read the first three pages several times, but had no idea what the book was about. She'd been too nervous, knowing that Thad was on his way over.

If she was half regretting her decision not to go to the movies with him before he arrived, she regretted it tenfold after. He looked better than a fudgy brownie standing at her door wearing a pair of snug, worn jeans and a golf shirt. She remembered that scrumptious body snug against hers, his mouth on her own, hungry and wet, and had a hot flash.

Damn hormones, she silently cursed.

"You sure you don't want to join us?" he asked, his crooked smile tempting her to forgive him, to trust him. "A nice movie, fresh popcorn, maybe an ice-cream sundae afterward?"

The ice cream almost got her, but Macy shook her head. She needed time to shore up her crumbling defenses. Thad wasn't an easy man to refuse. And it would be dark and late when they returned. Nights were difficult enough when she was only imagining his presence.

Maybe she should spend the next two hours going to the hardware store to purchase a dead bolt for her bedroom door.

"Have a great time," she said, giving the wriggling, excited Haley a kiss. Her daughter waved goodbye and promptly took Thad's hand to lead him away.

"We'll be back soon," he said, leaning close to add, as a whisper in her ear, "In the meantime, any chance you could dig out those silk pajamas you wore on our wedding night?"

Macy gulped and looked down at her rounded tummy. She just bet she'd make quite a sight in a size four at six months pregnant. But that didn't stop her from finding out, once they left. Standing in front of the mirror, she adjusted the beige silk shorts several times, but nothing she did made them look any better.

Unfortunately, none of her sexier lingerie, also leftovers from her first marriage, made much improvement. She had no waist. Now, breasts...well, breasts were another story. She'd gone up two bra sizes in the past three months.

But none of that mattered, right? Because Thad wasn't going to see her wearing anything but her mother's cast-off nightgown. Unless she could find one of Edna's many housecoats. One of those cotton snap numbers would be enough to drive the lascivious thoughts out of any man's head. Thad would take one glance at her, realize she looked more like June on *Leave it to Beaver* than she did his perfect, beloved, long-lost Valerie. And he'd run for the hills again.

Better that than to have him reject her while she was wearing something in which she felt cautiously hopeful. Then she'd feel completely unappealing, the way she did after the last incident. Only this time would be worse because she weighed an extra fifteen or twenty pounds.

The baby began to squirm inside her, and she smiled ruefully at her undulating middle. "I'm not blaming you," she said aloud, rubbing it affectionately. "It's just that daddy of yours. He makes me crazy."

Crazy in love, she admitted, but only to herself.

THAD HELD Haley on one knee during the movie so she could see over the row of people in front of them—and because he liked the feeling of being her dad. He'd fought for six long months to forget Macy and Haley, but getting them out of his blood had been virtually impossible.

Now he enjoyed the peace of giving in to his attraction. They belonged together. He believed that now. He believed that the time he'd spent feeling bereft and alone since Valerie's death was about to come to an end.

The animated characters on the screen burst into song, and Haley's smile widened, her eyes shining with rapt attention. Children were so easy to please. Thad only hoped Macy would prove as open to him as Haley had been. She'd once told him she loved him, and he'd thrown the words back in her face. That would be tough to forgive, but he was determined to make it up to her.

He glanced at his watch, suddenly impatient to get home. He wanted to crawl into bed with Macy, feel the skin he'd longed to touch for so long, have her turn to him and put her arms around his neck and let him make love to her for the first time. Then maybe he could dispel some of the fear that he'd lost her for good.

"Daddy?" Haley asked, twisting to face him.

"Hmm?" he responded, his thoughts still on Macy.

"Why does Grandma Edna call you a putz?"

Thad chuckled. "I guess your mom isn't the only one I have to win over again, huh?"

"OMIGOSH, I think he's here." Macy pulled the telephone cord with her as she crossed the living room to peek out the window. Sure enough, the headlights of Thad's car blinded her for a minute, then the purr of his engine died and the lights flashed off. "It *is* him. Oh, no! What am I going to do? I never made it to the hardware store."

"Calm down," Lisa told her. "You don't need a lock. You need a tranquilizer."

"Are you kidding? My mind has to be sharp. He said he's staying here tonight, and I just know that I'll sneak into his room if he doesn't sneak into mine."

"Macy, listen. You guys are married. It's about time you came to this. There's no reason to say no. Obviously, if Thad's back, he's ready for a more serious relationship."

"That isn't obvious to me at all. What if I scare him off again? When he gets close, or kisses me, he makes me say...things."

"Things?"

"Horrible things that come from somewhere deep inside me, somewhere I've never heard from before."

"Like?"

"Like 'I love you more than life itself,' and like 'I want to have your baby, do your laundry, scrub your back and pick up your underwear.'"

"Jeez, what's so horrible about that? Robert would love it if I said that."

"No! It makes Thad realize he doesn't feel the same about me. He doesn't want me out there buying curtains and messing up Valerie's fancy decor."

"I think telling him how you feel is the right way to go. At least you're being up front with him. At least he knows your terms from the onset. As a matter of fact, I admire him for not taking advantage of you six months ago."

"Lisa?"

"Yeah?"

"What if I *want* him to take advantage of me?"

"You said you're wearing your mother's housecoat. You must not want it too badly."

Macy could hear Haley's voice as they came up the walk. "I've got to go," she whispered, and slammed the phone down, wondering if she had time to dash to her bedroom before she had to open the door. She'd been lying about the housecoat. She was wearing her robe, but underneath she had on a sheer white nightie, a definite giveaway.

Jingling at the lock told Macy that Thad still had his key. She didn't need to answer the door. She could hide in her room. She started down the hall, then realized how cowardly it would appear for him to find her huddling beneath the quilts. She was a millennium woman, right? Sexually mature. She could handle this situation like an adult.

Clearing her throat, she turned on the light and smiled as Thad and Haley came through the door.

"Hi, Mommy!" Haley launched herself into her arms, taking Macy by surprise. She stepped back, but the force of the impact pulled her robe open a little in front, and Thad's gaze immediately dropped to a section of white lace that showed through.

He grinned. "It's not the silk pajamas, but I have a feeling I'm going to like it even better."

"It's flannel. It just looks like lace," Macy said, tightening the belt.

"Uh-huh."

Macy felt her cheeks heat and cursed her own weak will. "Anyway, I was just trying it on."

"Right. Should I put Haley to bed or should you?" he asked, moving in close, his breath smelling faintly like spearmint gum.

Taking her daughter by the hand, Macy retreated to the

bathroom, where she helped Haley brush her teeth. Then they moved to the bedroom, so Haley could put on her pajamas and say her prayers. Macy took an extra few minutes to read her a book, even though it was far past her bedtime, because part of her hoped Thad would fall asleep waiting for her.

The other part knew she'd kill him if he did.

When she shut Haley's door behind her, she found Thad in the living room, watching the sports news. He clicked off the television the moment he saw her standing in the hall.

"I put clean sheets on the bed in the guest room," she said.

"Uh-huh." He stood. His jeans clung to all the right places, but Macy tried not to notice.

"Let me know if you need anything."

"Uh-huh." He started down the hall toward her.

She swallowed, her throat suddenly dry, and held up a hand to keep him from getting too close. "I think I'll turn in."

"But you said to let you know if I need something. I do need something. In fact, I'm fairly certain I'll die without it." He took her hand and put one finger, then the next, into his mouth to tickle the sensitive pads with his tongue.

"What's that?" she managed to say, the sensation and its attendant wet warmth triggering other images in Macy's mind and making her breathing quicken.

"You."

"But...there's Haley. And I don't think...I don't think it would be wise to—"

He was close enough to put his arms around her and draw her to him. Instead, he slipped his hands inside her robe and beneath the sheer fabric of her nightie to reverently caress her protruding belly. He watched her as he touched her, a look of wonder claiming his face. "You're having my baby."

"Yes." Her voice was a hoarse whisper. "But Haley's just right down the hall—"

"And you're my wife."

"I know, but—"

"Mommies and daddies sleep together. I don't think Haley will have a problem with it." Lowering his mouth to her neck, he kissed her lightly all the way up to her ear. "God, you taste good. I think I've dreamed of claiming you as my own since the moment we first met."

His words added fuel to the fire smoldering low in Macy's stomach. She thought if he touched her again, she might melt into the floor.

He lifted his head from where he'd started to caress her breasts with his lips and pulled her robe open all the way so he could see her. "I don't think I've ever seen a more beautiful sight," he said. "You're gorgeous and you're mine, Macy Winters. We belong together."

Together sounded good, better than it ever had. Macy forgot her apprehension and self-consciousness. She could tell by the look on Thad's face that he was sincere. Pregnant or not, he desired her as much as she desired him.

Pulling his head toward her, she kissed him, letting her tongue meet his. Her hands lodged in his hair, tugging him closer, feeling the warmth and strength of him surround her. She wanted to feel him inside her. She wanted to wrap her legs around him and become one, and she knew she didn't want to wait very long to do it. It had been too long already.

As though her impatience had somehow communicated itself to him, he swung her into his arms and carried her through the hall and into her bedroom. He set her on the bed and quickly peeled her robe away, then feasted on the sight of her in her sexy lingerie. "How can you look even better to me than before?'' he whispered, gently teasing her hardened nipples through the sheer fabric of her top with his tongue.

"I'm not going to tell you I love you," she blurted, balling her hands into fists and trying to hang on to the anchor of that one thought amidst the onslaught of sensation coursing through her.

"What?'' His hands paused in stripping them both of their clothes, and he pulled back to look in her face.

"I'm not going to tell you I love you," she repeated stubbornly, meeting his gaze.

His eyes narrowed at the challenge as he ran a finger lightly over the swell of one breast all the way to its tip. She groaned and arched toward him when he pulled away, feeling as though he'd suddenly deprived her of air, and he grinned. "Oh, yeah?'' he whispered, rolling her carefully onto her back. "Then I'm going to make love to you until you do.''

THAD AWOKE EARLY, feeling more contented and relaxed than he had since Valerie died. He half expected some kind of remorse to hit him when he thought of her—he'd blown past all barriers and committed himself to Macy, with his heart, his soul, his body—but strangely enough, he felt only happiness.

Macy was nestled beside him, sleeping in the crook of his arm. Her wild, tousled hair made him smile. She'd been phenomenal last night. Passionate, responsive, soft, sexy. He loved her now more than ever, and he'd told her so, over and over again. The first time they made love, he'd whispered it in her ear with every thrust, until, at the very pinnacle of pleasure, she'd finally relented and moaned the same thing to him. In the aftermath, he'd cupped her face in his hands, kissed her eyes, her nose, her mouth and promised he'd never hurt her again.

"What are you smiling about?" Macy's eyes were open now, and she was staring up at him.

Thad traced the outline of her cheek with one finger. "You, last night."

She shyly returned his smile. "I've never experienced anything like what happened last night."

"It was perfect, because you're perfect." He kissed her, the beginning of desire flaring again at the feeling of her smooth legs entwined with his own. He wondered if they had time to do anything about it before Haley woke up and decided they probably didn't.

"You told me you loved me last night," she said, rolling up onto her elbows. "Did you mean it?"

He tweaked her nose. "How can you even ask me that? I must have told you a hundred times."

"I guess I'm just wondering what it means."

His hands worked their way up her firm backside and pulled her closer. "It means we're a family now. It means we share Haley and this baby, that we take turns with our son's midnight feedings and diaper changes—if I decide to let you help me," he teased, grinning up at her.

She arched a brow. "I'm going to nurse the baby, so you'd better be nice. You might need me more than you think."

"I already need you far more than I ever dreamed possible," he admitted. "I love you, Macy Winters. I'm glad you're my wife."

Macy smiled at that, but after a moment her smile disappeared and she started chewing her lip.

"What's wrong?" he asked.

"We don't have to live in your house, do we?"

He chuckled. "No. I put my house up for sale. I thought

I'd buy us something up here, close to the university, at least while you're finishing school. That way Haley can stay in the same elementary school.''

"That could be fun. I've never owned a house before.''

"Then I think you should get to pick it out.''

"We'll pick it out together. Something with lots of potential and character.''

"Oh, no!'' he groaned. "I can already see our weekends filled with sanding, painting and plastering.''

"It'll be fun.''

"As long as you give me plenty of incentive.''

"There will always be that.'' She delved her fingers into his hair. "Until then, will you stay here?''

"Every night.''

Her hand dropped to cup his whisker-roughened jaw. "You're something else. You know that? What made you change your mind about me?''

He nuzzled her neck, kissed her ear. "I never changed my mind, Macy. I just moved some things out of the way. And it feels right, don't you think?''

She nodded, but then her eyes clouded again. "You know how badly I want to become a doctor, right? You won't expect me to give that up?''

"I don't expect you to give up anything, except perhaps your medical-transcription work. I think, between the kids and school, remodeling a charming old house in the Avenues, and a demanding husband who'll want every extra minute you can give him, you'll have your hands full, don't you?'' He rolled her onto her back and kissed her belly, starting at her belly button and moving up through the valley of her breasts.

She played with his hair, twirling the locks around her fingers. "I don't know. All those hours of tedious typing might be tough to let go of.''

"Yeah, I can tell you're pretty broken up about it." His hand closed over one breast, and he groaned at how wonderful the weight of it felt in his palm. "What time does Haley normally wake up?"

"Seven."

Thad checked his watch. "Darn, it's past seven now."

Macy chuckled. "We could always tell her to watch a few cartoons," she suggested. "Or, if we're really quiet, maybe she'll sleep late."

He nestled his face in her breasts and breathed deeply. "I like the way you think," he said, his voice muffled, but before he could act on her invitation the phone rang.

They banged heads in their rush to answer it before it could wake Haley. Macy fell back, rubbing her forehead and laughing while Thad answered.

"Hello?"

Silence.

"Hello?"

"Thad, is that you?"

"Mom, what are you doing calling Macy at seven o'clock in the morning on a Saturday?" he demanded.

"I just wanted to see if she needs me to watch Haley while she studies for a few hours. What are you doing there?"

"I live here now." He winked at Macy, thinking that might throw his mother, but good old June didn't skip a beat.

"It's about time you came to your senses."

"Sometimes I'm a little slow."

She laughed. "Is that Macy I hear in the background?"

"Uh-huh. She wants me to thank you—"

"Mommy? Daddy?" Haley asked, her voice coming through the closed door.

Macy jumped out of bed to dress, and Thad sighed. "—for waking Haley."

"I could take her for the day, give you two some time alone," his mother said.

Thad got out of bed and pulled on his own clothes. "No, we appreciate the offer to baby-sit, but we have other plans today."

"We do?" Macy turned to look at him as she let Haley in.

Haley rushed right past her mother and threw her arms around Thad's legs. "You're still here!"

"I'm still here, angel," he said, mussing her hair. "And I'm not going anywhere."

"What are we going to do today?" Macy persisted.

"We're going to fly kites."

"Kites?" his mother echoed. "It's November."

"I don't care. I feel like flying kites."

"Just like in my dream!" Haley announced.

"Only better," he promised.

MACY STOOD at her dresser gazing into her jewelry box. Her body felt as light as a helium balloon after all that had transpired. Every time she thought of Thad and the tender, passionate way he'd made love to her, she smiled. Their initial relationship might have started out as a business deal, but she felt certain she'd gotten the better end of the bargain. Because of him, the doctors had been able to save Haley's life. Because of him, she was happier than she could imagine.

She almost wished she could thank Richard for running off. The past couple of years had been tough, but she and Haley had weathered the storm, and now they'd found a beautiful rainbow at the end of their journey.

Or was it just the beginning?

Turning sideways, she studied her pregnant profile, smiling faintly. *We're going to have a son. We're going to raise him together, with Haley.*

"Macy, are you coming?" Thad called from the living room. While she showered, he and Haley had been busy making a picnic lunch for their outing to the park. They were in a hurry to get going, but she was too content to move very fast.

"I'll be right there!" She dug in her jewelry box until she uncovered a soft velvet case. Snapping it open, she gazed at her wedding ring for a long time, thinking it more beautiful than ever before. The diamond had once been a symbol of Thad's generosity. Now it was a symbol of his love, of forever, she thought, and slipped it on her finger.

CHAPTER TWENTY-ONE

January

"IT'S TIME. You need to come get me."

"What?" Thad sat on the other end of the line, in his office, staring blankly at Kevin and the clients seated across from him. His secretary had just interrupted his meeting to say he had an emergency, but Macy wasn't due for another six weeks. What could she mean by "It's time"?

"The baby's coming. Hurry, Thad."

Macy had had a healthy, uneventful pregnancy, but the panic in her voice now made it difficult for him to breathe. "But it's too soon."

"I don't think our son cares. He's on his way."

"Oh, boy." Thad stood up, sat down, stood up again. Was something wrong with the baby? Why would it come early? "I'll be right there, Macy. Where are you? Don't try and walk anywhere. I'll come get you."

She chuckled. "What are you going to do, drive up on the lawn? I'm at the pay phones on campus, near the library, but I can make it to the front, where you usually pick me up. I'm just a little nervous. I've had so much backache with this pregnancy that I didn't realize I was in labor until the pains starting coming hard and fast." Her voice sounded strangled for a minute, then he heard her pant. "I'm afraid we don't have much time."

They'd been to Lamaze. Thad knew that pant meant she was having a contraction. "Honey, don't be frightened. I'll drive up on the lawn if I have to."

"I'll be waiting by the main entrance."

He slammed the phone down and started from the room, almost forgetting to explain himself. At the last minute, he said, "I have to go. My wife is having our baby." Then he ran to the elevators, cursed the damn things for taking so long, considered scaling the twenty stories to the ground floor via the stairs, and decided it would actually be quicker to wait.

As soon as the elevator doors sprang open, he hit the lobby button, descended and dashed to his car.

Macy was waiting at the main entrance, as she'd said, but he could tell by her face that all wasn't well. He pulled up, his heart in his throat, and ran around to help her into the car.

"You okay?"

"I think so." She reached out to squeeze his hand. "Just get me to the hospital."

"Maybe we should go to the University Hospital. It's right here."

"No, Dr. Biden can't deliver there. I've called her. She's already on her way to St. Joseph's."

"What if we don't make it?"

She grinned. "Then you'll get to deliver the baby yourself."

"We'll make it," he said.

Other than one construction delay, traffic wasn't a problem this afternoon. Thad wove through the streets, speeding when he could safely do so, and turned into the emergency entrance of St. Joseph's Hospital only fifteen minutes later.

Macy was in the middle of another labor pain. Her eyes were closed and her hands balled into fists.

"We're here," he said gently. "I'll be right back." He jumped out and jogged into the hospital to get a wheelchair, but Macy was already waddling in when he returned.

"Here you go," he said, helping her sit down.

They'd toured the hospital shortly after their Lamaze classes had ended. Thad knew exactly where to go. He wheeled Macy down a long corridor, turned left, passed through a set of double doors, and waved to get a nurse's attention as soon as they entered the maternity ward.

"What have we here?" The nurse's badge identified her as Nurse Somerset.

"My contractions are every two minutes or so apart," Macy said.

"When's your due date?"

"Next month."

She frowned. "Okay. Wait right here. I'll get you a room."

Minutes later, Nurse Somerset returned and showed Thad and Macy into one of the home-style birthing rooms they'd visited on their tour.

"Has Dr. Biden arrived yet?" Thad asked.

"Not yet. You've called her then?"

"Yes. She's on her way," Macy said.

"Good." The nurse handed her a gown. "Change into this. Then I'll check and see how far you've dilated. Has your water broken yet?"

"No. Is that good?"

"If we want to try and stop the labor, it is. Once your water breaks, stopping it isn't an option. But I'm not sure what Dr. Biden is going to do. She might want to let you go ahead and have it. You're what, thirty-four weeks?"

"Give or take a few days."

The nurse nodded and left.

Thad helped Macy change and get settled in bed. "The

doctor will be able to stop the labor if it's too early,'' he said, hoping to convince himself, as well as Macy, that they had nothing to worry about. "Even if we have the baby now, it should be all right. I mean, people have premature babies all the time, right?''

Macy was breathing deeply through her nose, at the tail end of another pain. When it released its hold on her body, she took his hand and kissed his palm. "I've never seen you so uptight,'' she said. "Everything's going to be fine.''

He nodded, but he'd lost too much in a hospital once before to relax now. "Should I have the nurse call an anesthesiologist?''

"Nope. We're going natural, remember?''

He grinned. "I thought you might change your mind.''

"Maybe I will,'' she said, giving him a rueful smile. "But I haven't yet.''

"What about Haley?'' He glanced at his watch. "She gets out of school in twenty minutes.''

"I called Lisa from campus. She's going to pick her up. Everything's been taken care of.''

"Did you call your mom? She needs some notice so she can make the drive from Vegas.''

"Not yet. You can call her if you want, but I'm not sure she'll talk to you. She's still convinced you're going to run out on me.''

Thad laughed. "She'll come around.'' *When I'm old and gray,* he added to himself.

He made the call, then alerted his own mother. "They're both on their way,'' he told Macy just as the nurse, who'd returned while he was on the phone, finished her examination.

"You've dilated to six,'' she told Macy. "At this point, I doubt Dr. Biden will try to stop labor.''

"Did I hear my name?'' Dr. Biden entered the room,

wearing street clothes, which she quickly covered with a blue smock the nurse gave her. "How you feeling?"

"Like I need to push," Macy said, panting through another contraction.

The doctor pulled on some latex gloves and checked her again. "This is going fast. Bring me a stool and get the bed ready."

"You're not going to stop it?" Thad asked.

"No. It's too late for that."

The nurse rolled a stool to the doctor and adjusted the bed so Dr. Biden could more easily reach Macy.

"I have to push," Macy grunted during the next contraction.

"Not yet," Dr. Biden warned. "You haven't dilated all the way. I don't want you to tear."

Macy gritted her teeth, letting Thad know the contractions were beginning to run together. "I have to push," she said again.

Dr. Biden quickly checked her cervix. "Hang on for just a few more contractions, Macy."

"Come on, sweetheart, you can do it," Thad said, trying to play his part as coach. But he'd never felt more helpless or useless in his life. His wife was lying on the bed, suffering, and the baby he'd wanted for so long was coming six weeks early. Would his son be whole? Healthy?

Suddenly blood gushed from Macy as though someone had turned on a faucet. Judging from the look of surprise on the doctor's face, it wasn't normal.

"We're going to need a transfusion here, stat," the doctor barked to the nurse. "And get an anesthesiologist. She's hemorrhaging. We'll do a C-section."

Thad stared at the growing pool of blood, the doctor's words echoing in his head. What did it mean? Surely

Macy's life wasn't in danger. The fear that it might be shot a pain right through his heart.

Oh, God, please, not again.

Other doctors and nurses flooded the room, working with quick efficiency. They ignored him until Dr. Biden cried, "Someone take him out while we move her to an operating room."

Thad ignored Biden and clung to Macy's hand, feeling naked and vulnerable and terrified.

"Thad?" Macy looked up at him, her eyes dazed by pain.

God, not Macy!

"I love you," she whispered. "No matter what happens, always remember that."

"Macy, don't leave me. I won't let you go," he said, but a nurse took him by the arm and dragged him away before she could respond.

THAD'S MOTHER joined him in the lobby of the hospital after thirty minutes of waiting. "What's the matter, son?" she asked as soon as she saw him.

Thad let her hug him, clung to her too long, perhaps, then made himself pull away. "She started hemorrhaging."

June's eyebrows knit in worry. "What did the doctor say?"

"Nothing. A nurse keeps coming out to say everything is going fine, but she won't get any more specific than that."

"And the baby?"

"I don't know. They're doing a cesarean."

Tears filled his mother's eyes, and Thad put an arm around her to comfort her. She talked to him, telling him she was sure everything would work out, but he wasn't listening. His thoughts revolved around the last time he'd had a wife and child in the hospital. The doctors had told him they couldn't save Valerie and her unborn child. He'd been forced to choose between them and lost them both, and afterwards, in his bitterness, he'd sworn there'd never be anyone else.

He'd been wrong about that. Even though his relationship with Macy had initially revolved around the baby he longed to have, he knew, if he had to make the same decision today he'd had to make with Valerie, his wife or the child, he'd choose Macy. He didn't understand the human heart or its capacity for love, but he knew Macy meant every bit as much to him as Valerie had. She was the cornerstone of his family now, and he prayed he wouldn't lose her.

"Mr. Winters?"

At the sight of Nurse Somerset, Thad jammed a hand through his hair and stood, his gut knotting in frightened anticipation. "Is she okay?" he asked.

She smiled. "Your wife is in stable condition."

He closed his eyes and let his breath seep out. "And my son?"

His mother took his hand and squeezed.

"He's beet-red and angry at the moment, but he's going to be fine. He weighed in at six pounds, two ounces, not a bad size for six weeks early."

Thad couldn't believe it. He stood staring at his mother for several seconds before he came to his senses enough to ask, "Can I see my wife?"

"They're still stitching her up. But you can come and hold your baby."

Thad felt a slow smile creep over his face. His baby. He finally had his baby. And he had Macy and Haley, too.

Feeling as if he was walking on air, he followed Nurse

Somerset to the nursery, where a rolling cradle just inside the entrance held an infant squalling at the top of its lungs.

The nurse lifted the tightly wrapped bundle and placed it in his arms. "Meet your son, Mr. Winters."

Glancing at his mother, who'd followed them, Thad smiled. Then he gazed down into the red, shriveled face of his son, smelled the sweet newness of him, kissed the fuzzy round head—and knew he'd never have to worry about clinging to the edge of the pool again. For Macy, Haley and his new son, he'd dive into the deepest part of the ocean.

EPILOGUE

"OPEN IT." Haley's excited face hovered above the gift in Macy's lap. She'd already unwrapped all of her own presents. A stack of games, Barbies and dress-up clothes teetered near the Christmas tree, and a shiny new bicycle from Santa waited next to the front door. Baby Joshua, who was crawling now and nearly able to walk, sat in the middle of the floor, cooing and gurgling and generally ignoring his own new toys while making an even bigger mess of the torn paper that littered the room. Thad was trying to make sure he didn't eat too much of it.

"Come here, little guy," he said, scooping up his son and settling next to Macy on the couch. "Mommy is about to open the present Daddy got her."

They were all in their nightclothes still, except Thad, who had tried on the new sweater Macy had given him and was wearing it with his pajama bottoms.

Macy set Lisa's gift aside—a certificate for dinner at Bellini's that had come with the wonderful but not surprising announcement of her and Robert's wedding in three weeks—and made a show of shaking Thad's gift. He'd placed it under the tree nearly three weeks ago, and she'd eyed it ever since. She'd also hefted it, shaken it and tried to peek through the paper at one end. But all her snooping had come to nothing. She had no idea what was in the box, only that Thad was excited to give it to her.

"Hmm…it's kind of heavy," she said.

Thad chuckled. "As if you didn't know that already."

"How would I know?" Macy asked innocently.

"Right." He rolled his eyes. "With the way you've been poking and prodding and shaking that thing, I'm surprised it's still wrapped."

Macy grimaced. Evidently, she hadn't been as sly as she'd thought. Giving up on her ruse, she ripped off the paper only to find another wrapped box beneath the first.

"A little guarantee," Thad boasted.

Haley laughed in delight at the sight of it. "I helped Daddy wrap them," she said proudly, letting Macy know there were more "guarantees" to come.

Thad pulled Haley onto his other knee for a quick kiss, but she was too excited to sit still. When Macy reached the third box, she slid off his lap and clapped at the sight of each new layer, as if her and Thad's trick was the finest joke in the world.

Macy enjoyed Haley's reaction almost as much as she enjoyed the anticipation of her gift—and the sight of her handsome husband watching her so expectantly.

The present was getting small. Now barely the size of her palm, Macy could guess what it was. The plush velvet box at the bottom of all the layers confirmed her guess.

"It's jewelry," she said.

"Open it," Thad prompted.

Macy snapped the lid open to find a gold chain with a pendant shaped like a mother cradling an infant. "It's beautiful," she breathed, her throat tightening as she recognized the added meaning in the symbol because of the way she and Thad had met.

"There's something on the back," Haley announced.

She turned the pendant over and saw two small words engraved on its back: *Forever—T.*

Tears burned behind Macy's eyes as she gazed at it.

A tentative smile curved Thad's lips. "Do you like it?"

She looked at him, and he must have seen what she was feeling in her eyes because he kissed the back of her hand, then pulled her into his arms for a kiss on the mouth. "I'm so glad I found you," he murmured. "I love you, Macy. Thanks for Haley. Thanks for Joshua. And thanks for trusting me enough to love me back."

"Do you like it, Mommy?" Haley echoed.

"I do," Macy assured her. "It's the best thing Daddy could have given me," she said, but she knew the love he gave her and their little family every day was far better still.